ANGER . . .
AND ATTRACTION

He swung round to face her, his eyes blazing with an emotion that caused Penelope to press back against the stall railing in alarm. "I am a Bellington, Penelope. Nothing will ever induce me to see your precious Ashington silver or portraits or anything else in that mausoleum of a house as anything but a monument to stiff-necked pride and arrogance. If I had my way, I would burn it all down to the ground."

He stopped abruptly, as if suddenly regretting his unguarded outburst. Quite unexpectedly, he reached out to touch her face.

The gesture took Penelope by surprise, and she stood mesmerized for several moments, acutely conscious of his fingers tracing the contours of her cheek with feather-light softness. When his hand came to rest beneath her chin and gently tilted her face, she realized with a jolt that he was about to kiss her . . .

The Rogue's Revenge

Olivia Fontayne

JOVE BOOKS, NEW YORK

THE ROGUE'S REVENGE

A Jove Book / published by arrangement with
the author

PRINTING HISTORY
Jove edition / August 1994

ISBN: 0-515-11374-3

A JOVE BOOK®
Jove Books are published by The Berkley Publishing Group,
200 Madison Avenue, New York, New York 10016.
JOVE and the "J" design are trademarks
belonging to Jove Publications, Inc.

PRINTED IN THE UNITED STATES OF AMERICA

10 9 8 7 6 5 4 3 2 1

The
Rogue's Revenge

(1066) duc de Saxe[3]

    /   /

Mathilde de Saxe[2]   Henri le Lion
m. Baron Charles Assolant[1]

- -

(c. 1700)

Caroline Ashington[4]   Francis John Ashington,
m. French officer   third Earl of Laughton,
                       m. Duke of Cornwall's daughter

         /

John Neville Ashington,
fourth Earl of Laughton,
m. Lady Amelia Pierce

/   /   /

Frederick Neville,   **Octavia**   **Henrietta**
fifth Earl of Laughton, spinster   m. Sir James Swathmore,
m. wife died early   baronet

/   /   /   /

Neville John,   **Penelope**[8] **Geoffrey** 4 sons
sixth Earl of Laughton, m. Sir Nicholas
m. Charlotte Hayward Bellington

1. Charles Assolant, first baron, knighted by William the Conqueror at Hasti
   1066.
2. Baron Assolant abducted the daughter of the duc de Saxe and married ⊾
   possibly for political reasons. He received the Abbey and the village of Ashing
   from William, duc of Normandy, as a wedding gift.
3. The duc de Saxe placed a curse on the Assolant (later Ashington) line to reve⊾
   his daughter's betrayal.
4. Lady Caroline Ashington ran away with a French officer and was disowned.
5. Adrian Bellington, a wealthy sea trader, purchased an obscure baronetcy
   Hampshire.

```
                          Sir Adrian Bellington, baronet⁵
                          m. Lucy Stanton
                                    /
```

David (2nd son)⁶ m. Ann Bellington	Ann Bellington m. David Ashington	Nicholas Bellington m. local girl
Elizabeth Ashington⁷ m. Andrew Bellington (cousin)		Andrew m. Elizabeth (cousin)

Nicholas Bellington,⁹
seventh Earl (temporarily),
m. Lady Penelope Ashington

- David Ashington made a mésalliance with a Cit's daughter and was disowned by his family.
- Elizabeth Ashington married her cousin, Andrew Bellington. Both died in a boating accident when Nicholas was five.
- Penelope Ashington was betrothed to Edward Hayward, Viscount Clayton, Charlotte's brother.
- Nicholas Bellington inherited his grandfather's small estate in Hampshire together with the title. Later he inherited Laughton Abbey and became the seventh Earl of Laughton.

PROLOGUE

The Letter

"But that is preposterous!" Lady Octavia Ashington exclaimed in shocked accents. "It cannot be true, my dear Penelope!" She paused to gaze repressively at her niece's pale face, her needlework momentarily forgotten in her ample lap.

"But it says so right here in the letter, Aunt," Lady Penelope Ashington insisted, her voice quavering slightly with suppressed emotion.

"Nonsense, child," Lady Octavia snorted. "There must be some mistake; take my word for it."

"I wish I could," Penelope replied in a low voice. "But Mr. Hamilton seems to be quite convinced of the authenticity of the information he received, Aunt. They are both dead," she added after an anguished pause, during which she read the solicitor's letter through again slowly, praying that in some miraculous way her aunt might be right.

"I simply refuse to believe that two vigorous, athletic English gentlemen such as your brother Neville and our dear Edward would allow themselves to be overcome by heathens, my love. So set your mind at rest. Before you know it, the two of them will be back at the Abbey and we can get on with your marriage plans. Yours and Charlotte's, too, naturally."

Penelope looked up, startled. "Charlotte!" she exclaimed. "How selfish of me. I had forgotten about poor Charlotte. However will I tell her that her brother and fiancé have been murdered by bandits out there in the Indian jungle?" The awful finality of these words dissolved her initial reluctance to accept

1

the tragic news contained in Mr. Hamilton's terse missive, and she felt a hot tear inch down her cheek.

Her aunt threw aside the cushion cover she was embroidering, pulled herself out of the deep armchair, and moved across to put a plump, motherly arm around her niece's shoulders. "There, there, child," she murmured, sitting down beside Penelope on the green chintz sofa. "Don't take on so, Penny, my love. It's probably all a hum, you know. Mr. Hamilton has doubtless got his facts mixed up. Here," she said bracingly, "let me have a look at his letter." She plucked the offending sheet from her niece's limp fingers and perused it carefully.

Penelope dabbed at her eyes with one of the delicate handkerchiefs her aunt embroidered for her every Christmas, and took a deep breath to steady her nerves. This simply could not be happening to her, she thought. How could Fate be so cruel as to take—in one fell swoop—both her beloved brother Neville—who had always seemed so indestructible, so steadfast and reliable—and her darling Edward. *Oh, Edward,* she thought, her mind going back to the last time she had seen the man with whom she had looked forward to spending the rest of her life. She felt again his strong, impulsive embrace—a rare occurrence in one who prided himself on his unimpeachable manners—on that last morning, and his whispered promise to come back to her soon. Penelope had always considered Edward Hayward, Viscount Clayton, quite impossibly handsome and unattainable—a blond Apollo who brightened her existence with his brilliant presence. She had been entranced with him since she was a little girl in pinafore and pigtails. And then the unexpected miracle had happened. Edward had come down from Oxford that summer of her nineteenth birthday and noticed her. Really *noticed* her, she thought, remembering the thrill of suddenly becoming the object of her dream lover's attention.

Penelope sighed. If Mr. Hamilton's news were true, her life might as well end now, she mused, this very afternoon, the fifteenth day of July, 1814. Visions of a solitary headstone in the ancient Ashington cemetery floated into her mind, and she was considering the touching effect her premature death might have on future generations of Ashingtons, when she recalled that there would be no more Ashingtons. Her brother Neville was the last of their line. Some stranger would undoubtedly inherit the title and move into Laughton Abbey. *Into her home!*

Penelope shuddered at the implications of such an eventuality. What would happen to her if the new earl were unfriendly? His wife—if he had one—would definitely not want an Ashington running loose in the Abbey. Actually two, she thought, because Aunt Octavia was an Ashington, too. What would become of them? She knew that her life at Laughton Abbey had been exceptionally placid, comfortable, and safe, and if occasionally she had quailed at the predictable perfection of her future with Edward, she had never felt the threat of uncertainty she did now. With Neville and Edward gone from her life, as Mr. Hamilton had insisted—and she was beginning to believe—they were, Penelope felt adrift and unprotected. This house that she loved so much would no longer be home to her, she realised with a shock. The new earl had every right to ask them to leave.

"Poppycock!" Lady Octavia exclaimed suddenly, startling her niece out of her unpleasant reverie.

Penelope glanced at her aunt, and the stern expression on Lady Octavia's comely face brought a chill to her heart. With sudden insight, she understood why her aunt was adamantly refusing to accept the solicitor's news. Laughton Abbey had been her aunt's only home for over forty years. She, too, had been born in the big bedroom on the third floor where Penelope herself had come into the world. Penelope felt an overpowering rush of affection for this woman who had been like a mother to her and Neville after the Countess of Laughton, their own beautiful, fragile mother, had succumbed to pneumonia when Penelope was twelve. With a fierce determination which surprised her, Penelope silently vowed that she would do whatever was necessary to ensure that her aunt would not have to leave the home of her childhood.

"Who is this Bellington fellow?" demanded Lady Octavia brusquely. "Never say that we are to have a total stranger thrust upon us? And a mushroom to boot, I wouldn't doubt," she added caustically.

This apparent capitulation to the inevitable caused a feeling of dread to seep into Penelope's heart. "So you think Mr.

Hamilton is correct?" she asked, more sharply than she had intended.

Her aunt looked at her speculatively. "I didn't say that, miss. And don't you go putting words in my mouth, young lady." She looked so affronted that Penelope smiled weakly.

"I confess that I did not pay attention to that part of Mr. Hamilton's letter, Aunt. What does he say about Mr. Bellington?"

"Sir Nicholas Bellington," her aunt corrected her, a hint of disdain in her voice. "Some obscure baronet from Hampshire, according to Hamilton. Apparently he is the next heir to the earldom."

"I always thought that Cousin Geoffrey was the next in line for the title," Penelope remarked, feeling guilty that they could be discussing Neville's replacement so casually.

"Geoffrey Swathmore? Well, so did I, come to think of it. Although I can't say I gave it much thought, of course. I had assumed that with Neville's marriage to Charlotte, we would soon have an army of little Ashingtons running about—" Her voice faltered, and Penelope realised belatedly that her aunt was more shaken by the news of Neville's death than she had appeared.

Impulsively, she reached out and clasped Lady Octavia's hands, only to find them cold and clammy. Resolutely pushing her own fears aside, Penelope set about comforting her beloved aunt.

"Aunt Henrietta always talks as though Geoffrey were the next in line," she remarked bracingly. "And of course, Geoffrey would like nothing better than to step into Neville's shoes. I can't say I would welcome him as the new master of Laughton Abbey, though. He is so impossibly pompous and condescending." She paused for a moment, her brow furrowed in thought.

"A weaseling Jackstraw if ever I saw one," Lady Octavia snapped with some of her natural asperity. "I can't for the life of me understand how a sweet-natured ninny like my sister Henrietta could have produced such a mincing dandy as that boy Geoffrey. Heaven help us all if the four younger lads turn out to be such simpering peacocks. Must be bad blood in Sir James's family somewhere, I don't doubt. That's what you get for marrying into the lower ranks," she added darkly. "But Henry would have him. Threw our poor Papa into the devil of a rage, she did." She paused in her diatribe—which Penelope had heard many times before—as if to savour the infrequent family upheavals in the placid unfolding of her life.

Penelope took advantage of the hiatus to steer her aunt in a more pertinent direction. "I wonder if Mr. Hamilton could have mistaken his facts, Aunt. I cannot recall ever hearing the name Bellington."

Lady Octavia was silent for so long that Penelope feared she had not heard her remark. "No, child," she said at last, her pale blue eyes clouding over with unhappy memories. "This Bellington fellow must indeed be the grandson of my Uncle David, just as Hamilton points out here." She waved the solicitor's letter vigorously. "It occurs to me that there may well be a streak of recklessness in the Ashingtons, my love." She turned to smile tentatively at her niece. "After all these years, I had forgotten all about Uncle David," she mused, almost to herself. "That's where Henrietta got her stubbornness, no doubt. From poor Uncle David."

She lapsed into another silent meditation that lasted until they were interrupted by the Ashington butler, who came into the small Yellow Saloon to enquire if the ladies were ready for their tea.

"Why, yes, Featherbow. That would be nice," Lady Octavia replied. "I did not realise it was getting so late."

As soon as the butler had closed the door, Penelope could not contain her curiosity. "What happened to poor Uncle David?"

Lady Octavia regarded her for several moments before replying. "He married beneath him," she said at last. "Just as Henrietta did. Only Uncle David's choice was much *much* worse than my sister's. At least Sir James's title had been in the family for several generations. David's father-in-law was a commoner, a mere Cit—there is no other word for it." Penelope saw her aunt's nose rise a fraction of an inch and smiled to herself. Lady Octavia was possessed of the same stiff-necked pride in her family lineage as all the Ashingtons. With the exception of those who fell from grace, Penelope mused. She herself had a fierce pride in her illustrious ancestors and was generally in accord with her aunt's sentiments, although she secretly considered her Aunt Henrietta's enduring passion for her sweet, affable Sir James infinitely romantic. Of course, Lady Penelope Ashington—she had often told herself—would never commit the ultimate indiscretion of falling in love with a gentleman so obviously ineligible as her Uncle James.

Another thought struck her. "But didn't you say that the new heir is *Sir* Nicholas? A baronet, I believe you said. How did that come about?"

Lady Octavia snorted her disgust. "The unconscionable mushroom actually *bought* his title," she explained. "Apparently the pretentious old fool was full of juice at the time."

"Aunt Octavia!" Penelope cried, amused—as she always was—at her aunt's frequent lapses into vulgarity. "Did you ever meet the Bellingtons?"

Her aunt stared at her in horror. "Of course not, child!" she exclaimed crossly. "Our Grandpapa disowned Uncle David entirely. We were forbidden to mention his name, let alone his reprehensible connexions. He never came back to Laughton Abbey again, you know. I cannot even remember what he looked like."

"How sad," Penelope remarked softly, wondering how this cousin she had never met, whose grandfather had been banished from the family estate, would feel about coming back to his ancestral home at last as lord and master. "He must hate us all," she murmured without realising she had spoken aloud.

"Now, don't you get any missish ideas into your head, Penelope," her aunt remarked shortly. "Bellington will undoubtedly gloat at the prospect of acquiring such an illustrious title. But as I said before, my dear, the whole thing is probably a hum and there is no need to fly into a pelter over something which may not even come to pass."

Privately Penelope was not so sure that her unknown cousin would be as awed by his new estate or as biddable as her aunt imagined. She felt a brief flash of pity for the almost unsurmountable obstacles this rustic stranger would encounter when he came to take possession of his title and lands. Unlike Neville, who had been raised with the expectation of one day stepping into his father's shoes, this newcomer would be like an intruder in a world which would be totally foreign to him. But then he *was* an intruder, wasn't he? she reminded herself. And why should she care if his table-manners were abominable or if he could not ride to hounds or drive a curricle to an inch as a gentleman should? After all, he was no gentleman and could not have set foot in White's or Boodle's; he would not belong to the Four-in-Hand Club or receive vouchers from the patronesses of Almack's. She smiled to herself at the very idea. He was no better than he ought to be, and it was the direst misfortune that had thrust him into a position of greatness he was ill-equipped to handle with anything approaching the dignity expected of the Earl of Langhton. She sighed. Aunt Octavia would be in her glory pointing out to the new earl how very short he fell of the elevated standards expected of an Ashington.

"But what if Mr. Hamilton is right, Aunt? Are we supposed to sit around waiting for this stranger to come and throw us out of our home?" she demanded. Some of her fears must have been revealed in her tone, for Lady Octavia glanced at her apprehensively.

"There is no need to upset yourself, dear. And I expect it will be many a month before this whole imbroglio is resolved. It says here," she flicked the solicitor's letter derisively, "that Bellington is stationed in Brussels at the moment. With Wellington's army, it seems, although the new duke himself is back in England, I understand. Now that Napoleon is safely exiled at Elba, we can expect to see our troops coming home, of course, but Hamilton says that will take some time. We may not see the new earl until Christmas."

"Never say that he is a foot soldier?" Penelope exclaimed, her worst fears about the respectability of their new relative taking sudden shape in her mind.

"Of course not, child," Lady Octavia responded tartly. "That would be the outside of enough. Fortunately for the reputation of the Ashingtons, the man seems to be an officer. Hamilton is not sure exactly what his rank is, but he—"

"Then he cannot be such a rudesby as we imagined, Aunt," Penelope interrupted. "From what I hear, it takes a considerable sum to purchase a commission in a respectable regiment."

"Who said anything about a respectable regiment?" Lady

Octavia cut in with brutal frankness. "That old reprobate of a grandfather of his would hardly have the connexions to get the boy into a crack regiment. We should be thankful that he is at least a lieutenant or captain or such and not taking the king's shilling as an ordinary soldier." This thought was evidently so distasteful to her aunt that Penelope was treated to one of Lady Octavia's more disdainful sneers and a fierce, quelling glance from that lady's piercing blue eyes.

For the second time since reading Mr. Hamilton's shattering news, Penelope felt it in her heart to pity the unsuspecting stranger. Before she could come to her absent cousin's defence, however, Featherbow arrived with the tea-tray, and by the time both ladies had consumed their first cup of China brew, Lady Octavia had brought their discussion closer to home.

"Tomorrow, if it is fine, we will drive over to Clayton Manor to inform poor Charlotte of this distressing news and make arrangements for a memorial service."

Penelope quailed at the thought of having to break her best friend's heart with the unhappy tidings of her double loss—she still shied away from thinking of Neville or her beloved Edward as dead—and much as she loved Charlotte, she dreaded the inevitable scene that awaited her on the morrow. Her own sense of loss was devastating, but her temperament forbade the hysterical weeping Charlotte would indulge in. She cringed at the thought of such a display of unbridled sensibility.

If only she could weep herself, Penelope thought as she prepared for bed that night, she might feel some relief from the overwhelming sense of sorrow that left her distraught. But Lady Penelope had never seen the use of tears except to make a lady's eyes red and unsightly, so tears did not come when she needed them. Instead, her heart was filled with an increasing fear that her quiet, predictable, comfortable life had been irrevocably threatened by dark forces beyond her control. What these forces were she could only guess, but they were real enough to keep her awake and restless far into the night.

CHAPTER ONE

Enemy Camp

By the time Christmas had come and gone at Laughton Abbey, no word had been received from the new master, and the Ashington ladies had long since become tired of waiting to welcome the mysterious stranger with the pomp and ceremony Lady Octavia considered fitting for the new Earl of Laughton.

"Perhaps he does not want to be an earl at all," Penelope had the temerity to suggest one morning at the breakfast table, after Featherbow had served her aunt her usual substantial helping of coddled eggs and York ham, and retired to the kitchen for a fresh pot of tea.

Lady Octavia looked up at her niece in astonishment. "Fiddlesticks!" she snapped. "What kind of sapskull would not want to be an earl, especially one with such an illustrious history as ours? You are being ridiculous, Penelope."

"Only think, Aunt," Penelope continued, quite as if Lady Octavia had not spoken. "What a sad letdown a quiet English existence must be after the exciting events on the Continent during these last few months. It's not every day that an emperor abdicates, as Napoleon did last April, followed by the signing of the Treaty of Paris in May. I wish I could have been there." Penelope sighed at the thought. "And the newspapers said that Wellington's staff was in Vienna with Lord Castlereagh for the opening of the Congress."

"It is highly unlikely that Bellington is a member of the duke's staff, my dear," her aunt scoffed. "Mr. Hamilton would have told us so. If you want my candid opinion, the scoundrel is deliberately shirking his responsibilities to the estate. The man's obviously a cursed care-for-nobody. It's not fair that you should have to bear the whole burden of managing this big estate, my love. That is a man's responsibility, and if Bellington had the slightest sense of what is due to his rank and position, he would have been here months ago to relieve you of this onerous task."

"It is not onerous in the least," Penelope protested automatically. She had had this same argument with her aunt many times since that afternoon last July when news of her brother's death had arrived to disrupt the placid tranquillity of life at Laughton Abbey. "I am as well versed in the running of the estate as Neville ever was. And as you well know, Aunt, that was one of the reasons poor Neville felt he could go off to India for a year, secure in the knowledge that Laughton Abbey would prosper in his absence. He trusted me and——"

"Yes," her aunt cut in. "But it is one thing to take care of things in your brother's absence, and quite another to lay out your own blunt to defray costs which should rightly be paid by the estate."

"Last year was not a profitable one," Penelope reminded her aunt. "And the tenants suffered from one of the coldest winters in history. Even in London the Thames froze over, they say. And then we had that smallpox epidemic in the village, and the roof blew off the church in that storm last November——"

"Enough, enough," Lady Octavia interrupted crossly. "I have heard all these woes before, dear, but there was no reason why you should have paid to have a new roof put up. No reason at all."

Penelope smiled. "Do you mean to tell me that you would have sat there every Sunday morning with the rain and sleet falling on your head, Aunt?" she asked, a mischievous twinkle in her lilac eyes. "I can't say I would have relished the discomfort myself." Penelope motioned to Featherbow to refill her cup with fresh tea.

"Now you are being ridiculous again, Penelope," her aunt scolded. "And changing the subject as you always do when I mention the depletion of your own fortune to cover estate expenses. Let this rogue Bellington pay his own bills," her aunt muttered with evident ill-humour. "If the blackguard ever deigns to come back to England to take up his responsibilities, of course."

Penelope had to laugh at her aunt's irrational dislike for the new head of the family. "We do not know that he is a rogue, Aunt," she said gently. "He may turn out to be perfectly respectable."

"And pigs will fly, no doubt," Lady Octavia snorted. "You are naive, child, if you believe that a Bellington could be either a gentleman or respectable. They are all encroaching peasants, believe me."

"He is a soldier," Penelope insisted stubbornly. "An English officer who has doubtless risked his life for his country. For the safety of English women and their children. For *you* and for *me*, Aunt." She paused, surprised at her sudden vehemence in defence of a man she knew nothing about, and whom she had every reason to fear. She laughed self-consciously. "Yes, I know what you will say, Aunt. I am being ridiculous again. And you may be right. But I cannot help feeling we are being unfair to this Nicholas Bellington, whoever he is."

At Laughton Abbey, winter gave way slowly to a late spring, and the delicate snowdrops bravely emerged in drifts from the banked snow, followed by phalanxes of squat crocuses in brilliant hues of blue and yellow. In March, this rural tranquillity was rudely shattered by the news that Napoleon had escaped from Elba and landed in France. The splendour of the golden daffodils had come and gone and April had run into May before the Ashington ladies heard that the Allied Forces were making a stand against the emperor's forces just outside Brussels. But it was not until the end of June, ten days after the event, that they received news of Napoleon's defeat at Waterloo and his second abdication on June 22.

By mutual consent they had refrained from mentioning Nicholas Bellington's name ever since news of the battle and the tremendous losses suffered by both sides had reached them. They avidly perused the seemingly unending lists of dead and wounded which reached them every week from various sources, but the new earl's name had not been there.

Which did not prove that Nicholas Bellington had survived, Penelope told herself several days later—for perhaps the twentieth time—as she cantered her mare Bluebelle back from an afternoon call on Charlotte Hayward. The absence of his name from those terrible, heartbreaking lists was no guarantee that he had not been killed in action. All she could do—and Penelope found herself doing so more often of late—was pray for her cousin's safe return.

The mare's suddenly pointed ears alerted Penelope to the presence of the two horsemen even before she noticed them disappearing round a bend in the driveway ahead of her. Something awkward about their appearance caused a frisson of alarm to run through her, and she urged the mare into a gallop. As she drew closer, she saw that her initial impression had been correct. The men rode close together and hunched in their saddles; the larger of the two seemed to be supporting the other as if he were in danger of toppling from the saddle. The horses walked with heads lowered, reins loosely dangling, hooves rhythmically swinging forward as if propelled by instinct rather than purpose. Neither men nor beasts paid the slightest heed to her, although they must have heard her approach from behind.

The two riders came to a halt before the shallow steps leading up to the double doors, which opened to reveal Featherbow staring uncertainly at the visitors. It was here that Penelope caught up with them. As she dismounted and threw the reins to a groom, she saw the larger of the two—a veritable giant of a man with a thick black brush of a beard—dismount awkwardly, keeping a firm grip on his younger companion, who seemed to be unconscious.

Penelope called to the butler to assist the strangers, but before Featherbow could do so, the black-bearded giant had lifted the other man from the saddle, as one would a very young boy, and stood him on his feet, a massive arm around his waist to support him when he swayed noticeably.

Only then did the giant turn a pair of shrewd black eyes towards Penelope. "Is this Laughton Abbey, ma'am?" he asked in a surprisingly soft voice touched with a Scottish lilt.

Jolted from her paralysis, Penelope stepped forward. "Indeed it is," she acknowledged. "It looks as though your companion is in dire need of medical attention." Even as she spoke, the younger man, whose chin was resting on his chest, sagged heavily against the giant, who held him upright effortlessly. Their clothes were thickly coated with the dust and grime of travel on English roads in summertime, but the younger wore a tattered officer's uniform, and Penelope guessed that he must be a gentleman.

"Aye, that he is, ma'am." The black eyes regarded her speculatively.

"Then we must do something about it," Penelope added briskly. "Featherbow, send for Dr. Kentwick immediately, and ask Mrs. Cooper to have a room prepared for the invalid in the guest wing. And send out a couple of footmen to help the gentleman upstairs."

The giant grinned down at her, his teeth flashing whitely among the black bristles of his beard. "That won't be necessary, thank ye kindly, ma'am. I can handle the lad well enough if you'll just tell me where to put him."

"Who is he?" Penelope asked, stepping closer to the drooping figure in an attempt to see his face. As she did so, the sick man raised his head, and Penelope drew in her breath sharply. He was older than he had seemed at first, definitely in his thirties, she thought. His eyes were dark and sunken and glazed with pain. They looked at her without seeing her. A thick black stubble covered his hollow cheeks and square jaw, and his neck—rising from the grubby collar of a shirt that had evidently not been changed recently—seemed to Penelope to be unnaturally thin and vulnerable. But the worst part about this stranger's ravaged face, the part that made Penelope feel slightly nauseated, was a hideous, gaping wound that started on his left temple and traversed his entire face, ending with a slight, incongruous curl beside his uncompromising mouth.

Penelope never knew how long she stood gazing in undisguised horror and pity at the dark stranger before his head fell forward again on his chest, and she noticed that his hair, tangled and in need of washing, was as dark and curly as his friend's beard. The thought flashed through her mind that it could well harbour colonies of lice, and she fought the urge to step back.

Her gaze swung away from the distressing sight before her and met the cool stare of the giant. Instinctively, Penelope realised that he had observed her examination of the sick man and read every thought that had passed through her head. She felt uncomfortable under the man's appraising stare and was about to reprimand him for his rudeness when he spoke again.

"He may be dying," he said simply, ignoring her question. He spoke as if dying were an everyday affair that should not cause her too much alarm. His tone was almost apologetic, as if he regretted the inconvenience of his friend's condition, and Penelope wondered what manner of man this giant was who could speak of dying with such calmness, as though Death's presence was a familiar part of his life.

And then she knew. Of course, she thought. He was a soldier, one who had seen battle and the death that always accompanied such feats of men. She glanced at the younger man again, and it seemed to her that he sagged more heavily against his friend's shoulder. Could he actually be about to die? she wondered. Here on her very doorstep? The thought appalled her, and she turned briskly back to the giant.

"Nonsense," she retorted, knowing that Lady Octavia would approve of her decisiveness. "Bring him inside," she ordered, once again in control of the situation. "We must make the poor man as comfortable as possible before Dr. Kentwick arrives."

She led the way into the house and up the sweeping marble staircase to the third floor, the bearded giant close on her heels, carrying the sick man like a baby cradled in his arms. They found the housekeeper overseeing the preparation of a guest-room in the west wing, while one of the upstairs maids took the chill off the freshly laid sheets with the warming-pan.

Penelope quailed inwardly when the big man laid his filthy burden on the pristine bed and stared to unbutton the younger man's shirt. The invalid's head had fallen back on the feather pillow, eyes now closed and thin lips relaxed as in sleep. Or in death, Penelope thought, deeply moved a second time by the pathetically ravaged face, split from brow to chin by the ugly wound. Even if this man lives, she thought—for the first time conscious of the possibility of his dying—that scar will mark him for the rest of his life, set him apart from other men as one whom Death has touched and passed on.

The sight of the giant pulling his friend's shirt out of his breeches reminded Penelope that she should not be standing there watching a man being undressed.

"I shall send in a footman to help you with that," she said quickly, turning to leave.

The giant straightened up and looked at her with something like censure in his black eyes, Penelope thought. He was reading her thoughts again, she realised.

"No need for that either," he said softly. "Me and the colonel have been through many a bad time together. Thank ye kindly, ma'am." He turned away as if she had ceased to exist.

This time she was certain that he was rebuking her. And somehow holding himself aloof. Holding them both aloof, for that matter, as though he were reluctant to allow her to encroach on the private male world they obviously shared. But he had let something slip, which she picked up instantly.

"Colonel?" she repeated, determined to break through this stranger's insolence. "Colonel who?"

The giant turned calculating eyes on her again, regarding her for several moments before replying.

"Colonel Nicholas Bellington," he said distinctly. "At your service, ma'am."

Penelope's eyes flew to the man on the bed. So this battered wreck of a creature was her Cousin Nicholas, was he? She had envisioned her long lost cousin's arrival at Laughton Abbey under many different circumstances, but never had she imagined that the new earl would arrive on his own doorstep accompanied by a great insolent ruffian, whose first comment would be that his master might be dying.

Penelope glared coldly at the big man, whose regard was far too penetrating for her comfort. "And I am Lady Penelope Ashington," she said, throwing all the force of her rank and breeding into the words. "I shall bring the doctor up as soon as he arrives."

So, she thought to herself as she descended to the small Yellow Saloon, where Lady Octavia would be sitting over her tea, the moment they had dreaded for almost a year had finally come.

The black sheep of the family had come home at last.

In the days that followed, Penelope often wondered how long her cousin would be destined to enjoy the comfort of his new residence. Dr. Kentwick had descended to the Yellow

Saloon with a somber expression on his weathered countenance after his initial examination of the patient that afternoon.

"Well, Doctor?" Penelope had urged impatiently, breaking the uneasy silence.

"I wish I had something encouraging to report, my lady," Kentwick replied, accepting Lady Octavia's offer of a cup of tea and taking up a stand before the empty hearth. "But unless his lordship is a good deal stronger than he appears at present, I am sorry to say that there is little likelihood of him surviving."

This plain speaking was greeted by an uncomfortable silence on the part of the two Ashington ladies, and the finality of the doctor's statement sent a chill down Penelope's spine.

"I know the wound on the colonel's face is serious and in danger of becoming putrid," she felt impelled to argue. "But surely even such a deep cut may be treated successfully? I remember how you saved the Turners' youngest boy last year when his leg was gored by Squire Rogers's prize Jersey bull." She paused, remembering all too vividly the child's bloody, mangled leg and his high-pitched keening cries, which had haunted her dreams for many months afterwards.

The doctor shot her a tired, commiserating glance. "If it were merely a matter of the face wound, my lady, I would be infinitely more optimistic about his lordship's recovery. But his left arm is broken in two places—apparently when he was thrown from his horse, his man tells me. He also has a considerable amount of shrapnel in his right thigh from a mortar explosion. The colonel must lead a charmed life," the doctor added thoughtfully. "He should have been blown to bits, but his horse took the brunt of the damage. And then there seems to be some internal bleeding, besides two broken ribs. It is not surprising that his lordship is burning up with fever. It appears they landed in Dover a week ago and have been on the road since then without proper medical attention."

The doctor's grim evaluation was followed by several moments of silence, broken eventually by Lady Octavia. "Are you saying that we have a dying man on our hands, Doctor?" she enquired bluntly.

"I am afraid so, my lady," Kentwick responded shortly. "His lordship's arm and ribs were set by an army doctor in Brussels, his man tells me. I have changed his dressings and cleaned out his facial wound, which was considered only superficial at the time. It has since become infected and will require stitches. However, what concerns me most is the mortar fragments in his thigh, which was so swollen and infected that I cannot be sure that I removed them all. And I don't like the fever he is running. It is unnaturally high, and I greatly fear that in his weakened condition, his lordship may not be able to withstand it much longer."

These grizzly details of her cousin's condition made Penelope cringe. The colonel had appeared already ravaged by fever upon his arrival several hours ago, and by now—if what Dr. Kentwick said was true—he would be fighting a final battle he was not likely to win.

"Is there nothing at all we can do, Doctor?" she heard her aunt enquire with her usual forcefulness. "Both Penelope and I are competent in the sick-room, as you well know. We cannot just sit still and let this young man die for want of trying."

"I was going to recommend sending for old Mrs. Henderson from the village," Dr. Kentwick replied, setting his empty cup down on the tea-tray. "The colonel will require round-the-clock nursing." The doctor paused briefly before adding, "If he lives through the night, that is."

Lady Octavia gave a small snort of impatience. "Of course he will," she said brusquely. "Penelope and I will see to it." She motioned to her niece to ring for Featherbow to remove the tea-tray. "Always the pessimist, aren't you, Kentwick? Why, I remember only last autumn you predicted that poor Polly Brewster's youngest would be carried off with the colic, and here the wee mite is, as healthy as anyone could wish. All it took was a bit of determination, as I told you at the time."

The doctor glanced at Penelope, wry amusement in his tired blue eyes. "Your aunt is right, of course. My diagnosis of little Mary Brewster was premature. But Lord Laughton is quite another matter, my lady. If you really wish to take on such formidable odds, I will leave some written instructions for you to follow."

"Of course, we are going to nurse the colonel," Lady Octavia insisted. "And send Mrs. Henderson over by all means."

"Very well," said the doctor, removing a small writing tablet from his pocket and jotting down a list of instructions. "I shall return this evening to take another look at that leg, and if Mrs. Henderson is free, I shall bring her with me."

After Dr. Kentwick had left, Penelope accompanied her aunt up to the sick-room, where they found the colonel's man—whose name Dr. Kentwick had told them was Samuel Hardy—bathing his master's burning forehead with a wet cloth. The sight of the giant man's huge hands occupied with such gentle duties was strangely touching, and the thought crossed Penelope's mind that these two men did indeed share a world of which she knew nothing at all. Mindful of the giant's previous insolence, Penelope smiled as she came into the room.

"Here, let me do that, Samuel," she said, taking the cloth from the big hands and dipping it into the bowl of cool lemon water. "You must be ready for a meal yourself. Lady Octavia and I will sit with the colonel while you go down to the kitchen. Then, I suggest you get some rest. Featherbow will show you where your room is."

Penelope had expected the giant to challenge her orders, and she found herself tensing for battle as she gently laid the damp cloth on the sick man's brow. She paused there for a moment before sliding it down his stubble-spiked cheek and under his forbiddingly square jaw.

She was unnaturally conscious of Samuel's looming presence beside her as she concentrated on the patient, but she deliberately ignored the tension she felt emanating from the giant man. If he chose to defy her, Penelope thought with unusual belligerence, he would discover quickly enough who was mistress of this house. At least she would continue in that position until the new earl was well enough—the alternatives could not bear considering—to decide her fate. Hers and Aunt Octavia's. Would he allow them to remain at Laughton Abbey, as tradition dictated a new titleholder would any unmarried females in his household? Or would he order them to remove to the Dower House, out of sight, out of mind?

As Penelope felt the roughness of her cousin's cheek under the pressure of the cloth, she wondered what kind of a man he really was. She already knew him to be unconcerned with establishing his position as the seventh Earl of Laughton. Most men would have arrived post-haste on the doorstep to seize the rank and everything it entailed. Nicholas Bellington had ignored his good fortune for an entire year and only arrived—perhaps under duress—on the point of death and in no fit condition to assume the rights and privileges of his new title. So what was he really like? she wondered.

Penelope examined her cousin's emaciated features and could find no hint of softness there. Even discounting the ravages of war, by no stretch of the imagination could this stranger be called handsome. There was something forbidding—almost threatening, she thought—about that square jaw and the thick black brows that occasionally drew together over his nose as if in response to a pain not entirely smothered by the laudanum Dr. Kentwick had administered earlier. No, her new cousin did not strike her as a man given to social niceties. He would be a hard man to deal with, she knew instinctively, and the thought was not comforting.

She sighed and glanced up. The giant still stood beside her, intently watching her ministrations, as if he were unsure of her capabilities. Torn between exasperation and a reluctant sympathy, Penelope smiled up at him.

"If you are to be any use to me in caring for my cousin," she said lightly, "you must get some food and rest, Samuel."

After an infinitesimal pause, during which Penelope felt that she was being measured against some unknown standard, his white teeth flashed briefly in the bramble of beard. "If you say so, milady," Samuel said in his soft Scottish drawl and silently left the room.

Penelope's gaze returned to the patient in the bed. If only she could manage the master as peacefully as she seemed to have managed the man, she thought, life at Laughton Abbey might flow on with nary a ripple.

Before this comfortable notion had time to crystallize, however, her cousin's black brows bunched in an unmistakable scowl, and Penelope suspected that any future harmony between the Ashingtons and this dark stranger was not written in the stars.

CHAPTER TWO

The Ancient Curse

Nicholas opened his eyes to a dark, unfamiliar world.

He lay completely still for several minutes, his body rigid with tension, trying to get his bearings. Where was he? he wondered. Not in his cluttered digs in Brussels, that was certain. Nor out in the field with his men; things were much too quiet for that to be the case. For one shattering moment it crossed his mind that he might be dead. Memories of his last conscious moments came crowding into his brain, jostling one another in a tangled morass of sensations. The incoherent shout from one of his men, causing him to whirl his horse, fast enough to evade death but not fast enough to duck the dexterous sabre thrust. With a shudder he relived the moment when he had turned to confront death—the French officer, sabre raised high in the air, face twisted into a grimace of killing lust. In the earsplitting racket of the pitched battle around him, Nicholas remembered the sudden imaginary silence in which the sword had sliced down—an endless, shimmering arc of death. A savage wrench on Hannibal's reins had put him out of range. Almost. The caressing sensation of the steel as it sliced through his cheek. The taste of salty sweetness as the blood and sweat ran down into his mouth. He shuddered.

He *must* be dead, he thought, not without a certain twinge of irony.

His first conscious sensation was one of being on fire, and this seemed appropriate enough. He had never given much credence to the traditional depiction of Hell, but he must have been wrong, he thought wryly. Fire and brimstone. That's where he was. In Hell.

He tried to stretch his cramped legs, and an unspeakable pain—so intense it made his parched lips peel back in a silent scream—shot through his right thigh. He struggled for several minutes to remain conscious, then lost the battle and slid back into darkness, amidst fading memories of deafening mortar fire, the shock of the direct hit, Hannibal's terrifying death scream as the horse shuddered under the impact, stumbled, and fell beneath him, his life escaping in a frightening whoosh of air. Yes, he must be dead. His last coherent thought.

When he again fought his way up from the depths of unconsciousness, the fires of Hell seemed to have abated. Nicholas felt a blessed coolness on his face. Someone—undoubtedly Sam—was bathing his brow and cheek with a lemon-scented cloth. What perversity had inspired the black rogue to use lemon-water? Nicholas wondered idly. He tried to smile, but his face hurt too much.

The cool caressing ceased abruptly.

"Are you awake, Colonel?"

A woman's voice, he thought, richly musical but tinged with apprehension. What was a woman doing in his lodgings? Colette? No, it couldn't be Colette, he thought. Not with a voice like that. Besides, he was no longer in Brussels.

And then it started to come back to him. The woefully inadequate hospital, the overworked army surgeons, the make-shift sick wards where rows and rows of wounded and dying soldiers were tended by volunteers from among the townsfolk. He had been brought there by Sam—who had miraculously emerged unscathed from the inferno of battle. His wounds, summarily patched up by a harried surgeon, had been pro-nounced superficial, and it had been left to Sam to change his dressings, bring him water, and finally get him out of there when his giant henchman had discovered young Rowland, a raw recruit from his own regiment, in dire need of a bed. Not that the medics could do much for the poor lad, Nicholas remembered. Both the boy's legs had been blown off. He would probably die anyway, and his eyes already held that secret knowledge even as his young face pleaded with his colonel to tell him that things would be all right.

Nicholas had done so and ordered the lad to report for duty when he was back on his feet. Neither he nor Sam had so much as glanced at the emptiness under the sheets where the boy's legs should have been. Rowland had been disproportionately grateful for his colonel's condescension and had even returned Nicholas's salute smartly as Sam escorted Nicholas outside.

"Colonel?" the woman's voice insisted, and Nicholas felt a small hand slip under his head as a glass of cool water was held to his dry lips.

He drank greedily, his mind still half submerged in the parching heat of the battlefield.

It was the scent of lilacs that chased the demon memories away from his feverish brain. There were no lilacs on the battlefield, of that Nicholas was quite certain. Nor in the dreary field-hospitals. That was one of the few things he could be certain of in this strange new world of lemon-water, and musical voices, and lilacs. For one wrenching moment, Nicholas imagined himself a child again at Bellington Hall, his grandmother's tidy little estate in Hampshire, where he had spent many a blissful summer hunting birds' nests among the massed rhododendrons along the driveway. And in the lilac bushes beside the handsome Tudor manor house, he remembered. Lilacs always reminded him of his beloved grandmother. Nicholas could still remember the desolation he had felt upon her death. In his loneliness, he had turned to his aging grandfather, who finally—after his wife's sudden death—complied with her wishes and bought his grandson a pair of colours in the 18th Hussars, the crack regiment he had himself belonged to as a young man.

The lilac perfume was closer now. He sensed the woman leaning over him to adjust his pillow. He breathed the scent in deeply and opened his eyes.

At first all Nicholas could discern was a pale halo of hair standing out in seductive disarray around a pixie face. The light from the window was behind her, and her hair glowed with a soft vibrancy he had never before seen in a woman.

As his eyes gradually focussed and became accustomed to the dim light, Nicholas found himself gazing into the delicate violet eyes above him. As he watched, mesmerized by their brilliance, he saw them widen in surprise, then dance with suppressed amusement, then shadow over with apprehension. He was hypnotized, lulled by the comforting nostalgia of his grandmother's world of love, and lilacs, and childhood memories, and only vaguely aware of the uncertainties which nagged at the back of his mind.

Unable to cope with the complexities of the present, Nicholas was about to let himself slip back into sleep when the woman spoke.

"Colonel Bellington?" she murmured softly, a hint of teasing in her voice. "Or perhaps I should call you Cousin Nicholas. Should I not?"

He was instantly jerked out of his nostalgic reverie. His eyes flew open, and he glared coldly up into the violet depths, the fierce hatred so strong in his heart that he spoke without conscious thought.

"You are an Ashington." It was a statement rather than a question, but for the briefest, most transient moment, Nicholas wished he might be mistaken.

The violet eyes registered perplexity, all amusement gone.

"Of course," she said, and Nicholas could almost hear the defiance, the pride, and insupportable condescension in her voice.

"I am Penelope Ashington. Your Cousin Penelope."

Nicholas felt a cold hand clamp down on his heart. So he was at Laughton Abbey at last, he thought bitterly. The Ashington empire. The sacred domain of generations of accursed Ashingtons. He closed his eyes and turned his head away. He wanted nothing to do with any of them, he thought viciously. Especially Ashington females with lilac eyes and golden hair. They were nothing to him. Not even the great-grandfather he shared with this unwanted cousin—that third Earl of Laughton of infamous reputation—could make him wish to acknowledge the connexion.

He would prefer to destroy every last one of them. As a boy he had sworn to do so, ever since he had heard the story of the third earl's perverse cruelty to his younger son David, Nicholas's grandfather. He would not be swayed by the uncanny resemblance between his beloved grandmother and this unwanted cousin with the lilac eyes. He would not be such a fool.

"Get out," he snarled with as much force as he could muster.

When his cousin made no move to go, he repeated his command.

"I said get out," he mumbled, feeling the rage subsiding as he began to slip into darkness again. "Sam? Send Sam."

Nicholas kept his eyes firmly closed, but he heard her light steps move towards the door. They paused for a moment before he heard the door open and close gently behind her.

He took a deep breath of relief. He was temporarily free of them, he thought. Only the faint scent of lilac lingering in the room reminded him, as he slipped once again into unconsciousness, that he was not really free at all.

"Well?" Lady Octavia demanded in her brusque fashion when Penelope walked into the breakfast-room a few moments later. "How is our invalid doing this morning?"

Penelope examined the contents of the chafing dishes on the ancient oak side-board with something less than her usual enthusiasm. Her cousin's first words to her since his arrival in a comatose state a week ago had disturbed her more than she cared to admit, even to herself. She looked with distaste at the dish of coddled eggs, her aunt's favourite, and replaced the cover. No, she thought, she was not in the mood for food this morning. She was more interested in explanations. Why had Cousin Nicholas's dark eyes changed so abruptly from a dreamy, relaxed expression to cold rejection? There could be little doubt that the mention of her name had triggered the reaction in the earl, but Penelope was at a loss to imagine why she had aroused his ire.

"He is still feverish, Aunt," she replied, pouring herself a cup of tea from the squat silver tea-pot. "But he was lucid for the first time this morning and seems to have taken an instant dislike to me."

"What rubbish you do talk, Penelope," her aunt scolded. "The unfortunate man does not know you, so how could he take you in dislike? Thank you, Featherbow," she added, as the butler appeared with a dish of clotted cream. "I know I should not eat cream, of course, but it is so hard to resist with strawberries, I always say." She shot a guilty look at her niece.

Penelope smiled at her aunt's ingenuous excuse for indulging her weakness for rich foods, which Dr. Kentwick had forbidden her to eat. "Besides," she teased, "we all know that clotted cream was invented expressly to eat with strawberries for breakfast, don't we, Aunt?"

"That's enough impertinence from you, miss," Lady Octavia said sternly. "And I'll thank you to say nothing to the good doctor about this lapse of mine, Penelope. Now, tell me, child, what did the colonel say to put you in the hips?"

"He called for Sam, Aunt. Which reminds me, Featherbow," she continued, turning to the butler, "please send Hardy up to his master at once. The colonel seems to be awake and might be induced to take some nourishment."

"And what else?" Lady Octavia demanded, as soon as the butler had closed the door.

Penelope smiled at her aunt, marveling at the intuition which permitted the elder woman to sense the agitation beneath her niece's carefully serene exterior. She had always felt a deep love and admiration for her aunt, but as Penelope grew into womanhood, she had come to depend on her for friendship and guidance as well as affection. Under her bluff exterior, Lady Octavia concealed an understanding heart and a sharp intelligence which Penelope valued highly.

"He growled at me. Told me to get out of his room, in fact," she said simply, knowing that her aunt would take this eccentric behaviour in her stride. She debated trying to explain to Lady Octavia the unsettling sensations she had experienced during that odd exchange with her cousin, and decided against it. Her aunt would accuse her of being missish. Yet Penelope knew she was anything but missish; she also knew what she had felt as she gazed into her cousin's eyes and saw his expression change so suddenly to one of dislike. No, she corrected herself. The colonel's eyes had been full of a much stronger emotion. If it were not so preposterous, she might have called it hatred.

"And what else?" her aunt repeated, without taking her eyes from the cream she was pouring over her dish of strawberries. "Something has upset you, child. I can feel it." She set the cream down with apparent reluctance and took up her spoon. "Tell your old auntie all about it."

Penelope laughed aloud at the expression her aunt had always used with her as a child when something had gone wrong in her sheltered life at Laughton Abbey. "You are *not* old, Aunt."

"And you are avoiding the question, dear. What did your precious colonel do to upset you?"

Penelope sighed. "I got the distinct impression that he hates me, Aunt," she replied, glad to share with her aunt the mystery of her cousin's strange behaviour.

She had expected Lady Octavia to use her favorite expletive and tell her she was being ridiculous. But her aunt surprised her.

"And well he might," she said slowly, a spoonful of strawberries arrested in midair. "And well he might, child." She sighed and returned her attention to the fruit. "Old hatreds die hard," she added after a pause. "More's the pity."

Penelope stared at her in amazement. "Whatever do you mean, Aunt?"

Lady Octavia scooped up the last drop of cream from her dish and put her spoon down carefully. "As you know, there is an old legend in our family, my love—and I don't know how much truth there is to it—which tells of a time way back when our ancestors were rogue Norman barons under William the Conqueror. The first baron received his title at the hands of the Normal Bastard himself on the battlefield at Hastings. During the thick of battle, our records claim, our ancestor gave up his horse to replace one of the three that were killed from under the Conqueror."

"Yes, so I've heard," Penelope said. "A title for a horse." She laughed at the incongruity of men. "A fair exchange, indeed."

"So William must have thought," her aunt remarked. "It probably saved his life into the bargain. Before that—so the story goes—they were roving knights with a small holding near Amiens. But after the first Ashington—or Assolant as the family was called back then—became a baron, he wished to improve his influence with William, so he looked high for a bride."

"The unfortunate daughter of the duc de Saxe, sister to the infamous Henri le Lion," Penelope interjected, caught up in the story she had known since childhood. "He abducted her, the heartless rogue. I've always wondered if it was truly a love-match as the legend claims, or merely a political move on our astute ancestor's part to consolidate his power."

"Probably the latter," her aunt replied pragmatically. "Marriages were even more politically motivated in those days than they are now, so I don't doubt that Assolant had his eye on the future. In any case, the duc never forgave the baron's effrontery, although William pardoned him, of course. The Conqueror had need of audacious men to help him hold sway in England. And the baron did benefit enormously through this alliance, of course. He received the Abbey and the village of Ashington as a wedding present from his king. But this is not the end of the story, child."

"You mean they did not lived happily ever after?" Penelope enquired with a mischievous twinkle in her lilac eyes.

"You might say they did. At least prosperously, at any rate," Lady Octavia replied. "But as I said before, the duc de Saxe never forgave the upstart baron. And when his daughter Mathilde—whom he banished from his sight forever—gave birth to her first child, the duc pronounced a curse on the House of Assolant, a curse that appears to have come down to us through the generations of Ashingtons who followed."

Penelope stared at her aunt in surprise. "I have heard nothing of any curse, Aunt. Are you hoaxing me?"

"You have not heard of it because it is a closely kept family secret, dear. Only your father became privy to it, after his marriage to your mother had actually taken place. You see, the outraged duc chose a truly diabolical curse, one which would undermine the future honour and prestige of the House of Assolant. He swore that in every generation, one member of the family would bring disgrace and dishonour to the family name by marrying far beneath the appropriate rank."

Penelope eyed her aunt askance. Lady Octavia was not given to fanciful inventions, but this tale of vengeance and ancient curses smacked too much of the kind of melodrama one found between the pages of Gothic romances to be credible.

"Why haven't I heard of this curse before?"

Lady Octavia smiled indulgently. "For obvious reasons, my child. Your father did not want to put any nonsensical ideas into your head, that's why."

"Did Neville know?"

"No. The titleholder usually passed the story of the curse down to his son after an eligible match was consummated. I imagine your father would have told Neville after his marriage to Charlotte. Had either of them lived that long, of course. I was tempted to forget the whole thing and let it die a natural death."

"I'm glad you did nothing so poor-spirited, Aunt. How did *you* know about the curse?" Penelope wanted to know.

"Your father told me shortly before he died."

"And you were supposed to tell Neville?"

"Yes. But now that is a moot point, isn't it? With Neville gone, the Ashington line is broken. Perhaps the curse will be broken, too."

Penelope felt oddly affected by her aunt's revelation. She began to understand more clearly the reason for Lady Octavia's fierce pride in the Ashington honour. Her father had been equally intolerant of mushrooms and other lesser forms of gentility, she remembered. And then an odd thought struck her.

"What about Cousin Nicholas?" she asked. "Do you think he knows about this curse?"

"Oh, I am quite sure he does," her aunt replied calmly. "He is, after all, a product of it, living proof that the duc de Saxe's revenge against the Ashingtons is still in force. I know nothing of his father, of course, but his grandfather, my Uncle David, brought the wrath of the family down on his head when he eloped with his Cit's daughter. And in the generation before, his own father's youngest sister—my great aunt Caroline— ran away one summer with a French officer of very questionable parentage. They say she died in childbirth in some remote French village, poor thing, but I cannot say for certain."

"And I suppose you mean to tell me that Aunt Henrietta is the black sheep of your generation, Aunt?" Penelope scoffed at the notion of that label in connexion with her gentle, warm-hearted aunt. She was vastly intrigued by the legend of the curse but unwilling to acknowledge its relevance in her own life.

"Of course, dear." Lady Octavia's glance was decidedly reproving. "Our dear Sir James—however sweet-tempered you may find him, and I agree he is that—is hardly a suitable, much less a brilliant match for my sister. Especially when you consider that she turned down an offer from the Duke of Sutherland's heir to marry Sir James. My poor grandfather nearly died of apoplexy when he found out."

"I think you are being very stuffy over this whole affair," Penelope exclaimed. "And which Ashington in the present generation is destined to continue the infamous duc's curse?" she enquired rather caustically. "As you say, my dear brother is gone, and his engagement to Charlotte Hayward was entirely respectable, in any case. That leaves me." She laughed. "Do you see me in that role of reprobate, Aunt? I trust I am too much my father's daughter to do anything so outlandish as run away with an undergroom or one of the gardeners. And what about Cousin Nicholas? Must we keep all the milkmaids and innkeepers' daughters out of his sight in case he succumbs to their ineligible charms? I think we are talking about coincidences and the vagaries of love rather than curses, Aunt. I truly do."

Her aunt glanced at her speculatively, an unaccustomed frown on her cherubic countenance.

"We shall see, child," she remarked tersely. "We shall see."

During the tedious weeks of sick-bed care that followed, Penelope's thoughts often returned to Lady Octavia's story of the long-ago curse placed on her ancestors by an irascible father wishing to punish a runaway daughter. After some consideration, Penelope had rejected the notion that the formidable duc de Saxe's daughter had been motivated by anything but love for the brash, freshly minted baron who stole her away.

As she sat by the colonel's bed late at night, after the household had settled into silence, Penelope would examine the gaunt, ravaged face of her cousin and speculate on which of his features he might have inherited from that rogue baron of long ago. The dark colouring definitely came from their Norman ancestor, she concluded. Her brother Neville was also dark as their father and other Ashington men had been, although Neville's hair had been more closely cropped and less inclined to curl around his ears than the colonel's. Her cousin's complexion was darker than Neville's, more weather-beaten by army life, she supposed. But the more she scrutinized the colonel, the more convinced she became that he was a closer replica of that warrior ancestor than her brother had ever been. Whatever suspect blood her great-uncle David had introduced into the line when he married his little Cit had done nothing to dilute the strength of the wild Norman blood that ran in Ashington veins.

The thought that her cousin was as much an Assolant as any of them, in spite of the duc's curse, gave her a perverse pleasure. Penelope smiled gently as her eyes roved over the still form in the wide bed beside her. As soon as it had become obvious that the colonel was not in danger of imminent death, as Dr. Kentwick had predicted, she had ordered the new earl removed from the small guest-room in the west wing and installed in the master bedroom on the third floor. The imposing suite had been designed by the third earl upon the momentous occasion of his nuptials to the only daughter of the Duke of Cornwall. Although the family history had recorded this prestigious alliance with understandable pride, rumour had hinted at the new countess's dissatisfaction with her sumptuous rooms overlooking the extensive Home Park and artificial lake. Penelope had always found the prospect delightful, and she and Charlotte had spent many a rainy afternoon in happier times discussing the changes the latest countess might want to make upon her marriage to the sixth earl.

Penelope sighed. All these girlish plans had come to naught, of course, and Charlotte had refused to set foot in the master-suite again since learning of Neville's death. Penelope herself came here regularly. Even after Neville's evening coats and hunting jackets, his frilled shirts and starched neckcloths, London-made boots and red Morocco slippers, breeches and other unmentionables had been removed from the clothes-presses in the spacious dressing-room and packed away in the attic, Penelope had continued to visit the suite. The very air in the richly appointed rooms seemed to be redolent with history, and Penelope liked nothing better than to recline on the delicate French chaise-longue in the countess's chamber, breathing in the spirit of her ancestors and speculating on their joys, their dreams, their sorrows and disappointments.

Cousin Nicholas's wayward grandfather had been born in

the countess's immense four-poster bed, as had her own. But what different fates had awaited these two innocent little boys, she thought, springing from the self-same womb yet doomed to be separated by a father's rigid pursuit of family honour. Or could it be, she mused, her gaze lingering on the rugged face in the bed beside her, that Lady Octavia was right, and the curse of another irate father so long ago had struck again at the House of Ashington?

So engrossed was she in these historical speculations that it came as a shock to find herself the object of a cold examination by the man in the bed. Penelope experienced a frisson of fear as her gaze locked with the colonel's dark, hostile eyes. To hide her nervousness, she rose to her feet and stepped closer to the bed.

"I'm glad to see you are awake, Cousin," she said, attempting a cheerfulness she did not feel. "I need not disturb Samuel to help me give you your potion."

"What day is it?" the patient enquired harshly.

"Tuesday," Penelope replied shortly, uncorking the bottle of tonic Dr. Kentwick had left the day before and measuring out a spoonful of the thick green liquid.

"I meant the date," came the impatient response.

Penelope bent over the patient and slipped her right arm under the colonel's head. "Then you should have said so," she remarked, resting the spoon against his tightly closed lips. "Today is the tenth of August, 1815," she added, returning his stare unflinchingly. "Now, open your mouth like a good boy."

Penelope never knew what prompted her to address the colonel so condescendingly, but the result was everything she should have known it would be. A low growl of rage issued from his throat, and his mouth relaxed briefly into a sneer. The distraction was all Penelope needed to force the spoon between his curling lips and pour half the liquid into the colonel's mouth. The other half ran down his chin and splattered the pillow as he jerked his head violently away.

"The devil take you, wench," he snarled, after his coughing had subsided. "What muck are you dosing me with, for God's sake?"

"The devil may well take you, too, Colonel," Penelope snapped back, her temper aroused by this cavalier treatment from the man she had helped to nurse back from the brink of death. "And you are wasting your breath calling on the good Lord, I might add. If you wish to recover, you had best do as you are told." She glared down in exasperation at his averted head and the soiled linen. "And I intend to see that you do. So resign yourself to swallowing this medicine that Dr. Kentwick has instructed me to give you." She poured another spoonful from the bottle and bent to raise the patient's head. Before she could do so, however, the colonel's right hand shot out from beneath the covers and grasped her painfully by the wrist.

"I said desist, girl," he snarled, glaring at her so ferociously that Penelope wondered fleetingly if he had taken leave of his senses.

"And I said you will take this potion, Colonel," she responded coolly. "Now, stop acting like a cantankerous old curmudgeon and open your mouth."

His fingers tightened on her wrist, and Penelope grimaced. A fraction more pressure and she might well find herself with a broken wrist, she thought. Already the pain was almost more than she could bear.

"You are either deaf or stupid, woman," he growled.

"And you are a rag-mannered heathen," she retorted. "You had best make up your mind to do as I say."

"No woman tells me what to do." His eyes were pits of black rage, and Penelope had to steel herself to look into them without trembling.

She forced a smile. "If you believe that, Colonel, you are even more of a sapskull than I had imagined," she said calmly. "Now, will you take your medicine without a fuss, or must I employ drastic measures?"

"I will not."

"Very well. Don't say afterwards that I didn't warn you."

Before he could guess what she was about, Penelope brought her left arm forward and poured the contents of the spoon over the astonished colonel's mouth and chin. His cousin released her right wrist and made a grab for the spoon, but he was too late. The damage was done. A thick, sticky green liquid moved sluggishly down his face and neck to soak the collar of his nightshirt.

Penelope stepped back and regarded him, laughter trembling

on her lips. "You do look funny, Colonel," she said, gingerly massaging her bruised wrist. "The first green-faced colonel I've ever seen. I think you would have done better to take your medicine like a man."

Colonel Nicholas Bellington let out a sting of muttered oaths which brought a flush to Penelope's cheeks.

"Colonel!" came a shocked exclamation from the doorway. "There are ladies present, sir."

Penelope turned to meet Sergeant Hardy's mortified gaze. He advanced into the room and stood looking down at the colonel, a dazed expression on his bearded face.

"Get that bitch out of here," the colonel roared.

Samuel looked apprehensively from his master's green-smeared face to Penelope's amused one, his face suddenly tinged pink with embarrassment.

"You had best leave, milady," he murmured.

"And don't bother to come back," the colonel added viciously.

Penelope laughed outright. "His lordship seems to be on the mend, Samuel," she remarked, as if nothing out of the ordinary had occurred. "But he has refused to take his medicine," she added, unwilling to let the obstreperous colonel have the last word.

"He also needs his face washed. See to it, will you, Samuel," she threw over her shoulder as she swept out of the room and closed the door with a satisfying click behind her.

CHAPTER THREE

Clash of Wills

Nicholas glared at the closed door for several moments after Lady Penelope's departure before turning his furious gaze on his manservant.

"Don't stand there like a great dim-witted looby," he snarled. "Get me some breakfast. I'm starved."

Samuel moved towards the bed, his white teeth glinting through his beard. "Glad to see ye're feeling more the thing, Colonel," he murmured in his soft drawl. "You do look a sight, though, sir. The lady was right. You need your face washed."

The colonel gave a snort of disgust. "Didn't I tell you to keep that managing female out of my room?"

Samuel wrung out the cloth in the blue Staffordshire bowl on the bedside table and wiped his master's sticky chin. "Aye, sir, to be sure you did. But it's a wise man who knows when to advance and when it's best to retreat. And you can take my word for it, Colonel, when Lady Penelope sets her mind to a course of action, a whole regiment of Light Bobs ain't going to stop her, and that's a fact." He rinsed out the cloth and wiped more of the green syrup from the colonel's neck.

Nicholas collapsed into the softness of the down pillow and glared at his sergeant. He hated to admit it, but his recent altercation with his cousin had exhausted him, and he felt torn between an insidious drowsiness and the gnawing hunger in his belly.

"What time is it?" he said gruffly, ignoring his henchman's unexpected praise for his cousin.

34

"Going on eight o'clock, sir."

"No wonder I'm hungry," Nicholas muttered. "I can't remember when I had my last decent meal. And don't bring me any more of that pap you've been feeding me. I want a couple of slices of ham—thick ones mind you—with scrambled eggs, sausages, toast, a mug of ale, and— "

"Whoa there, sir," the sergeant cut in, a wide grin on his bristly face. "Ye'll be dreaming, Colonel, if ye think Lady Penelope will countenance any such orgy. Mighty strict about the victuals the cook is allowed to send upstairs, she is. I don't think she'll take kindly to— "

"The devil fly away with that interfering harridan," Nicholas snapped, his patience showing signs of severe strain. "Damned if I'll be ordered about by any skitterbrained archwife with no more sense than to starve a man to death." He glowered at his sergeant as if daring him to argue the point. "Now, get down to the kitchen and rustle up a decent meal. And stop fussing at me with that blasted cloth." Impatiently he brushed Samuel's hand away from his face.

The sergeant regarded him with a glimmer of amusement. "No sense getting on yer high horse, sir," he remarked. "That fall must have addled yer brains besides breaking yer bones, m'lad. And ye're daft, I tell ye, if ye ain't noticed that her ladyship is no harridan. No sir. Even a blind man would see that. Plain as a pikestaff. A sight for sore eyes is her ladyship, and no mistake. As pretty a lass as you could— "

"If you'll stop this nauseating raving and get me some nourishment, I'll overlook the impertinence, Sergeant," Nicholas interrupted harshly. His head had begun to ache, and he could feel one of his black moods coming on. He was in no condition to tolerate his henchman's customary informality.

"You had better take yer medicine first, Colonel," Samuel replied, showing no sign of being affected by his master's rebuke.

"Over my dead body," Nicholas growled, closing his eyes against the early morning sunlight streaming in the French windows.

"It might well have come to that if her ladyship had not been so set on saving yer hide, Colonel. Though why she should have troubled her pretty head over an ungrateful gudgeon I can't for the life of me understand."

Nicholas opened his eyes. "Do you mean to tell me that I've been at the mercy of that harridan for . . . How many days has it been now?"

"Weeks, sir. Not days. Going on five weeks now, it is. And ye can thank yer lucky stars for stubborn females like their ladyships. If it had been left up to the old sawbones, ye'd have been dead a month ago."

"Ladyships?" Nicholas repeated sharply. "Do you mean to say a whole army of fidgety females has been in and out of my room while I was too weak to defend myself?"

"Only two, sir," came the amused response.

"That's two too many, Sergeant. I absolutely forbid you to allow another female inside this room. Is that understood, Sam?"

As if in defiance of this explicit order, the door flew open and a plump, merry-faced lady bustled into the room. She was followed by a footman carrying a tray with covered dishes on it.

"Put it down here, Robert," the lady ordered, indicating a delicate gate-legged table near the window.

"And how is our favourite patient this morning?" she asked, turning a bright inquisitive smile on the colonel. "Oh!" she exclaimed, glancing sharply at the green splashes on the pillow-case and the greenish water by the bedside. "What has been going on here?" she demanded, favouring the sergeant with a reproving stare. "And where is my niece, Samuel?"

"Lady Penelope has gone off to rest, milady," the sergeant replied with what Nicholas considered entirely too much meekness. "And this, milady," he made a sweeping gesture at the soiled bed linen, "this is the result of a minor skirmish—shall we say—over a dose of syrup."

The plump lady seemed to take in the situation at a glance. "Are you telling me that the colonel has not had his medicine this morning?"

"And I don't intend to," Nicholas cut in. "And who are you, may I ask? I'm getting mighty tired of these streams of busybodies traipsing through my bed-chamber. Sergeant, see this lady out at once."

Samuel glanced apologetically at the plump lady. "Begging yer pardon, milady. His lordship is a mite testy this morning."

The plump lady smiled at him with nauseating cheerfulness. "Any fool can see that, lad," she said dryly. "To answer your question, Colonel, I am Lady Octavia Ashington. Penelope's aunt. Your grandfather David was my uncle, my boy." She gazed at him with shrewd blue eyes as though she were assessing the effect of her words. "Now then," she continued bracingly, "we can't have this testiness, as the good sergeant calls it. I would call it plain cantankerousness myself. But then, I believe in calling a horse a horse. Or is that a spade? Never mind, my boy. We'll have those linens changed in a jiffy. And a clean night-shirt you'll be needing, too. Samuel," she commanded, pointing a finger at the giant sergeant, who seemed to be cowering behind a large wing-back chair. "Where does the colonel keep his night-shirts? Get me a clean one, if you please, while I give the lad his medicine."

Nicholas cringed at the thought of having his night-shirt changed by this unflappable female who was obviously capable of anything. He caught his sergeant's eye over the small lady's head as she stood by the bedside, pouring the green liquid into a spoon. Samuel shrugged his huge shoulders eloquently and disappeared into the dressing-room.

Lady Octavia bent over Nicholas and slipped a plump arm beneath his head. "There now," she said soothingly, "open up, there's a good lad. Let's have no more of this nonsense."

Nicholas had the fleeting urge to tell her ladyship that she had taken on the wrong man to bamboozle with her overbearing ways, but at the last moment, he caught a flicker of compassion in her lively blue eyes, and before he could plan a defensive tactic, the spoon was in his mouth, and he had swallowed the vile green syrup without a murmur of protest.

The cherubic face broke into a bland smile. "Now, that wasn't so bad, was it?" Lady Octavia chided. "And as a reward I have brought you something a little more substantial for breakfast. Penelope will no doubt be cross with me, but I have a weakness for good hearty food myself. And besides, it's high time you started to get your strength back, my boy. You'll be wanting to be up and learning how to run the estate, I warrant. Can't do that on chicken broth and dry toast, now, can we?"

He must really be losing his grip, Nicholas thought disgust-edly, to allow himself to be bullied by a female—an Ashington female into the bargain. But the thought of a decent meal caused him to overlook her blatant condescension and submit meekly to having his bed-linen changed by a red-faced maid and a fresh night-shirt pulled over his head by Lady Octavia herself.

In the days that followed his first real encounter with the Ashington ladies, Nicholas discovered, to his chagrin, that he did indeed owe his recovery to the very females he was determined to despise. Samuel never tired of pointing out, every time Nicholas cursed his benefactresses for some fresh indignity, that if the colonel had wished to quit this earth, he should have stayed in Brussels, where the army surgeons would have made quite sure that he got his wish.

This indebtedness did nothing to sweeten the colonel's temper. Indeed, it had quite the opposite effect. When Nicholas made his first painful excursion down to the Yellow Saloon one afternoon, he had to grit his teeth to avoid insulting Lady Octavia, whose condescending airs he found hard to bear.

Both ladies had risen upon his entrance on Samuel's arm, and by the time that they had settled him on the gold brocade settee, plumped his cushions, arranged a table conveniently by his side, and insisted on pouring him a cup of China tea—a brew he heartily despised—Nicholas was fit to be tied.

"I don't drink tea," he said flatly.

Lady Octavia dismissed this objection with an airy wave of her plump, be-ringed hand. "My dear boy, pray don't be nonsensical. Tea is a most invigorating beverage. It will settle your nerves."

"There is nothing wrong with my nerves," he snapped. "Featherbow," he turned to the portly butler who was setting out the silver tea-set, "pour me a glass of sherry."

"That is quite out of the question, Colonel," Lady Penelope cut in firmly. "No strong liquor until you are completely healed, Dr. Kentwick says."

Nicholas glared at her. "Sherry is hardly strong liquor," he retorted, thinking—as he had so often in the past few days—

how unfortunate it was that Lady Penelope Ashington reminded him so forcibly of his beloved grandmother.

"It is alcohol, nevertheless," Lady Octavia remarked with a ring of finality. "And that is still a nasty swelling you have on your face, my boy."

Nicholas wanted to point out that he was not—by any stretch of the imagination—her boy, but he gritted his teeth again. He also resented any reference to the angry red sabre slash on his cheek. It was only recently that Samuel had finally allowed his master to look at himself in the mirror, and Nicholas had been appalled and faintly disgusted at the disfigurement he had suffered. Since neither of the Ashington ladies or Dr. Kentwick, or even Samuel himself, had so much as flinched at his appearance, Nicholas was unprepared for the sight of the ugly distortion. Although he had never considered himself handsome in the usual sense, he had been well pleased by the regular, strong-jawed masculinity of his features. Lady Octavia's casual mention of his swollen face reminded Nicholas that one stroke of a French sabre had turned him into a virtual monster.

"The condition of my face need hardly concern you, my lady," he said icily, straining for a politeness that he did not feel.

"You are off the mark there, Colonel," his cousin said with an amused gleam in her lilac eyes. "Both my aunt and I have invested heavily in your recovery and would be very cast down if you were to suffer a relapse."

"Besides which," Lady Octavia added, "we are most anxious for you to take up your responsibilities to the estate, my boy. You can hardly expect Penelope to carry the burden much longer. She has already done far too much, as I am always telling her."

"Oh, do hush, Aunt," Penelope interrupted quickly. "There is time enough for our cousin to take over the running of the Abbey when he is completely restored to health. Let's not worry him with such details now."

Nicholas could have sworn that Lady Octavia's remark had made his cousin uneasy, and as he stared at the delicate blush that suffused her cheeks, emphasizing her ethereal, fairylike beauty, he wondered why a gently bred, single young female had involved herself in the running of an estate as large as Laughton Abbey was reputed to be.

Although the question remained unasked, it was not forgotten, and as the days went by Nicholas became more determined than ever to regain his strength and take full possession of his inheritance. Much against his sergeant's advice, one afternoon in late August he ventured down to the stables.

"Ye'll not be thinking of straddling a horse, Colonel?" his sergeant enquired in considerable alarm. "Lady Penelope would surely put a stop to that flight of fancy if she knew."

"Well, she ain't going to know," Nicholas snapped, his anger always ready to explode at any mention of interference by the Ashington females. "And I can do what I like on my own land, I trust." His words sounded petulant even to his own ears, and this made him even more determined to have his way.

"You there," he shouted at a young groom who was busy currying a big bay gelding in the stable-yard. "What's your name?"

The boy turned and touched his forelock respectfully. "Jeremy, milord."

"Who's in charge here?"

"Mr. Gerald Langly is, milord. Mr. Langly has been headgroom at Laughton Abbey for nigh on thirty years, milord." The lad glanced apprehensively over his shoulder. "Shall I fetch him, milord?"

The search for Mr. Langly was unnecessary, however, for at that moment the head groom came out of a stall leading one of the neatest bits of horseflesh Nicholas had ever seen, and made himself known to the new earl. The animal, a tall black gelding with a deep chest and muscular hind-quarter, was evidently in prime condition, and Nicholas forgot his ill-humour as he examined the horse. The head groom was only too pleased to discuss the animal's breeding and reputation as a prime goer on the hunting field.

"There's not a gentleman in the district who has not tried to buy Bluedevil at one time or another, milord," Mr. Langly announced proudly.

"Well, I'm glad to see they didn't succeed," Nicholas remarked, his spirits roused at the spectacle of such magnificent horseflesh. "Have him saddled for me, will you, Langly. I think I'll take a turn in the meadow to try out his paces."

Mr. Langly stared at the earl, consternation written all over his homely face. "Oh, I couldn't do that, milord," he said apologetically.

It was Nicholas's turn to stare. "Why the devil can't you, man?" he demanded, his temper simmering again. Were even his own servant bent on questioning his authority? he wondered. Could this be part and parcel of the Ashingtons' attempts to thwart him?

"Well, you see, sir, nobody rides Bluedevil but her ladyship. Most particular she is about it. A rare dust she would raise if I dared to put any but her own saddle on his back, milord. Those are my orders, begging your pardon, milord." The man looked highly uncomfortable under Nicholas's black stare, but he stood firm.

"I'm sure Lady Octavia would have no objection to my taking the horse for a canter in the meadow, Langly."

The head-groom's face split into a grin. "Oh, no, milord. Lady Octavia has nothing to do with Bluedevil, sir. A rare handful he is when he takes it into his head to kick up his heels. He's Lady Penelope's horse, milord. A bruising rider she is, too, if you'll pardon the expression."

"Are you saying that this horse belongs to my cousin?"

"Yes, milord. Raised him from a foal she did."

Nicholas held the groom's steady gaze for a moment, before turning to the gelding Jeremy had just finished currying. "What about the bay over there? He looks as though he might be up to my weight."

Mr. Langly coughed nervously. "I'm sorry, milord, but Merrylegs is another of Lady Penelope's horses."

"And she forbids anyone to ride him? Am I correct?"

"Yes, milord," the groom murmured apologetically.

Nicholas felt a huge wave of rage welling up inside him. He had been prepared for opposition and resentment from the Ashingtons. There was no way—he had told himself when he received the shattering news of his accession to the title—that his grandfather's stiff-necked family would welcome him with open arms into its midst. Indeed, the Ashingtons must despise him almost as much as he despised them if all the stories he had heard about his grandfather's treatment at their hands were true. And Nicholas had no reason in the world to believe otherwise. Not only had the old Lord Ashington refused to countenance his son's marriage, but the family had dared to insult his beloved grandmother—a crime far more heinous in Nicholas's eyes. And all because the third earl's wife—a cold, proud Beauty of impeccable lineage, he had heard—had declared his sweet, unassuming grandmother to be irrevocably beneath her notice. The aristocratic bitch had turned them away from the door when his grandfather had brought his newborn daughter back to his family a year later. After that rejection from his own mother, David Ashington had never gone back home again.

Nicholas broke out of his reverie to find three pairs of eyes regarding him warily.

"If ye'll forgive me, Colonel," Samuel ventured. "I don't think this is such a good idea—"

Nicholas ignored him and turned his glacial gaze on the head-groom. "Have the goodness to show me which horses are *mine,* Langly," he said in a tone which his subordinate officers of the 18th Hussars would have recognised immediately.

The groom, who had never even heard of the Colonel's crack regiment, nevertheless recognised the hint of steel in the new earl's words and shuffled his feet uneasily.

"Most of the young master's hunters have been sold off, milord," he began apologetically. "Eating their 'eads off they were, milord, and nobody to ride 'em after Master Neville got himself killed by those heathens." He glanced nervously at the earl, and Nicholas felt a flicker of compassion for the groom. His anger should be directed at the insufferable Lady Penelope, he told himself. Langly would do whatever that managing female told him to do, Nicholas had no doubt of it. He found himself looking forward to a clash of wills with the woman who seemed to be bent on making his life a misery.

He did not have to wait long. Nicholas barely had time to catch the flash of relief in Langly's eyes before a clatter of hooves on the cobble-stones heralded the approach of a rider. He whirled around in time to see Lady Penelope pull a neatish, highly spirited dappled-grey mare to a prancing halt beside the group gathered in the stableyard.

Nicholas's first reaction was to catch his breath at the vision of health and vitality before him. And pure, unadulterated loveliness, he acknowledged, albeit reluctantly, cursing himself as this unwanted thought intruded on his consciousness. Accustomed as he was to the company of the most fashionable ladies Brussels had to offer, Nicholas was impressed, in spite of himself, by the spectacle of feminine beauty before him. Lady Penelope sat her mare with an easy, unconscious grace, and Nicholas could see at a glance that his cousin's midnight-blue riding habit, with its flaring skirt and snugly fitted frogged jacket, was in the first stare of elegance. Lady Penelope's crowning attraction, however, was an absurdly jaunty blue shako perched precariously on her pale curls, its single feather curling flirtatiously beside her perfect cheek.

Nicholas scowled up at her, his lips taut with irritation.

"Good afternoon, Colonel," Lady Penelope said, her musical voice and condescending smile grating on Nicholas's nerves. "I trust you are not contemplating riding just yet, are you? I would not recommend it. In fact, I am sure Dr. Kentwick would frown upon such unnecessary exertion so soon after leaving the sick-room."

"It hardly matters whether I intended to ride or not," he answered brusquely. "It appears I haven't a decent horse to my name." He glowered up at her and was unreasonably annoyed when Lady Penelope broke into an amused laugh. She was even lovelier when she laughed, Nicholas thought dispassionately, and hated her all the more fiercely for not looking like the harridan she undoubtedly was.

"Now, that is farradiddle if ever I heard any," she said lightly, dismounting from the mare in a flurry of blue skirts and handing the reins to Jeremy, who had been standing in readiness since her arrival, gazing worshipfully up at his mistress.

"I told his lordship that Master Neville's hunters have been sold off, milady," Langly explained. "But there are still several hacks available. Caesar, for example, or Mr. Nobody—"

Nicholas's hackles rose instantly. "No doubt it would amuse you to see me mounted on a horse with such a name," he interrupted harshly. "I decline the honour, however—"

"Mr. Nobody has carried Ashingtons most successfully in

many a hunt during the past twelve years," Lady Penelope put in calmly. "He is not a horse to be sneered at, my lord."

"He will not be carrying any Bellingtons, take my word for it." Nicholas glanced irritably at Bluedevil, who was nibbling playfully at his mistress's sleeve. "How many other animals of yours are eating their heads off at my expense, Cousin?"

He noticed that the amusement had left her face and her lilac eyes now regarded him coolly. "Only Bluedevil and Merrylegs." She gestured towards the bay. "And Bluebelle here, of course." She leaned forward to caress the grey mare affectionately. "Then I have a team of greys for my curricle," she added defiantly. "That's all, my lord. I don't count the Duchess, who is my aunt's mount."

"What does a female need with a curricle?" Nicholas demanded, reminded that he himself had lacked the funds for such a sporting vehicle for too long now.

"Her ladyship is a famous whip, sir." Jeremy broke in, a totally besotted look on his boyish face. "Drives to an inch, she does, too, milord."

"Hush, Jeremy," Lady Penelope intervened, with a quick smile for the stable-lad. "Lord Laughton can hardly be interested in my poor driving skills."

Nicholas glared at her. If the artful baggage thought to outmanoeuvre Colonel Bellington, her wits had gone begging, he thought viciously. For reasons he did not care to examine too closely, Nicholas fiercely resented the fact that this pampered, overbearing female had enjoyed a luxury which in the Bellington household had been considered an unnecessary extravagance.

He made her a curt bow. "Not at all, Cousin," he retorted. "Quite the contrary, in fact. I have always had a hankering to be driven around the countryside by a famous whip." His lip curled as he spoke, and he saw Lady Penelope's face pale as she registered the thinly veiled insult. "Perhaps you would oblige me." As he had intended, the request sounded more like an order than a question, and he smiled at the parade of emotions that flickered across the lady's face.

"It would be my pleasure, Colonel," she said, after an awkward pause. "Perhaps tomorrow afternoon—"

"Why not now?"

It was Lady Penelope's turn to glare at him, but as he had anticipated, she did not argue in front of the servants.

"Have my team put to, will you please, Langly?" she ordered. "And Jeremy, give Bluebelle a rub-down, will you?

"I hope that Dr. Kentwick does not have my hide when he hears of this foolishness," Lady Penelope remarked, slanting an accusing look up at Nicholas from beneath thick lashes.

"The devil may fly away with the good doctor with my blessing," he shot back. He was feeling a strange elation at his easy victory over his cousin's scruples. "And besides," he added mendaciously, "I trust you to take good care of me, Cousin."

She made no reply to this facetious remark, and Nicholas was soon distracted by the reappearance of Langly, leading two magnificent grey Welsh-breds, who showed unmistakable signs of restlessness. He was wondering idly if he had perhaps been too hasty in entrusting himself to a female driving this mettlesome pair, when another groom emerged from the stable, leading an identical, equally restless pair.

Nicholas did not want to believe what his eyes were telling him.

"You drive four-in-hand, Cousin?"

Lady Penelope smiled sweetly. "Yes, indeed," she replied. "And I know what you are about to say, Colonel. It *is* highly pretentious of me, I'll admit. But there is no greater thrill that I know of than tooling down our narrow country lanes behind a team like mine, never knowing what might be around the next curve in the road." She smiled at him mischievously, and Nicholas felt a reluctant glow of pleasure as he gazed down at the sparkle in her lilac eyes.

He wondered if the saucy baggage was being deliberately reckless to provoke him into crying off. Her next words confirmed his suspicion and caused him to reject any notion of retreat.

"Would you prefer me to take a single team, Colonel? I could do so, if you wish, although it is only half the fun."

"Not on my account," he retorted shortly, wondering at this sudden recklessness which had overcome his soldier's caution.

He was given no second chance to change his mind. Before he could examine his own chaotic feelings on the subject,

Nicholas found himself seated in the precarious sporting vehicle, his thigh pressed against his cousin's in unsettling intimacy. Lady Penelope expertly flicked the long whip over the leaders' ears, and they swept out of the stable-yard and bowled down the long driveway at a pace calculated to chill any but the stoutest blood.

CHAPTER FOUR

Open Warfare

Penelope was on her mettle and none too pleased at having allowed herself to be bullied into showing off her driving skills. She knew herself to be a very competent whip, but the presence at her side of the disapproving colonel disturbed her more than she cared to admit. Her nervousness transmitted itself instantly to her highly bred horses, who did not need any further encouragement to give rein to their bottled-up energies. She was well aware that four spirited horses were difficult enough at the best of times to control with any degree of flair, but when those same horses took it into their heads to shy at every bird in the hedgerow, break their stride at the least faltering of her hands on the ribbons, and generally behave like the temperamental creatures they were, Penelope fervently wished the colonel in Jericho.

As the racing curricle approached the stone entrance to the Abbey at a pace calculated to freeze the blood, Penelope felt the colonel tense beside her and smiled to herself. It gave her a glimmer of satisfaction to know that her cousin was not as phlegmatic as he appeared. Perhaps he was at that very moment hoping that she would embarrass herself by begging his assistance in stemming the wild rush of her runaway team. She could well imagine the cutting remarks she would have to endure if she were foolish enough to succumb to such missishness. The thought of confirming the colonel's already low opinion of her stiffened Penelope's determination not to falter, and she checked the ribbons a fraction, calling out firmly

to her right leader as she did so. She breathed a silent sigh of
relief when Jason acknowledged her command by flicking his
ear back and checking his headlong pace fractionally. Taking
advantage of having caught her lead horse's attention, Penelope increased the pressure on the ribbons and was gratified
when the unruly team dropped down to a spanking yet more
seemly gait.

Penelope smiled complacently as she manoeuvred her team
smartly through the gates and into the narrow lane that
bordered the estate for several miles. That should show him,
she thought, unexpectedly overcome by a strong desire to
bridge the antagonism her cousin had displayed towards her
since he had awakened from his feverish coma. She glanced at
him, a tentative smile on her lips, and found him gazing at her
with none of his usual hostility.

"Nice piece of driving, Cousin," he remarked, and for once
Penelope could detect no sarcasm in his tone.

Her smile broadened, and she felt ridiculously pleased with
herself. "Why, thank you, Colonel." She laughed. "I do believe
that is the first time I have heard a word of approval from you
since you arrived at the Abbey."

When she saw the familiar frown draw his heavy brows
together, she wished she had responded more demurely to his
compliment, as a well-bred young lady should. "I must
confess, however," she hurried on, anxious to restore the
unusual softness to his glance, "that I did wonder for a moment
there whether we would not both land in the hedge. I have not
had them out for nearly a week, and they don't take kindly to
kicking their heels in their stalls." She was silent for a moment,
then added, "I fear they miss my brother. Neville used to take
them up to London occasionally to get the fidgets out of them."

"Am I to understand that you actually allowed a mere man
to handle your cattle?"

Penelope could not tell from his tone whether the colonel
was roasting her or not, and when she glanced up at him, his
eyes were hooded.

"As a rule I don't like anyone to use my horses," she said
slowly, feeling her way. "But I had no objection to Neville
taking the greys out once in a while. He was never allowed on
Bluedevil, however." She laughed at the recollection of her

brother's only attempt to sneak a ride on the black colt. "The one time he did take Bluedevil out when I was away, he was thrown and broke an arm." She glanced at her companion and saw that he was amused. "He never tried it again, I can assure you," she added, her attention momentarily diverted as the greys threatened to take exception to a flock of white geese browsing by the roadside.

"I was informed by Mr. Hamilton," the colonel remarked suddenly, "that there was a steward in charge of the estate." He regarded her quizzically.

"There was," she said defensively. "That is to say, there still is, but Matthew Stevens is old now and laid up with his rheumatism much of the time."

"Then he should be pensioned off and replaced. Why hasn't that been done?"

"You may do so yourself, if you wish," Penelope replied sharply. "Now that you are master of the Abbey, you can do as you like, I suppose." She paused in dismay at the bitterness in her voice. What must he think of her? she thought, trying to control the sudden flash of emotion which had betrayed her. "I do beg your pardon," she murmured, thoroughly mortified at her rag-mannered outburst. "It's just that Matthew has been with us since my father was a boy. And besides . . ." She stopped abruptly, suddenly appalled at what she had been about to say. Was there, she wondered, a polite way of telling a stranger to his face that he could know nothing of the bonds of duty and responsibility between master and retainer on an estate such as Laughton Abbey? She seriously doubted it.

"Besides what?" His voice was soft but filled with the suggestion of steel.

Penelope glanced at him and saw that he was regarding her steadily, his brows pulled down in the familiar frown.

"Nothing that won't wait until we get back, Colonel," she said lightly. "Let us try to enjoy an hour or two of sunshine without coming to cuffs, shall we?" She flashed him one of her most brilliant smiles and pointed out the lane dividing the Ashington lands from the Haywards' smaller estate.

"Don't change the subject," he said in the same steely tone, as though she had not spoken. "I want to hear you say what you almost did just now. Before you thought better of it, of course."

Penelope felt a tremor of apprehension. The man was intolerably rude to badger her thus. She had apologised for her own outburst, hadn't she? Why couldn't he let it drop as a gentleman should?

"I must drive you over one afternoon to pay a call on Charlotte Hayward," she said brightly, as though her companion had not committed an unforgivable faux pas. "But only if you will promise to drink tea in a civilised manner," she added, slanting a teasing glance at him from under her lashes, to show that she was willing to overlook his shortcomings.

Her efforts went entirely unacknowledged by the man at her side, and after that one quick glance, Penelope averted her eyes. His harsh face was set in a pale, frozen mask highlighted by the ugly red gash across his left cheek. And his eyes . . . Penelope shuddered at the bleakness she had glimpsed in their dark depths. What could she say to a man like this strange cousin of hers who seemed to be the antithesis of everything she knew and valued in the world?

His next words confirmed her growing suspicion that he had read her mind.

"You resent the idea of a Bellington being master here, no doubt," the colonel remarked coolly, as though he cared not a jot for her opinion. "Instead of one of your precious Ashingtons. No, don't deny it," he added when she turned to protest his bald accusation. "I expected no less from your family, my dear." Penelope knew instinctively that the endearment was meant as an insult, and her chin went up defiantly.

"Ah," he said in the same cold voice that chilled Penelope's blood. "You and your aunt may look down those famous Ashington noses at me all you choose, Cousin. Nothing will alter the fact that I am master here and intend to remain so. I wish it were otherwise," he added bitterly. "But your aunt has taken every opportunity to impress upon me that I have a sacred duty to perform here. At least she seems to believe it is a sacred trust to hold the Laughton title. I'm not at all convinced of it myself, but that is neither here nor there. What do you think, Penelope? I presume that, as head of the family, I may take that liberty?"

Paralysed by the depth of bitterness she detected in the colonel's voice, Penelope strove to deny the brutally frank assessment he had made of the awkward situation at the Abbey. Her aunt would perhaps not have phrased it so starkly, but Penelope had little doubt that Lady Octavia would agree with the new earl's sentiments.

"You are mistaken, Colonel," she began stiffly.

He interrupted her with a harsh laugh. "I think not. And I can hardly blame you, I suppose. It cannot have been pleasant to discover that the hallowed Laughton title had suddenly devolved upon the black sheep of the family. One that had been safely banished from the fold long ago and never thought of again. Am I not correct, Penelope?"

"No, you are not," she responded sharply. "And you have no right to pick a quarrel with me over something that happened so long ago," she added. "If you insist on being odious, Colonel, I shall take you home."

When he made no reply, Penelope suited her actions to her words and swung her team around in the narrow lane, urging them forward with more than her usual recklessness.

Dinner that evening was an awkward affair. Penelope was still smarting from the colonel's attack and was in no mood for polite conversation. It fell to Lady Octavia to maintain a semblance of socially acceptable chatter, but even her ladyship's natural garrulousness had worn perilously thin by the time the last course was removed and the ladies rose to repair to the drawing-room.

Penelope had not exchanged a single word with the colonel during the entire meal, and the only glance she had thrown his way had encountered such a stony stare from beneath his lowered brows that she had not been tempted to look at him again. She was therefore surprised when he addressed her as she rose from the dinner-table.

"I would like a few words with you, Cousin, if you please," he said in a tone that Penelope had long since identified as his military command voice. She had learned that he would not be lightly refused when he used that particular tone of authority. She paused in the doorway and glanced at him enquiringly.

"Perhaps you would care to take your tea in the library with me?" He had followed the ladies out into the hall and now stood regarding her with a faintly ironic twist to his lips. It occurred to Penelope that the deep scar on the colonel's face—still pink and painfully raw—made him look decidedly sinister. Even when he smiled—if the slight lift of his lips could be called a smile—the effect was more devilish than inviting. And the curl of the scar beside his mouth twitched disturbingly. She withdrew her gaze with an effort and gave him the smallest possible smile.

"Only if you promise not to ring another peal over my head," she said. "I cannot say I enjoy having my sins thrown in my face."

"Then you admit I was on the mark?"

"Would it make any difference if I denied it?" she countered, turning on her heel and walking down the hall towards the library. "What is it you wish to see me about, Colonel?"

He followed her into the leather-scented room and took up his place behind her grandfather's carved oaken desk. It seemed odd to see a stranger there—she still caught herself thinking of him as a stranger—where she herself had sat for the past three years to reconcile the estate accounts. Even before Neville had left for India, he had been glad to accept her offer to see to the minutia of running Laughton Abbey after their father died, and Penelope had enjoyed doing her part in holding the big estate together.

Now, as Nicholas Bellington stood behind the old desk and stared at her, Penelope was suddenly shocked afresh by the realisation that her brother was truly gone and that—however much she might wish it otherwise—the Abbey would never be the same again. A lump formed in her throat, and she looked away before her eyes might reveal her nostalgia.

To regain her composure, Penelope settled herself in a green leather armchair before the desk, wondering if the colonel had yet discovered just how dipped the estate was at present. If he had, she thought ruefully, she had better resign herself to another round of recriminations.

His first words confirmed her fears.

"Your aunt informs me that you have been in charge of the accounts for several years now. I have been examining the books," he said, tapping the open ledger that lay on the desk before him. "And I find that the expenses seem to outweigh the income from the estate. In some cases, by considerable amounts. Particularly over the past year."

"Yes, that's true," she replied noncommittally. She would be damned in Hell, she thought crossly, before she would offer any justification for drawing upon her own funds to cover the servants' wages and other miscellaneous expenses over the years she had been in charge of the Laughton affairs. She had taken enough recriminations already from Mr. Hamilton in London, and from her aunt. She was determined not to take any from Colonel Bellington.

She returned his stare blandly.

He raised a quizzical eyebrow. "Can you explain to me, Penelope, how it is that an estate which—according to Hamilton's estimation—is worth well over thirty thousand pounds a year, can be operating at a loss?"

Penelope sighed. "Well, as Mr. Hamilton might have told you, Colonel, the past few years, and last year in particular, have not been profitable ones. Last year the harvests were disappointing, and the tenants suffered greatly with a smallpox epidemic which broke out over in Ashington Village."

"Hamilton told me nothing of this," he interrupted brusquely. "But that does not explain why no rents were paid during the last quarter. As far as I can see, there is nothing left in the account to draw on at all."

Penelope gazed at the colonel's face, which had taken on a chiselled expression. The curled scar beside his mouth was jumping nervously again. "It is not quite that bad," she argued. "Next quarter's rent will soon be coming in, and there is the interest due in December on the money Papa invested for Neville in the Funds. And if you are worried about the feed bill, you need not be; I take care of that myself," she added defiantly.

"I am more concerned about the wages for the next quarter. I hadn't realized the staff here was so large. Where is that sum to come from?"

Penelope forced herself to meet his dark gaze calmly. He would have to know sooner or later, she thought resignedly, although she would have preferred not to be the one to break the news. "I have been taking care of that, too, Cousin," she explained in a low voice. "There are so many demands on the estate, that it seemed only fair—"

"You *what*?" he demanded harshly. "Am I to understand that you are spending your own pin-money on the estate? Paying off my bills?"

She could not resist a smile at his misconception of her finances. "Hardly pin-money, Colonel. You see, I inherited a tidy legacy from my grandmother when I was fifteen, and it has been growing steadily since then. So now I feel justified in spending some of it on my home and the people who have served me for so long. I see nothing wrong in that—"

"Well, I do," the earl snapped, his face suffused with rage. "I will not have a female paying my bills, do you hear me," he shouted. "While you remain under my roof, girl, you will do as I say. And in the future you will confine yourself to household matters and leave the running of the estate to me. Is that clear?"

Penelope had risen to her feet during this tirade, her temper dangerously aroused. "Perfectly clear, Colonel," she said coldly. "But you should consider that, as it now stands, the estate will not bear any extra burdens for some time. I trust you are not a gambler, Colonel. Or prone to sartorial extravagances." She flashed him a sardonic smile. "Because if you had expected to come into a large fortune with the title, I regret that you will be sadly disappointed, my lord."

"Do you indeed?" the colonel said between gritted teeth. "We shall soon see about that."

"I could have told you how it would be, Penny," Charlotte remarked, with a complaisancy which set Penelope's teeth on edge. "The fellow is nothing but an encroaching mushroom, just as dear Lady Octavia predicted last summer when we first heard that the rogue was to step into my darling Neville's place. A sad day it was, indeed, when such things were allowed to happen."

"You are being unfair, Charlotte," Penelope interrupted, before her friend could get started on another tirade against the man who had supplanted her betrothed as the Earl of Laughton. "It is hardly Colonel Bellington's fault that he was the next in line for the title."

Penelope regarded her best friend with barely disguised

irritation. She had ridden over to Clayton Manor that afternoon expressly to find some relief from the tension that had developed between her cousin and herself since their quarrel two days ago. In her need to confide in her childhood friend, Penelope had looked forward to a comforting hour or two listening to Charlotte confirm her every misgiving about the new master of the Abbey. She had certainly not expected to find herself defending the odious wretch who had so rudely informed her what she could and could not do in her own home. Of course, it was no longer really her home, she mused, glad of the interruption when the Hayward butler came in with a plate of fresh lemon tartlets.

"Cook sends these up with her compliments, Lady Penelope," the old retainer said. "Knowing as how your ladyship is so fond of lemon tarts." He set the plate down with an expectant smile.

"Thank you, Jeffers," Penelope replied. "Please tell Mrs. Mason that I appreciate her thoughtfulness."

"I could have borne it better had Geoffrey been the rightful heir," Charlotte murmured, her lips drawn into a disgruntled pout as they so often were these days. "But to have a pretentious nobody as master of the Abbey is beyond anything disagreeable, Penny. I simple cannot bear it."

"I seem to remember a time when you could not bear Geoffrey either," Penelope pointed out impatiently. Her willowy, effete cousin, Geoffrey Swathmore, had been a persistent visitor at Laughton Abbey over the years and had at one time declared himself desperately enamoured of the chestnut-haired Lady Charlotte. After Charlotte's engagement to Neville became official, Geoffrey transferred his amorous attentions to his cousin Penelope, who had told him, in her blunt way, not to be a ninny.

As Penelope rode back to the Abbey, she asked herself, for the umpteenth time since receiving that disastrous letter which had changed all their lives, what had happened to the bright, biddable girl who had been her friend and confidante ever since she could remember. Neville's death had done something terrible to Charlotte, changed her cheerful nature in many subtle ways. Try as she might, Penelope could no longer spend an hour in her company without becoming impatient with her friend's refusal to let go of the past. Neville was dead. That was an irrevocable truth. So was her own dear Edward. But while Charlotte fretted and whined away her days lamenting what might have been, Penelope had long since put her love for Edward and her dreams of spending the rest of her life blissfully at his side away in a remote corner of her heart.

Penelope dismounted in front of the wide doors and tossed her reins to a groom. She was so absorbed by her troubling thoughts that she had traversed half the spacious entrance hall before she noticed anything amiss. She came to an abrupt halt and stood gazing in amazement at the stack of oil paintings propped against the wall near the stairs. At that moment a small cavalcade consisting of two of their burliest footmen came down the wide marble staircase, led by Featherbow.

When the butler saw his mistress, his usually impassive face showed signs of distress. He motioned the footmen to put their load down, and Penelope saw that it consisted of more paintings, one of which she recognized as the prized likeness of her mother in a rural setting, done by Joshua Reynolds many years ago.

"Whatever is going on, Featherbow?" Penelope demanded, pulling off her riding gloves and removing the jaunty beaver she wore on her blond curls.

"His lordship's orders, milady," the butler replied tersely, sending the footmen up the stairs again with a curt gesture.

Penelope stared at him in amazement. "But why . . . why bring all the paintings down here, Featherbow? What does he mean to do with them?"

Featherbow stared ahead woodenly. "His lordship told me to clear the Long Gallery of all this . . . this rubbish. His very words, milady." The butler's face twisted as if in physical pain.

There must be some logical explanation for the colonel's strange order, Penelope thought, but her confused brain refused to come up with one.

"If the colonel wished the Long Gallery to be cleaned, he should have applied to me," she murmured at last.

The butler cast her an anguished look. "No, milady. It appears that his lordship wishes to send all these paintings"—he made a hopeless gesture with his arm towards countless generations of Ashington history—"up to London to be auctioned off. Leastwise that is what his lordship told me, milady. I couldn't rightly say—" He paused, his face crumpling alarmingly until Penelope felt the unfortunate man would burst into tears. "I can't rightly say, milady—" Again, the butler seemed unable to complete his sentence.

Penelope took pity on him. "That's all right, Featherbow. Where is my cousin? I will find out the meaning of this outrage."

"In the library, milady," Featherbow seemed to pull himself together with a visible effort. "His lordship just called for a bottle of the French brandy." He made this perfectly natural request sound like an unpardonable breach of etiquette.

"He did, did he?" Feeling her fury mounting uncontrollably, Penelope threw her gloves and beaver down on the hall table, gathered her habit over her arm, and marched down the hall.

If it was war the rogue wanted, she thought, grasping the knob of the library door and flinging it open, war he would most certainly get.

CHAPTER FIVE

The Rogue's Revenge

Nicholas had been looking forward to the impending confrontation with the hoity-toity Lady Penelope all afternoon. There was no doubt in his mind that she would react—perhaps violently—to his deliberate provocation, and he wanted to witness her discomposure. He even admitted to a perverse sense of satisfaction in knowing that he had attacked her in her most vulnerable position. As it behooved any military commander worth his salt, the colonel had observed his enemy carefully during the past few weeks of their uneasy relationship. And ever since that fateful afternoon when she had driven him out in her fancy curricle, Nicholas had known where an attack from him would do the most damage.

He grinned wolfishly at his reflection in the gilded mirror over the mantelpiece and took another sip of the excellent brandy. The idea had come to him that very afternoon when Lady Octavia—operating no doubt under the assumption that the rudesby colonel needed to have the illustrious heritage of the Ashingtons rubbed in his face—had graciously offered to give him a tour of the Long Gallery. Nicholas had deliberately avoided entering this holy sanctuary of aristocratic relics. He had no intention of worshiping at a shrine which included that starched-up harridan—the great-grandmother he had never acknowledged and never would—who had banished his grandfather and insulted his adored grandmother. The thought that they were all up there in the Long Gallery, condescending smirks still lingering on their supercilious dead faces, made him want to throw a saddle on his horse—the only one in the stables he felt was truly his—and ride off into the bright October afternoon without a backward glance.

The face in the mirror glared back at him, pale and drawn, a hint of savagery in the dark eyes. Nicholas instinctively raised a hand to still the wildly twitching curl of mutilated flesh beside his taut lips. It was lucky he had never had any ambitions in the petticoat line, he thought ruefully. That face would hardly be a welcome addition to a lady's drawing-room. The scar was healing slowly, but the tortured pink gash down the length of his face would always be unsightly. He traced it idly with his finger, pausing at the incongruous curl beside his mouth. No, he thought without regret, he would never be a lady's man with a face like this.

The thought of women brought him back to his present situation. The preservation of the family heritage seemed to be of primary concern to the Ashington ladies. Lady Octavia had thrown out any number of broad hints about the importance of assuring the continuance of the original line. She had even had the temerity to mention a neighbourhood chit—a female who had been selected by his predecessor as the next countess—as a likely and highly eligible *parti*.

Nicholas grinned mirthlessly at his reflection. He had been forced to step into Neville Ashington's shoes as the titleholder, but he'd be damned in Hell before he accepted his predecessor's choice of women. It would serve them all right if he took one of the upstairs maids into his bed, or Lady Penelope's rosy-cheeked abigail, Alice. The wench had adopted the same faintly condescending air towards him as her mistress, but Nicholas wondered just how strong her loyalty would prove if he offered to set her up as his countess. It amused him to think of Penelope's chagrin and mortification at such an eventuality. She would undoubtedly leave the Abbey in a flurry of self-righteous condemnation.

Of course, his present course of action promised to achieve the same results with less inconvenience to himself. He had given the order as soon as he had declined Lady Octavia's invitation to join her in the Long Gallery. The old butler had gone rigid with indignation, of course, and pretended not to understand the colonel's crisply issued command. Eventually

Featherbow had bowed to superior force, but from his extreme pallor and agitation, the butler had given every indication of suffering an imminent seizure and had withdrawn in disarray. A while later, Nicholas had heard the unmistakable sounds of heavy steps coming and going on the main staircase. With any luck, Lady Penelope would trip over the blasted portraits when she returned from her afternoon ride.

He would not have long to wait now, he thought, taking a long pull at the amber liquid in his exquisitely cut crystal glass. And when she came, he would be ready.

There was a sudden, violent crash behind him, and Nicholas paused to wipe the satisfied smile off his face before turning to face the enemy.

She had come, all right, and although she was indisputably the enemy, and Nicholas had vowed to destroy her and every vestige of her Ashington pride, he could not repress a tremor of admiration at her magnificence.

Lady Penelope reminded him of nothing so much as a tigress on the rampage. She stood glaring fiercely at him, sleek, and poised, and dangerously tensed for the attack. Nicholas instantly recognised the look that glittered in the depths of her lilac eyes. He had seen that exact same look many times before. Most recently he had glimpsed that killer-lust in the blood-shot gaze of the French officer who had nearly put paid to his existence at Waterloo. The lady's eyes were not blood-shot, but deep in their lilac orbs Nicholas recognised the fighting fury he had sought in instill in his troops before each battle. He knew that if Lady Penelope had had a sabre in her fist at that moment, he would have been in danger for his life. Instead, she held her riding-crop, and Nicholas wondered if she planned to use it on him.

Time stretched out interminably as she faced him, eyes locked with his in a challenge so palpably belligerent that Nicholas felt the hairs at the back of his neck rise in response. Finally, Lady Penelope reached behind her to slam the library door and stepped further into the room.

Nicholas allowed his gaze to drift insolently over her rigid form, moving from the delightfully disordered crown of pale curls, down her aristocratic Ashington nose, pausing briefly on her shapely mouth, drawn taut with fury. His eyes dropped to the white column of her throat and passed down to her breast, provocatively moulded in the deep blue jacket of her riding habit. He paused again, conscious of the agitated rise and fall of her small breasts beneath the clinging habit. He smiled wryly at the voluptuous visions—so foreign to his plans for this particular female that he was quite taken by surprise— which assailed him at the thought of placing his hands on those shapely female hips which flared quite wantonly beneath her small waist.

Abruptly, she broke the spell. "I fail to see anything amusing in what you are doing, Colonel. And I would like an explanation of this mad start of yours. If you please," she added, as an afterthought.

Nicholas's smile broadened. "I was merely admiring the charming picture you present, Cousin," he replied softly, glad of the chance to mock her. "I swear you quite take my breath away."

He caught a flash of bewilderment in her eyes, before she could veil them. Then she stamped her foot angrily. "You are being quite ridiculous," she exclaimed crossly. "Quite deliberately so, I don't doubt it. I was referring to the outrageous orders you have given to poor Featherbow. I can only assume that he has misunderstood you, Colonel."

"Really? I very much doubt that, Penelope. My orders were particularly clear, or so I thought." He paused to savour the moment of triumph. "What is he doing that has alarmed you?" he added innocently.

"You know perfectly well what he is doing," she snapped. "He is bringing down all the family portraits from the Long Gallery and stacking them in the front hall." Her eyes begged him to reassure her that this atrocity was not happening in her privileged, protected world, although Nicholas knew that no such words would pass her lips.

For the briefest of moments, Nicholas wavered, his lust for revenge pierced by the intensity of those lilac eyes. The moment passed, however, and he raised quizzical brows. "That is exactly what I instructed him to do," he admitted, striving to keep the unholy satisfaction out of his voice.

"But why?" she cried. "You had only to tell me if you wanted the Gallery cleaned and I would have—"

"I don't care a fig what happens to the damned Gallery," he interrupted coldly. "You may store hay there with my blessing."

He noticed that Penelope had gone very pale and had clutched at the back of a wing-chair for support, her riding-crop hanging limply from her wrist. The chit has courage, he thought, impressed in spite of himself.

"Featherbow informs me that you have ordered the paintings sent up to London," she said through lips that quivered slightly.

Nicholas observed them dispassionately. He was usually immune to feminine wiles, but Penelope's distress was much more profound than he had bargained for. He deliberately thought of his grandmother's shame, and the moment of weakness passed.

"Yes," he said calmly, taking a fortifying draught of the brandy. "It seemed to me that I should be able to get a better price for them in London. What do you think, Cousin?"

"You . . . you cannot be serious, Colonel." Her voice was barely audible.

Nicholas noticed that her knuckles showed starkly white against the red damask of the chair. He stared at her, waiting for the thrill of triumph he had expected to feel when the top-lofty Lady Penelope finally realised that she was about to lose her precious ancestors, but the triumph was strangely muted.

"Of course I'm serious, you silly chit," he said impatiently. "Why else would I say so?"

Penelope stared at him for several moments, her magnificent eyes clouded with warring emotions. "You are mad," she whispered at last. "Utterly mad, Cousin. How can you possibly consider selling your heritage to the highest bidder? The very notion is obscene."

"They are not my ancestors," he retorted coldly. "They are nothing to me at all."

"Oh, but they are your *family*. Your own *grandfather* is in one of the paintings," Penelope pleaded, the hint of desperation in her voice filling him with perverse pleasure.

"My father is not there," he said, all the old resentments rising to the surface of his mind with familiar clarity. "Nor my grandmother, God bless her sweet soul. She was not good enough for the Ashingtons, of course." Nicholas could hear the bitterness in his voice at the mention of his grandmother. "And neither am I." He laughed, a strange harsh sound which startled him. "I never will be either. Not if I have anything to say in the matter."

He turned his back, strangely reluctant to witness the suffering in her distraught expression, and poured himself another brandy from the decanter on the mantelpiece. His face, when he glanced up at it in the mirror, was almost as pale as hers, and his eyes seemed to have become deep wells of dark, turbulent emotions. Her voice, when it came, dragged him back from the edge of this unfamiliar abyss of half-formed regrets.

"How much did you expect to get for them?"

The timbre of her voice should have warned him. He swung around and found himself facing a metamorphosed woman. Gone was the pleading expression, gone the pale, anguished stare filled with the terrifying realisation that her world had trembled. No longer did Lady Penelope's small hands clasp the chair for support. She stood quietly, an expression of dignity tinged with hauteur on her tranquil face. She had the look of a woman who had faced horror and survived. Nicholas had seen that expression before, too. It startled him to see it in the eyes of a woman whose spirit he had thought to break. He let out a crack of harsh laughter. This chit was turning out to be a worthy adversary.

"Anywhere from three to five thousand pounds." He imagined that the sum would wipe the calm serenity from her lovely face and set her to begging again. But again, she surprised him.

"I shall give you four thousand," she said, quite as though she were discussing the price of eggs. "I shall instruct Featherbow to have the paintings stored in the Dower House." She turned to leave, and her calm assumption that he would accept her terms nettled him.

"And if I do not agree to your price?"

She turned, a small secretive smile on her lips. "Oh, but you will, Colonel," she assured him confidently. "Unless, of course, you wish to admit openly that you are indeed the rogue you seem to imagine we take you for."

When he made no reply—what could he say that would not confirm her opinion of him?—she turned and swept out of the room, leaving Nicholas with a distinct impression that although

he seemed to have won this skirmish, he had better look sharp
if he intended to win the war.

Penelope was still trembling with mingled fury and disgust
long after she had retreated to her room, allowed Alice to
remove the blue riding-habit, and stretched out on her bed to
recover from her shattering encounter with the colonel in the
library. At her abigail's insistence, she had submitted to having
her face bathed with lavender water, but these tender ministrations did nothing to alleviate the quaking of her limbs and the
terrifying feeling that her life at Ashington Abbey would never
be the same again.

"Shall I bring you up a cup of tea, milady?" Alice enquired
gently after she had settled her mistress in the big four-poster,
her eyes covered by the damp cloth.

"No, thank you, Alice," Penelope replied. "It will soon be
time to dress for dinner. Where is my aunt?" She had not seen
Lady Octavia since her return from visiting Clayton Manor,
and for this she was grateful. Sooner or later her ladyship
would have to know that they had a real enemy in their midst,
one who was evidently bent on destroying them. One who, in
fact, had revealed himself to be every inch the rogue her aunt
had claimed he would be. But for now, Penelope needed time
to gather her strength for what promised to be a pitched battle
for the survival of everything the Ashingtons had held sacred
from that glorious day so long ago when William, Duke of
Normandy, had conferred the first barony on that warlike
Norman knight.

"Her ladyship is resting, milady. She has not left her
sitting-room all afternoon."

Penelope sighed in relief. "Then my aunt is unaware that his
lordship has ordered the family portraits removed from the
Long Gallery?" There was no use pretending that the servants
were not fully informed about the new earl's eccentricities, she
thought, seeing that her question came as no surprise to her
abigail. Before the day was out even the remotest tenants
would know that open warfare had broken out between the lord
of the manor and the Ashington ladies.

"Oh, no, milady. You can be easy on that head. Her ladyship
offered to give Lord Laughton a tour of the Gallery after lunch,

but his lordship was somewhat abrupt with her, or so I heard, because Lady Octavia retired to her room immediately."

Penelope removed the damp cloth from her eyes and stared at her abigail in surprise. "Who told you all this, Alice?" she demanded and was further astonished when Alice turned a bright pink.

"I heard it from Mr. Samuel, milady," Alice murmured, her eyes lowered demurely.

So, Penelope mused, the black-bearded giant had made a conquest of her level-headed maid. She experienced a pang of alarm, and the ungenerous thought occurred to her that perhaps the huge sergeant had been deliberately sent to infiltrate the enemy camp. "I wouldn't trust that bearded heathen if I were you, Alice," she felt obliged to warn her abigail. "Remember that his loyalty is with the colonel, not to us."

Alice's gaze showed her uneasiness, but her voice was firm. "Oh, you have nothing to fear from Samuel, milady. He is a great hulk of a man to be sure, but gentle and kind, take me word for it, milady. Not like his lordship at all."

Penelope was not so sure, but she held her peace. "I think I will wear my new green silk this evening," she said, determined to show that monstrous rogue that she was unimpressed by his malevolent manoeuvres to upset her. "And perhaps my mother's emeralds."

It was Alice's turn to stare at her mistress in astonishment. "You'll be going down to dinner, milady?" she blurted, her brown eyes round with alarm. "Wouldn't it be best to have a tray sent up, milady?" she added coaxingly. "You'll feel ever so much better for an early night and a good rest, believe me, you will."

"I am sure you are right, Alice," Penelope replied. "But if that rogue thinks I intend to cower in my room, he will soon find he is sadly mistaken. Do you want him to suppose he can ride roughshod over this household with nobody to say him nay?" So incensed was she at the thought of the colonel gloating over her supposed defeat, that Penelope found she was no longer trembling. She flung the covers off and slid out of bed.

"Give me my robe, Alice. I intend to have a serious talk with Lady Octavia." If there was to be a war, she thought, slipping

into the blue silk dressing-gown Alice held ready for her, the
Ashington ladies would be wise to plan a defensive strategy.

Lady Octavia agreed heartily with this decision when
Penelope entered the private sitting-room they shared several
minutes later. To her surprise and relief, her aunt did not
embark on her favourite sermon against the evils of the
encroaching lower classes, nor did she waste time in fruitless
recriminations. Privately, Penelope suspected that the news of
the colonel's iniquity had overset her aunt more than she cared
to admit. Her usually ruddy cheeks had paled at Penelope's
graphic description of the new earl's unprecedented attack on
the Ashington heritage.

"The black-hearted, bloody bastard!" she exclaimed as soon
as the audacity of the upstart's action had penetrated her
befuddled brain. "A pox on the rogue! A vulgar make-bait and
cursed lickpenny, if ever I saw one!"

"Aunt Octavia!" Penelope intervened with a reluctant grin.
"Such language is unworthy of you, dearest. And if you intend
to use it on the colonel, you had best be warned that he is much
better at it than you will ever be, believe me."

Lady Octavia snorted rudely. "It is most satisfying to be able
to vent one's feelings, Penelope, as you will discover before
you are much older." She regarded her niece curiously.
"However do you know so much about that rogue's vocabu-
lary? Never tell me that he has used it on you?"

Penelope smiled ruefully at the memory of her cousin's rage
during their first skirmish over his medicine. "As a matter of
fact, he did, Aunt. When I poured that green syrup all over his
face. I admit that it was a ramshackle thing to do, and I
deserved it, but he did react rather more violently than I had
expected."

"Like the true barbarian he is," Lady Octavia muttered. "But
you can depend on me to help you, Penelope. I suggest that we
maintain an icy silence during dinner. That should put the
pretentious mushroom in his place."

She should have known, she thought angrily, the morning
after that uncomfortably silent dinner, when she discovered
that the enormous silver epergne was missing from the
sideboard in the state dining-room. Yes, she should have

known that the colonel would not capitulate quite so tamely. A cursory examination of the silver cupboards revealed that many of the heavy pieces which had graced the Ashingtons' tables throughout the generations were also missing. A closer perusal convinced her that serious inroads had been made into the family silver, including the solid dinner plates which were reputed to have been used by Queen Bess herself while visiting the Abbey on one of her progresses throughout the land.

When she failed to find Featherbow at his usual post in the front hall, Penelope surmised that the butler was deliberately avoiding her. Resolutely, she made her way down to the kitchens and discovered that she was right: Featherbow was sitting dejectedly at the huge kitchen table, moodily staring into a tankard of ale.

He leapt to his feet at her appearance, a guilty expression on his weathered face.

"Ah, Featherbow," Penelope said in a level voice. "I believe you have something to tell me about the silver. Am I right?"

The butler looked as though he had swallowed something unpleasant, and his eyes slid nervously around the room. "Yes, milady," he said finally. "The earl has seen fit to have most of the silver boxed up and stored in one of the guest-rooms in the West Wing. It was the first thing he said to me when he came down to breakfast this morning, milady." He looked at her helplessly. "There weren't nothing I could do. Nothing at all. He wouldn't listen to reason, milady, and that's a fact."

The idea of the ancient butler trying to reason with that pig-headed scoundrel made Penelope smile in spite of herself. "Do you mean you had the temerity to tell the colonel he was being unreasonable?" she enquired. "I congratulate you, Featherbow. I hardly dare do so myself."

"He threatened to let me go without a reference, milady." The butler ran a gnarled hand over his face. "I never thought to live to see the day when a Featherbow would receive such treatment in this house," he muttered. "After nearly fifty years of service, too."

Penelope's temper suddenly flared again. "Have no fear, Featherbow," she said calmly. "Your position at the Abbey is as safe as mine, so don't you worry." She refrained from pointing out that her position was considerably shaky and would

undoubtedly be more so as soon as she could find the colonel
and give him a piece of her mind.

She was unable to vent her fury upon the colonel until
mid-afternoon, however, because he had driven out to visit a
tenant with old Matthew Stevens in the gig. When Featherbow
brought the tea-tray up to the sitting-room where Penelope sat
with her aunt discussing the latest iniquity committed by the
earl, he had news of the colonel's return.

"Jeremy sent up word from the stables that his lordship has
just driven in, milady," the butler said in his most toneless
voice. "Shall I request his lordship to wait upon you, milady?"

Penelope glanced at her aunt and decided against this line of
action. If she summoned him, he would know she had
discovered the missing silver. It would be far better to surprise
him, Penelope thought, picking up her Norwich shawl and
making for the door.

"No, thank you, Featherbow," she said. "I won't be long,
Aunt," she added, her thoughts already on the unpleasant
interview ahead of her.

The stables lay but a short walk from the house, and when
Penelope arrived in the stable-yard, she saw the gig still
standing there, although Jeremy had unhitched the horse and
was giving him a vigorous rub-down. The lad touched his
forelock as soon as he saw her.

Penelope strode purposefully into the horse barn and looked
right and left along the long line of stalls. They were distress-
ingly empty these days, she thought, as she wandered through
the dim, sweet-smelling stable. Would they ever be filled with
scores of hunters and bustling grooms again? she wondered. As
in the days when her father held regular meets at the Abbey?
Those had been happy, fun-filled days, she remembered, and as
the horse-mad daughter of the house, she had been at the centre
of all that exciting activity. Today a black threat hung over her
beloved home, and for the first time, Penelope questioned her
ability to stave off the ruin which the new earl seemed
determined to bring down on their heads.

Halfway down the length of the barn she came across the
first occupied stall. A huge raw-boned chestnut swung his head
up nervously as she stopped to peer into the gloom of the stall.
She recognised the enormous animal as the gelding Sergeant

Hardy had ridden up the driveway the day her cousin arrived at the Abbey. Had she known the disaster the colonel would unleash upon her family, she mused, would she have acted any differently? Would she have been quite so determined to save his ugly hide from the Grim Reaper?

She shuddered at the thought and what it implied. It was unworthy of her, she decided, reaching into the stall to stroke the soft muzzle of the tall horse.

"I wouldn't do that if I were ye, lass," came a softly lilting voice from behind her, making her jump round in surprise. "Old Dogbones here can be mighty temperamental when he takes a dislike to someone."

Penelope smiled up at the bearded face towering above her. "Do you suppose he has taken me in dislike, Sergeant?" she enquired. "And who can blame the poor animal for being testy with a name like that? Shame on you, Sergeant, for calling a perfectly good horse by such a degrading name."

"He was a bag of bones when I got him, milady," the soft voice continued. "And when ye get right down to it, lassie, one name is pretty much like any other, wouldn't ye say?"

"I doubt you will ever get her ladyship to agree to such a heresy as that, Sam," a deep, amused voice remarked from behind her. "The very idea that there is no difference between being born an Ashington, let's say, and being someone as plebeian as a Hardy, or a Morgan, or even a Bellington, is close to blasphemy. Wouldn't you agree, Cousin?"

Penelope ignored him.

"Thank you for introducing me to your horse, Sergeant," she said, bestowing a deliberately charming smile on the bearded giant. "Perhaps the name is fitting after all," she added impulsively. "Not every horse can be blue-blooded can it? And blood will always tell in the end."

The sergeant threw her a speculating glance from beneath his heavy brows before taking his leave and striding away down the length of the barn, his feet echoing softly in the straw.

CHAPTER SIX

Frontal Attack

Penelope stood for a full minute, watching the giant shape disappear soundlessly into the dimness of the barn. She was acutely conscious of the presence of the man behind her, an immovable force she must face and try to convince that the course he had chosen was ruinous to all of them. In destroying the Ashingtons and the heritage of the earls of Laughton, the seventh earl was destroying himself, too. Of course, he could never sell the land or the Abbey, but he could mortgage them and put the family so deeply in debt that it might take another two or three generations to recover. If they ever did. Penelope was not quite certain about the legality of what the colonel had done with the portraits from the Long Gallery. She had always considered them part of the estate and hence entailed, as she had the silver. The huge epergne, she recalled, had been a gift from a grateful Bolingbrook, Earl of Lancaster, before he became Henry IV to an earlier Ashington, presumably—or so the family history claimed—for unspecified assistance in wresting the throne from Richard II. No, she thought resolutely, she could not stand by and allow this unprincipled rogue to strip her of everything she treasured.

She swung round to face him and paused, suddenly aware of the seemingly impossible task she had set herself. The colonel lounged against Dogbones's stall, his left arm—freed of its sling—resting along the top rail and his right hand thrust casually into the pocket of his buckskin breeches. Her eyes were drawn to the powerful muscles of his thighs beneath the tightly stretched cloth and the breadth of his shoulders encased in the plainly cut brown coat, and for the first time it struck her that Colonel Bellington would be considered a fine figure of a man in many circles. Except for his face, of course. She raised her gaze to examine the scar that would always disfigure what might have once been called a handsome face. Did he feel any bitterness at the mutilation? she wondered fleetingly. Had she been in his place, she would have been devastated, but then perhaps it was different for a man. No, she amended quickly, it was different for some men. The sudden picture of her cousin Geoffrey's consternation had his petulant good looks suffered such a mutilation made her smile.

"You find my appearance amusing, Penelope?"

His voice was deep and faintly melodious, she realised with surprise. In fact, it was rather pleasing to the ear in a disturbing kind of way, which she could not fathom. And his mouth was relaxed into that half-mocking smile he often wore when he looked at her. It was an extraordinarily inviting month, she thought abstractedly, full and generous, yet firm to the touch. Or so she imagined. Her mind skittered to a stop, embarrassed at the wantonness of her thoughts. In the half-lighted stable, her senses lulled by the sweet-smelling straw and the familiar sounds of horses munching in their stalls, Penelope found herself suddenly awash with emotions and yearnings she had never experienced before. Their intensity frightened her, and she saw from the flicker of amusement in the colonel's eyes that he had guessed her momentary weakness.

"Not at all, Colonel," she replied crisply, thrusting all softer emotions from her mind. "I do not find anything about you amusing, if you want the truth. Quite the contrary." She paused, strangely reluctant to break the fragile peace between them by insulting him.

"What *do* you find me, then? Besides an encroaching mushroom unworthy of the position thrust upon me, of course." His voice was almost gentle, but Penelope distinctly heard the underlying touch of sarcasm.

"I have never said anything of the kind," she protested.

"But you have thought it? Am I not right?"

What could she say to that, she wondered, short of an outright lie? "I'll admit to certain reservations about your willingness to accept the responsibilities of the title," she countered carefully. "At least at first."

"And now?"

She looked into his eyes and wondered—not for the first time—exactly what kind of a man the colonel really was. Not one that she had ever encountered before; that had been evident from the day they met. He was nothing like her brother, whom she had been able to tease or bully or cajole into doing practically anything. Nor was he like Edward. The very notion of comparing the dark, slightly sinister man before her with her dear Edward was ludicrous, of course. Edward had been all that was agreeable, attentive, and adoring. No other man could ever hope to meet his standards.

Penelope sighed and brought her attention back to the man in front of her, observing her with dark, unreadable eyes.

"Now?" she repeated. "Now I believe you could well do so if you put your mind to it." She ventured a tentative smile. "You would have to put all the silver back, of course."

"I am sorry to disoblige you, my dear," the colonel drawled, evidently amused at her attempt to deflect him from his goal.

"You plan to sell that, too, I presume?" Penelope felt her previous illusion of well-being in the company of her cousin slipping away.

He only smiled, as if the question were too obvious to need an answer.

"How much?" Penelope demanded shortly, determined not to give this man the satisfaction of seeing her beg for anything, even to save the family silver.

The colonel laughed outright. "I'm glad to see we are beginning to understand each other better, Penelope. I imagine three or four thousand would be all I could get for such old-fashioned pieces."

Penelope felt herself start to tremble with anger and frustration at this crass disregard for the symbols of the most glorious moments of her family's past. "I cannot understand you," she whispered, unable to put into words her utter incomprehension of the new earl's lack of pride in their shared heritage. "I have tried," she continued, keeping her voice low and reasonable, "but I find your actions truly outrageous and perverse."

The colonel's grin widened. "Of course, you do not understand me, my dear," he drawled with what seemed to Penelope deliberate sarcasm. "You are an Ashington, Penelope, and live in a rarified world removed from the realities of life. You will never understand me while you continue to see life through those lovely Ashington eyes of yours." He paused, and Penelope felt the sudden heat of his dark eyes devouring her face. She felt inexplicable dizzy and put out a hand to the rail on Dogbones's stall to steady herself.

"How can you expect me to be anything else but an Ashington?" she asked, her anger suspended by the unexpected compliment—the first she had ever heard from him. "That's what I am, after all."

"That's exactly my point." He glared down at her as if willing her to understand his argument. "But I am not, you see. So don't expect me to behave like one. Don't ask me to see and feel what simply is not there for me." He paused again, and his eyes left her face to wander off into the dimness of the barn. "I don't belong here, Penelope. That's the truth of the matter." The bitterness was back in his voice, and his mouth lifted derisively, stretching the pink scar into a twisted curl of disgust or self-loathing. Penelope could not tell which.

"There is no truth in that whatsoever!" she exclaimed sharply and without in the least meaning to come to his defence. All she knew was that this stern man's unexpected admission had touched her deeply. "Ashington blood runs in your veins just as strongly as it does in mine."

She was totally unprepared for the ferocious look he turned upon her. "I would prefer not to be subjected to your insults, Penelope," he snarled in a voice so full of repressed fury that it caused her to grasp the rail more tightly for support. Even Dogbones raised his head to stare at them, sensing the tension in the air.

"I didn't mean—" she began.

"No, of course, you didn't mean to insult me," he cut in savagely. "That is precisely why it is doubly offensive." He turned away from her impatiently to run his hand down the velvety muzzle of the startled horse.

Penelope was lost. "I don't quite see—"

Again the colonel interrupted her, his attention still on the horse. "No, how could you? How could it ever occur to you that Ashington blood means nothing to me?" he said harshly. "If I could drain every last drop of it out of my veins, I would do so." He swung round to face her, his eyes blazing with an emotion that caused Penelope to press back against the stall railing in alarm. "I am a Bellington, Penelope. Nothing will ever induce me to see your precious Ashington silver or portraits or anything else in that mausoleum of a house as anything but a monument to stiff-necked pride and arrogance. If I had my way, I would burn it all down to the ground."

He stopped abruptly, as if suddenly regretting his unguarded outburst. With a visible effort, he pulled his lips into a taut grin. Quite unexpectedly, he reached out to touch her face.

The gesture took Penelope by surprise, and she stood mesmerized for several moments, acutely conscious of his fingers tracing the contours of her cheek with feather-light softness. When his hand came to rest beneath her chin and gently tilted her face, she realised with a jolt that he was about to kiss her. The notion was utterly preposterous, but the enigmatic glitter in his dark eyes flustered her into stepping abruptly away. She must have been mistaken, she thought, her blood pulsing wildly in her veins. This man hated her, she reminded herself firmly. He was merely trying to humiliate her or amuse himself at her expense. This rational explanation of the dangerously seductive moment calmed her racing pulses, and she glanced at him through her lashes.

"Poor little Penelope," he murmured softly, thrusting the offending hand back into his pocket. "I have shocked your gentle sensibilities, have I not? Do not tease yourself, my dear. I promise not to burn the Abbey down about your head. Word of a soldier, if not a gentleman."

Since no apology seemed to be forthcoming for the other shock he had given her, Penelope pulled the shawl closer about her shoulders and met his gaze defiantly. "It is unkind of you to roast me, my lord," she said stiffly, hoping that her voice did not betray her emotional upheaval. "Will you accept three thousand pounds for the silver?"

"Is that all you are offering, my dear?" She was quite certain that he was mocking her but refused to rise to the bait.

"Just so."

"In that case, it is yours, Penelope. And I wish you joy of it."

Without another word, the colonel turned away from her and walked off into the dim recesses of the barn.

Nicholas was more than usually blue-deviled when he came upstairs to dress for dinner that evening. He had come within a hair's-breadth of kissing the silly chit, he thought, wondering what maggot had got into his head to contemplate such folly. Not that he had actually contemplated it for a moment, of course. He had been quite thrown off stride by his own vehement tirade against the Ashingtons, and she had looked up at him with those wonderful lilac eyes full of shock. But it had been the flicker of alarm which had quite melted his rage, and then his hand—seemingly of its own accord—had been trailing down the soft curve of her cheek. And when it reached her chin, it had seemed so natural to tilt her face up. Her lips had been parted, he remembered vividly, as if enticing him to take further liberties. He recalled the velvety fullness of them and the anticipation of their sweet warmth which had triggered the familiar stab of desire.

And then she had stiffened and stepped back. Thank God that one of them had shown some particle of sense, he thought. He had been spared the humiliation of making a cake of himself with the one female in the whole country he had sworn to bring to her knees.

This distracting thought caused him to ruin another starched neckcloth, which he tore off and flung to the floor in an uncharacteristic display of temper.

"Here, sir, you'd best let Mr. Bates do that or we'll never get you downstairs on time," his sergeant remarked from behind him, where he stood with another pristine cravat over his brawny arm.

Nicholas grunted in disgust but allowed the elderly valet to place the last cravat round his neck and tie it in a simple but elegant fall. He did not like being waited on, so had never called upon Bates, the late earl's valet, to assist him in dressing, although he tolerated the valet's insistence upon keeping his new masters' sparse wardrobe in order.

"I see you have been badgering that poor wee lass again," Samuel remarked with the casual familiarity that had always existed between the two men. The sergeant glanced specula-

tively at the colonel, and Nicholas thought he detected a hint of
censure in his batman's soft voice. He picked up the second
bank-draft, which had been delivered an hour ago by Featherbow. Penelope's handwriting was firm and round and decisive,
much like herself, Nicholas thought with a flash of amusement.

As he made his way down to the drawing-room twenty
minutes later, Nicholas found himself hoping that Penelope had
chosen to wear her green grown again this evening. Last
week—after their first set-to—she had been defiantly dazzling
in it, the green silk providing the perfect foil for her pale gold
hair. He had meant to tell her so, but her chilly reserve had put
an effective damper on their brief encounter before dinner.

Now, as he approached the drawing-room, he heard the
sound of music and smiled. So, he thought, the tiresome chit
was feeling cheerful in spite of having had to part with three
thousand pounds. He stopped just inside the door and saw—
with a glimmer of satisfaction he quickly repressed—that
Penelope was alone. She wore a blue dress tonight, cut low
over her small bosom and tied beneath her breasts with a sash
in a darker shade. The white expanse of her throat was
enhanced by a single strand of pearls. Such perfect skin
merited an adornment more voluptuous than a simple necklace,
he thought, struck by the incongruity of the notion.

Lady Penelope seemed to sense his examination for she
stopped in mid-phrase and raised her eyes.

"Please continue," Nicholas said, strolling over to the
pianoforte. "I did not mean to disturb you."

"I am a mediocre player," she replied, her hands idle in her
lap. Nicholas knew from what he had heard that Penelope was
lying, but he had the distinct impression that she would not
play again even if he got down on his knees to beg her, which
naturally he had no intention of doing.

So, he thought, the wench was bent on defying him, was
she? Well, he would see about that. He smiled and examined
the elegant rosewood instrument intently, running his palm
over the polished surface and then standing back to admire it.
"Hmm," he murmured conversationally. "I wonder how much
an instrument like this would bring in London?"

Lady Penelope's response was everything that he could have
wished. Her lilac eyes widened as the implications of his

remark sank in. Her alarmed gaze met his amused one, and Nicholas found himself half seduced again by the brilliance reflected there.

"You are not serious, I trust, my lord?" she said with a coolness he had to admire.

"Why shouldn't I be, my lady?" he shot back.

He saw her take a deep breath to steady her nerves. "Because this instrument belonged to my mother. It was a wedding present from my father, and now belongs to *me*." She glared at him. "You have absolutely no right to dispose of it on some capricious whim."

He felt a frisson of unholy satisfaction. The wench had taken a direct hit, he thought. He pressed his advantage. "Indeed?" he said, imitating her coolness. "You know how little history matters to me, Penelope. Perhaps you would do well to consider how much—in monetary terms, not sentimental ones, of course—the instrument is worth to you."

Penelope sprang to her feet, her eyes blazing, face pale as the pearls she wore. "You are odious on all points, Colonel," she said, ice dripping from every word. "An insensitive Jackstraw," she stormed. "A barbarous, uncouth oaf, with no more notion of what it means to be a gentleman than that bearded blackguard who is forever skulking around—"

"Penelope!" Lady Octavia's scandalised cry startled them both. "What is the meaning of this hoydenish conduct?"

Nicholas was gratified to see a deep blush suffuse his cousin's perfect cheeks. He grinned at her. "How much, my dear?" he murmured before turning to greet Lady Octavia.

"Well?" that lady demanded, advancing into the room. "I am waiting for an answer, Penelope."

Something in the stubborn set of his cousin's head, the slight tremble he perceived in her tightly clasped hands, and the unnatural brightness of her eyes warned Nicholas that Lady Penelope was quite capable of sending them all to the devil and storming out of the room. He took pity on her and guided Lady Octavia to her usual place on the settee and murmured soothingly that her niece had merely displayed some spirited reluctance to his request that she play for them after dinner.

Lady Octavia looked at him oddly, but chose to accept his explanation. "Oh, I see no reason why she should be skittish about that," she remarked, settling herself comfortably. "Penelope is an excellent pianist and much in demand at evening gatherings."

Nicholas took his place before the hearth, looking across Lady Octavia's head to lock gazes with a pair of wrathful lilac eyes. What excuse would his cousin find, he wondered, to avoid playing for them after dinner?

CHAPTER SEVEN

Brighton Retreat

"Oh, fiddle!" Lady Octavia exclaimed energetically as the heavy travelling coach made its way laboriously along the winter-ravaged Sussex road. "I can think of a dozen worse things the rogue could have done to us besides selling off the furniture and the horses. So cheer up, dear. We will do very well in Brighton, even though the Regent is not in residence at this time of year."

Penelope sighed and made a valiant attempt to pull herself out of the brown study she had fallen into ever since leaving Laughton Abbey earlier that morning. "Tell me a single one, Aunt, and perhaps I will believe you."

"He could have filled the house with a bevy of light-skirts and opera dancers," her aunt replied, evidently finding a certain grim pleasure in attributing this particular form of depravity to the seventh Earl of Laughton. "Or invited a whole company of his military cronies to indulge in drunken orgies. Or he could have done both, my dear, and then we would have been forced to witness an endless succession of half-clad nymphs running up and down the stairs pursued by drunken soldiers."

"Nymphs?" Penelope repeated, intrigued as always by her aunt's fertile imagination. "I thought you said they were light-skirts and opera dancers?"

Lady Octavia shrugged her ample shoulders. "It's one and the same," she insisted. "Everyone knows what opera dancers are."

"They do?" Penelope stared at her aunt in astonishment.

"I'm sure I know no such thing, Aunt. And I would like to know how you came by this interesting bit of information."

When Lady Octavia did not respond, Penelope laughed, momentarily distracted from her melancholy. "There, it's just as I thought. You haven't the least idea how opera dancers go on, do you, Aunt?"

"Indeed, I do," Lady Octavia said indignantly. "If you must know, your father nearly ruined us all by running off with one." When she saw she had Penelope's startled attention, she continued complacently. "My brother Freddy really made a cake of himself, my dear. He was besotted with the creature, but luckily your grandfather was able to convince the hussy that five thousand pounds was of more immediate benefit to her than tying herself to a young cub almost half her age."

Penelope had heard vague rumours of an indiscretion in her father's salad days, but this was the first time she had heard any of the details.

"Why didn't you tell me all this long ago, Aunt?" she demanded. "I declare, it is monstrously entertaining." She gave her aunt a roguish grin. "And it proves that the curse of the duc de Saxe is still very much with us, don't you agree?"

"Of course, it is," Lady Octavia replied sharply. "And don't you forget it, my girl. It can strike when you least expect it." She glared at her niece as if daring Penelope to contradict her. "Now," she said, with determined cheerfulness after a few moments of silence. "Let us consider how we shall amuse ourselves in Brighton, my dear. I vow I am quite looking forward to seeing all our old friends again."

The thought of Brighton brought Penelope abruptly back to the present. It was the week after Christmas, a time when the Ashington household would normally be preparing feverishly for the New Year's Eve ball at the Abbey. Yet here they were, she thought disconsolately, jouncing around in the big coach on a cold winter day, all their personal belongings in two smaller carriages behind them, leaving their comfortable home forever. It was enough to make her want to cry, a weakness she heartily disapproved of.

"I cannot think of a single thing that would amuse me in Brighton," she remarked with uncharacteristic petulance. "And most of our friends are no doubt comfortably rusticating in their country homes at this time of year. As *we* should be." She turned to gaze morosely out at the bleak hedgerows, devoid of their summer splendour, and the unfairness of her fate seemed suddenly too much to bear. "Oh, Aunt," she wailed, "perhaps if I hadn't thrown that Chinese vase at him, the colonel might not have demanded that we remove to the Dower House. And I know it's all my fault that he left the Abbey so abruptly. I *know* it is."

"Fiddlesticks!" Lady Octavia exclaimed. "You did exactly as you ought, my love. Although I am glad your dear mother was not here to witness it, of course. And I would have given anything to see that scoundrel's face when you shattered the vase at his feet. Even though it was one of my favourites," she added philosophically. "And how many times must I repeat to you, Penelope Ashington, that it is fruitless to repine over what cannot be mended?"

Penelope gulped back the tears that threatened to overcome her, and attempted a wobbly smile. If truth were told, she had been surprised at Lady Octavia's reaction to her appalling behaviour during that last disastrous interview she had endured with the irate colonel. She could not recall precisely what he had said that had pushed her into that unladylike display of temper. After all, she had held up reasonably well under his previous attacks against her family treasures, hadn't she? During the six months since the colonel's first appearance at the Abbey, she had been forced to purchase not only the family portraits and silver, the carriages and horses, but all the oriental rugs from the Abbey drawing-rooms, her mother's favourite boudoir furniture, and many antique pieces collected by her grandmother. Perhaps it had been his arrogance in assuming that she would submit tamely to his continued threats to dismantle her home, she thought, snuggling deeper into the plaid woolen rug she had wrapped around her shoulders to stave off the damp December chill. Or perhaps it was her own desperation at being forced to choose between expending her own fortune to save her family heirlooms and begging the rogue to desist from his ruinous course of action.

And Lady Penelope Ashington would definitely not beg. She had decided that the moment she had divined his intention of breaking her will. No, she thought resentfully, that was one battle the obnoxious colonel would never win. He had obviously thought to coerce her into submission by his blatant attacks on her heritage, and she had deflected disaster by acceding to his demands. Until that afternoon in mid-December when he had pushed her too far and her patience had snapped. She still remembered clearly the liberating sensation which had flooded through her when she had said no, this is as far as she would go in this farcical charade.

They were alone in the drawing-room at the time, and the colonel had made some snide remark about the cost of two Chinese vases sitting on their low tables on either side of the hearth. The familiar prickle of fear at the humiliating scene which would ensue had made her angrier than usual. Instead of entering into the charade of bartering for the priceless objects, she had picked up the nearest vase, acutely conscious of the centuries-old fragility of the porcelain under her fingertips. She had met his eyes and recognised the gleam of triumph in their dark depths. She had lifted the vase above her head . . . Time seemed to stand still. And then the vase lay shattered on the hearth, and his look of victory vanished, replaced by shock and some intangible emotion which made her reckless with euphoria. She had laughed then, and seized a Dresden shepherdess from the mantel and tossed it after the vase, intoxicated by a new sense of freedom as the shattered pieces flew out onto the carpet at his feet.

It was that evening after dinner that the colonel had banished both Ashington ladies to the Dower House. And the following morning he was gone from the Abbey, not carousing to London as Penelope had at first supposed, but to his home in Hampshire. At least that was what Alice had been able to glean from Sergeant Hardy before the two men rode off at daybreak. No one had seen them since.

"You are right, as always, Aunt," Penelope admitted, after Lady Octavia had repeated her question for the second time. "But I do wish I knew what the colonel's intentions are regarding the Abbey. Perhaps we should have stayed at the Dower House after all, just to keep an eye on things."

Lady Octavia sighed audibly. "Much as I regret to say this, Penelope, the Abbey is no longer any concern of ours. And as for moving into the Dower House, let me tell you, my girl, that only under the direst circumstances would I ever consider living in that mausoleum. We will be much happier in Brighton, so make up your mind to it, dear."

Whether this was true or not, Penelope told herself firmly, there was no going back now.

As the weeks went by, Penelope had to agree with her aunt that the Brighton residence, which Lady Amelia Pierce—her grandmother on her father's side—had bequeathed to her many years ago, was infinitely superior in every way to the Dower House. Situated on the fashionable Steyne, the elegant residence was within comfortable walking distance of the Pump Room and other local attractions, but was in dire need of refurbishing, a task the two ladies threw themselves into with noticeable vigour. Between sending off to London for the latest samples, deciding upon new wallpaper for the formal drawing-room, and hiring extra staff for the kitchens, Penelope found herself beginning to enjoy the prospect of being absolute mistress of her own establishment. It was only occasionally, as she sat playing on her mother's pianoforte—which she had, in a last act of defiance, ordered carted down to Brighton—that Penelope's thoughts returned to her childhood home, and she would wonder what new outrage the infamous earl was committing against Laughton Abbey.

"I do hope he has not turned off any of the staff," she remarked one evening towards the end of February, while the two ladies sat by the roaring fire in the cozy Chinese drawing-room, waiting for the butler to bring in the tea-tray.

"Nonsense, child!" exclaimed Lady Octavia, instantly recognising the cause of her niece's worried frown. "You worry too much, my dear, as I have told you many times already. Featherbow is quite capable of sending any servants who are unhappy at the Abbey over to us in Brighton. Now, tell me what you wish me to do about Henrietta's invitation to spend March over at Swathmore Hall with her, Penny. I received a second note from her this morning, and she urged me for a reply."

"I would rather put off any visits until we are quite settled in here. That is, if you agree, Aunt? Besides, I would rather not be subjected to Cousin Geoffrey for such an extended period, if I can possibly avoid it. His attentions are becoming quite marked again, and I do not wish to give him any encouragement."

"I am relieved to hear you say so, dear. Poor dear Geoffrey may be my nephew and believes himself to be all the crack, but he is not my favourite gentleman by any means. But that reminds me," she continued, glancing archly at her niece. "As soon as the weather becomes warmer, we must start planning quite another campaign, love."

Penelope paused in the Schubert lieder she was practising to regard her aunt with surprise. "I am quite tired of these military manoeuvres, Aunt. It reminds me too vividly of the tactics a certain colonel employed to force us to retreat from the Abbey."

"Pooh! The rogue miscalculated badly there, if you ask me," Lady Octavia replied. "I don't doubt that he is heartily sorry for pushing you to take a retaliatory position, dear."

This comment brought a smile to Penelope's lips. "*Must* you talk as though you actually enjoyed being routed by that military rogue?"

"Oh, but we were hardly routed, dear. Look at it this way. The colonel ordered us to retreat to the Dower House, but what did you do? You spiked his guns, Penny, by deploying our forces to Brighton, quite out of his range. So, in a way, we have outmanoeuvred him after all. He must be terribly frustrated at not having us to bully any more."

"I do believe you *are* enjoying this so-called campaign against the colonel, Aunt. Don't you regret having to leave home?" she added wistfully.

"Of course, I do, my pet. I miss it a great deal, but it is no use repining over the oddities of fate, I always say. And I am beginning to feel that we will be very comfortable here. We are so much closer to the shops, and in the summer we can attend the assembles at Castle Inn, visit the Pavilion, and perhaps we might even dine there if you catch the Regent's eye, Penny. Which reminds me, we must visit Madame Dumont's salon next week to look at the new fashions. It is high time you had a whole new wardrobe, my love. I can't bear to see you looking dowdy."

Penelope looked at her aunt in surprise. "I wasn't aware I

looked dowdy, Aunt. My green silk is brand new. I've only worn it once."

"Yes, I know, dear," her aunt replied. "And perhaps that's just as well."

At Penelope's startled reaction, Lady Octavia added obscurely, "The colonel liked it far too well on you for my peace of mind, dear."

"And what on earth do you mean by that?" Penelope demanded, annoyed at herself for the sudden elation her aunt's words had caused.

"Oh, nothing, really. Except that we should not underestimate that rogue, Penelope. He will stop at nothing to obtain whatever twisted design he has in mind. We are free of him for the moment, of course. But I doubt that he will be content to let things rest as they are."

Her aunt's enigmatic prognosis filled Penelope with vague, disturbing feelings of alarm. What could her cousin do, she wondered, to upset the peaceful life the two Ashington ladies had begun to carve out for themselves in Brighton? Even if her aunt was right, and he had felt thwarted at their removal, not merely from the Abbey, but from the estate itself, what fresh attack could he launch that they could not shrug off? Having convinced herself—with a twinge of reluctance she refused to acknowledge—that the colonel had been neatly excluded from their lives, Penelope put the thought out of her head and went down to the kitchen to consult with their new cook.

By mid-March, those members of the ton who, for one reason or another, preferred not to remove to London for the Season, began to arrive in Town, and the Ashington ladies found themselves quite inundated with invitations to various dinners, musicales, and card parties. Unless the weather was particularly cold or wet, Penelope rarely missed her morning ride along the Steyne on Bluedevil, and it was on one such morning that she heard a familiar voice hailing her from one of the fashionable carriages on the parade.

"I say, Penny," Geoffrey Swathmore called out, "I'm dashed glad to see you. Have a message for you from my mother."

Much as she would have liked to, Penelope could hardly ignore him, and she brought Bluedevil alongside the bright yellow sporting curricle her cousin had recently acquired. She noted with disapproval that the two rangy chestnuts he drove were lathered with sweat and fidgeted nervously under his constant twitching at the ribbons.

"Your off wheeler is racked up too tightly, Geoffrey," she pointed out, knowing that the criticism would throw her cousin into a fit of the sulks. "And why must you always drive them into the ground?"

But her cousin didn't answer. He was staring over her shoulder, and as she watched, Penelope saw the familiar petulant expression distort his handsome features into a scowl. "The devil take the scoundrel!" he muttered beneath his breath. "What is that dashed encroaching Jackstraw doing in Brighton? He ain't badgering you again, is he, Coz?"

Penelope looked startled for a moment, and then suddenly she knew whom the object of Geoffrey's scorn must be. An unexpectedly pleasant wave of excitement shook her as she realised that by turning her head, she would see the colonel again. Was it her imagination, or could she actually feel him observing her? She did not pause to analyse this utterly nonsensical thought, but swung Bluedevil around and met the colonel's eyes instantly.

She tried to restrain the glad smile that slipped unannounced across her lips, but it was too late. Colonel Bellington had seen it and changed his direction. As he approached her, his giant black shadow riding closely behind him on a fresh-looking Dogbones, Penelope wondered if he had been about to ride by without acknowledging her presence. The thought distressed her.

The parade along the Steyne was far from crowded on a morning so early in the Season, and Nicholas had instantly recognised the pale gold halo of curls under the jaunty blue beaver. He had ridden behind her for some time, admiring her seat on the tall black gelding, and the long length of leg and thigh beneath the voluminous folds of her riding-habit. He saw young Swathmore hail her from his curricle and thought he detected a hint of reluctance in her response. But stop she did, and Nicholas found himself anticipating the moment when Lady Penelope Ashington's lilac eyes would light on him again.

He had not anticipated the impulsive smile. It caught him off-guard, and he was startled to realise how easily she had broached his defences with that single friendly gesture. He resisted the inclination to return the smile, although he was sure she must have detected the silent admiration in his gaze, for she blushed prettily as she gave him her small gloved hand.

Swathmore must have seen it, too, for the frown which marred his sharply elegant face deepened into a petulant scowl, and his nod of greeting was barely civil.

"Morning, Swathmore," the colonel said, brushing the cub with his disinterested gaze before turning back to Penelope. "You are looking in high gig this morning, Penelope," he drawled, his lips quirking into a smile. "I trust I find you and Lady Octavia in good health?"

Was that a dimple that had flashed fleetingly beside her mouth? he wondered, oddly perturbed by the possibility. And if so, why hadn't he noticed it before? He had seen at their first encounter that Lady Penelope Ashington was a fine enough looking female, but her crowning beauty of sun-bleached curls and lilac eyes, so like his grandmother's, had always drawn his attention away from the classical proportions of her face. The dimple—or had he imagined it?—had emphasized the delicate femininity of her mouth, and he found himself remembering the lost moment in the stable when he might have tasted the soft, velvety texture of her lips.

He was jerked out of this reverie by Swathmore, whose curt tone told Nicholas more clearly than any words that the cub still fancied his chances with his cousin, Penelope. Nicholas found the notion amusing.

"Come into Brighton to enjoy the petticoat company, Laughton?" Swathmore enquired with a deliberately impertinent innuendo. "I fear you could have saved yourself the trouble. It's too early in the Season for the real dashers, and I have yet to see a single chit who would appeal to a Town Beau." He regarded Nicholas with a smug grin at his own witticism, which the colonel ignored.

"I wonder you can say so, Swathmore, with Lady Penelope sitting here before you," he answered glibly, reluctant to give the cub the set-down he richly deserved for speaking so intemperately before a lady. He was rewarded by a grateful glance from Penelope, which only made Swathmore more belligerent.

"Why have you come, then?" he demanded rudely.

"That is none of your business, Geoffrey," Penelope said sharply, a blush of mortification staining her cheeks. "Pray forgive my cousin's uncouth manners, Colonel." She turned the full barrage of her magnificent eyes upon him, and Nicholas— while recognising with a glint of cynicism this instinctive feminine offensive—allowed himself to be seduced by it.

"There is no secret about my journey into Brighton," he said smoothly, deciding, on the spur of the moment as he had done so often on the battle-field, that a direct attack was his best move. "I came to see you, Penelope. I had hoped to call on you this afternoon."

"Devil a bit, man!" exclaimed the startled dandy, jerking his ribbons in agitation and causing his team to sidle nervously. "Is there to be no end to this badgering? First you throw my cousin out of her own home and then—"

"Lord Laughton did nothing of the sort, Geoffrey!" Penelope interrupted angrily. "I cannot conceive how you came by such addle-pated notions. You quite put me to the blush. Where I choose to live is my decision, and if I choose Brighton, it is none of your concern. And I will thank you to keep your odious comments to yourself."

With her colour still high, and her eyes flashing dangerously, she looked magnificent, Nicholas thought, and he found himself perversely enjoying the younger man's discomfiture.

"If you are going to be obnoxious, you can forget I invited you to dine with us tonight, for, I don't mind telling you, I intend to invite my other cousin, too." She glanced at Nicholas apprehensively. "That is if you can stand to be in the company of such a rag-mannered brat, Colonel?"

Nicholas had no trouble at all accepting this invitation, especially since he noticed that Swathmore's face turned absolutely livid with rage at Penelope's uninhibited censure. And besides, he thought as he took his leave and rode on, it was rather fortuitous that he had run his quarry to earth so soon after his arrival in Brighton. He would be able to initiate his next campaign that much faster.

For the first time since it had occurred to him last January,

Nicholas felt a twinge of uneasiness about the line of attack he had decided to employ against the Ashingtons. It had taken him some time to admit, even to himself, that in their last encounter, Penelope had soundly routed him. He had come to enjoy besting her at the game he had initiated with the ancient gewgaws of the family honour she held in such high esteem. He had grown almost addicted to their private struggle, and had anticipated just such another victory when he idly brought up the subject of the Chinese vases. He had watched with perverse pleasure for the progression of emotions that flashed across her lovely face every time he baited her.

But Lady Penelope had surprised him. She had picked up the delicate artifact and held it in front of her, glaring defiantly across its opalescent beauty into his eyes. Her own had been filled with the familiar frustration and impotent rage which his attacks usually provoked. Then all of a sudden a change had come over her countenance, starting as a flicker of surprise in her eye and expanding to engulf her entire expression. It had taken him a second to recognise it for what it was: the unholy gleam of victory in the eyes of the enemy. Unprepared as he had been for her counter-attack, he had been paralysed for those vital seconds which on the battlefield often meant the difference between life and death. And then it was too late. The Chinese vase lay shattered on the hearth, shards of porcelain littering the rug at his feet. The destruction of the Dresden figurine, which had followed the vase into oblivion, was an act of pure defiance and exultation, as was the silent, triumphant exit Lady Penelope had made, lilac eyes flashing with a passion he understood all too well, but had never expected to see in a gently bred female.

The shock of being beaten at his own game had struck so intensely at his pride that Nicholas had promptly banished both ladies to the Dower House. He had repented as soon as the curt command had been given after dinner that evening, but the colonel could not bring himself to recant. Even when Samuel offered to be his emissary, he had refused to relent. Instead, he had taken a perverse delight in ordering his henchmen to prepare to depart the Abbey at daybreak for an extended visit to Hampshire.

It was not until he was installed beside the comfortable

library fire in Bellington Hall two days later, that an unpalatable notion had struck him. Might not his unannounced departure from the Abbey be construed as a retreat? he wondered. In spite of this unpleasant thought, Nicholas had deliberately stayed away for the holidays, knowing that his absence would disrupt the planned celebrations at Laughton Abbey. What did he care for the traditional New Year's Eve ball? He had been away from home too long for such sentimental festivities to affect him, hadn't he? But as Christmas day approached, he found himself wondering what Penelope was doing. He felt a twinge of guilt at the thought of leaving her burdened with the task of supervising the gifts and traditional Christmas dinner for the staff and tenants of the huge estate.

As the old year faded into the new, Nicholas had walked in his grandmother's dark, silent, snow-covered rose garden trying to understand his own feelings about the last six months spent as master of his grandfather's childhood home. Laughton Abbey, he mused. Why, even the name held reverberations of times long gone; times when the Abbey had hosted kings and queens of England in its vast, stately halls; times when pomp and ceremony had held sway, as they doubtless had in his grandfather's day, that day, too, now gone with him to his grave on the hill overlooking Bellington Hall. Had his grandfather wished, in the secret corners of his Ashington soul, to be laid out in his allotted place beside the dozens of other Ashingtons in the carefully tended plot set aside to receive such hallowed bones? Or had he been content to lie here on the green hills of Hampshire next to his beloved Annie Bellington.

As Nicholas listened to the church bells in nearby Alton ring in the New Year, he knew, as certainly as he lived and breathed that he wanted to be buried here with his grandmother's people. His duty—as he had grudgingly come to accept it over the past few months—lay in Sussex, as the seventh Earl of Laughton but his heart lay here in Hampshire at Bellington Hall. Now, if only he could reconcile the two, he thought; duty and heart should not be thus divided.

And it was then, in the first chill, frosty hours of the New Year, that Nicholas saw his way clearly. Yes, he thought amazed at the simplicity of the solution which had been there before him all this time. He had it in his power to avenge his grandmother in a manner that would undoubtedly have appealed to her lively sense of the ridiculous. He would do his duty to the Ashingtons, as his grandfather would have wanted him to, regardless of the rancour that David Ashington had preserved intact up to the day of his death.

But Nicholas would destroy them, too. As he had sworn to do the day he first learned his grandmother's story. He would obliterate the last Ashington from the face of the earth. And he could do it in such a way that Lady Penelope Ashington would know, beyond a shadow of a doubt, that she had been finally defeated. Defeated by a Bellington, no less. He had some of the most powerful weapons at his disposal; he had the title, he had Laughton Abbey. Weapons which would be useless against someone like himself, but against Penelope they would be mortal. These were things she valued above all else; hadn't she demonstrated it to him time and again?

So he would give all these things to her. It would be a truce she would understand fully, a pact her world accepted every day without question. He would make her a countess, and in doing so, he would also make her a Bellington. The final defeat for that pride he had so often seen glittering in her lilac eyes. She would live and die a Bellington, possibly even here at Bellington Hall, and lie beside the great-uncle she never knew, rejected by her family so long ago.

And beside his gentle grandmother, who would have loved her, loved her and forgiven her, he realised intuitively, conscious of a sudden feeling of uneasiness at the diabolical simplicity of his plan.

The uneasiness passed, and Nicholas went to his bed savouring the irony of Fate that had placed victory and vengeance so neatly in his hand.

CHAPTER EIGHT

Proposed Alliance

"Mark my words, Penelope," Lady Octavia remarked with no little complacency, when her niece brought home the news of Colonel Bellington's arrival in Brighton. "That rogue is up to no good. So don't be taken in by this sudden concern for our health and comfort. Where was the rascal when we could have used an escort into Brighton last December, can you tell me? And why has he not shown his face here before now? That's three months, child. You'll not convince me that he has the least concern for our welfare in that black heart of his. More than likely, the scoundrel has some new trick up his sleeve to extort more blunt from you."

Penelope laughed at this stern assessment of the new earl's motives, which she was reluctant to share. "It was hardly extortion, Aunt," she corrected gently. "I got more than fair exchange for any monies I laid out at the Abbey."

"I cannot imagine what *else* you would call it, then," Lady Octavia snorted dismissively. "And as for fair exchange, that's highly debatable. Now here he comes to plague us again. I'll wager you ten pounds, lass, that this Captain Sharp is about to launch another of his military campaigns. Must have been bored silly all by himself there in that big house with no females around to intimidate with his domineering ways."

"I do not recall you complaining about any domineering manner at the time, Aunt," Penelope could not resist pointing out. "In fact, I distinctly remember you gloating when the colonel took himself off after the episode of the Chinese vase."

"Pooh! Don't argue with me, child. I can tell a rogue when I see one, let me tell you. Now, which of your new gowns are you planning to wear this evening?" she added, changing the subject so abruptly that Penelope blinked.

"I hadn't planned to take particular pains with my appearance, Aunt," she replied, wondering what her aunt was getting at. "I don't want to encourage Geoffrey, especially when he made it so plain that his object in coming to Town is to inflict his attention upon me again."

Lady Octavia waved her plump hand dismissively. "But the colonel will be here, child. I suggest the lilac silk as your best choice. It matches your eyes, love, and men always notice that kind of thing."

Penelope could not hide her astonishment at the implications of her aunt's suggestion. "What maggot has got into your head, Aunt?" she exclaimed, her cheeks glowing with annoyance. "And why should I care whether the colonel notices the colour of my eyes?" The notion was so disturbing that Penelope got up abruptly and strode over to the morning-room window, presenting a rigid back to her companion. She knew that her eyes were her best feature, and this morning the colonel's gaze had held a glint of unmistakable admiration. At least so it had appeared to her at the time. How could her aunt possible suspect . . . but no, these were the very missish fantasies that she had so despised in her friends at Miss Brady's Brighton Academy for Young Ladies when she was a mere schoolroom chit herself. Even at that early age, Penelope had been bound emotionally to the young Edward Hayward, the paragon of her dreams. She had never even considered looking at another man, much less playing one man off against another to amuse herself. Her aunt's next words brought her down to earth rather abruptly.

"I should rather hope you wouldn't be such a silly goose, dear," Lady Octavia replied easily. "If you did fancy the colonel, we would be in a pelter indeed. But then, he is not your run-of-the-mill ladies' man by any stretch of the imagination. And the poor man's face is a disaster with that dreadful scar slicing through it. But he does have a certain air about him; and when he smiles, he can be quite charming."

Penelope could do little but gape at her aunt's frank

assessment of the seventh earl's attractions. Or lack of them, she corrected herself, for that scar had taken what masculine beauty he might have had and turned it into a caricature of a face. Rather an attractive face at times, she thought, mindful of the way his smile had trembled in the curling scar beside his mouth this morning.

She had turned during her aunt's odd speech and stood looking down at her shrewd blue eyes, wondering what freakish start Lady Octavia would think of next.

"Ah, I see you have noticed that, too, Penny," she declared, a troubled frown marring the serenity of her comely face. "But do not be deceived for a moment by that smooth-talking rogue. He is an enemy to the Ashingtons, dear. I sensed it from the beginning. It wouldn't surprise me if he were driven by some corkbrained notion of righting the wrongs of the past. And of course, that is plain foolishness. He can no more change what is done than I can, and believe me, love, sometimes I heartily wish I could."

Penelope sank down on the elegant French settee as though her bones would no longer hold her upright. In her forthright manner, her aunt had put her finger on the heart of the matter. These same fears had plagued her during her dealings with Colonel Bellington at the Abbey, but she could not bring herself to admit that a man of his bearing, a man so closely related to them both, would sink to such treachery. No, she thought stubbornly, this time her aunt must be mistaken. Had he set out to ruin her, he might have asked ten times the price he had for the Ashington treasures.

She shook her head in disbelief. "What a bag of moonshine, Aunt," she said at last, standing up and brushing the creases from her modish morning gown. "Now, will you please tell me why I should wear the lilac silk tonight, dearest?"

Lady Octavia looked at her niece and sighed. "If you cannot figure that out for yourself, my love, you are even more of a peagoose than I had imagined." She paused, then a conspiratorial grin widened her generous mouth. "I was thinking in terms of diversionary tactics, dear. There is more to the colonel's innocent little excursion into Brighton than meets the eye. I am sure of it. If we can distract him with a small skirmish here and there, we might discover what his intentions are." Her blue eyes twinkled with such unholy enthusiasm that Penelope had to laugh.

"And *I* am to be the diversion, am I?" she concluded, amused in spite of herself. "What my father would have said at the spectacle of his favourite sister actually encouraging his only daughter to throw out *lures* to a gentleman of dubious reputation hardly bears thinking about, Aunt. I can only hope that this is a passing aberration and that by dinner-time you will be feeling more yourself again."

Her aunt only smiled. "Hardly anything so vulgar as lures, my love. But you *will* wear the lilac gown, won't you? Humour me, Penny. There's a good girl."

So Penelope wore the new lilac silk gown, with its scooped neckline hugging her bare shoulders above the tiny sleeves, its fashionable lines unmarred by ruffles, or bows, or floating ribands, its slim skirt falling away in clinging waves of colour from the pearl-studded sash beneath her breast, to hint at the seductive curve of a hip and thigh as she moved. Madame Dumont's only concession to frippery had been the single dark violet satin flounce at the hem, which gave the gown a distinctive rhythm and rustle when in motion.

"I feel like one of your precious opera dancers, Aunt," she remarked, preening in front of Lady Octavia's cheval mirror shortly before their visitors arrived. "Are you sure this is wise? I hate to imagine what Geoffrey's reaction will be. He is sure to imagine that I wish to attract his notice."

"Never mind that rackety moonling," her aunt replied impatiently. "It is that pesky colonel we want to hoodwink. One glimpse of you in that gown, my dear Penelope, and that rogue will forget he was ever in the King's army at all. And if we are lucky, he may even forget that the third earl's countess cast his grandmother's breeding—or lack of it—in her face."

"That would be a major victory, Aunt. But don't count on it."

From the earl's demeanour during dinner and in the drawing-room afterwards, one would never have guessed that an angry word had ever passed his lips, Penelope thought. He was impeccably dressed in a dark evening coat, evidently cut by a master, for it hugged his broad shoulders with nary a crease to tell it was not moulded to his tall body. His cream unmention-

ables and white cravat, the latter tied neatly in a modified
Mathematical, made Geoffrey's flamboyant green jacket,
nipped in at the waist, his green and silver striped waistcoat,
highly starched cravat, and lemon-yellow pantaloons look like
a caricature out of one of the London dailies.

Colonel Bellington arrived at precisely half past five, and
when he was ushered into the drawing-room, Penelope was
able to catch the unmistakable flare of admiration in his eyes
before he came across the Oriental carpet—one of those so
recently removed from his own drawing-rooms—to bow over
Lady Octavia's hand. She could not catch his murmured words,
but whatever it was brought an unfamiliar flush of pleasure to
her aunt's face. The devil take the man, she thought, watching
with some amusement as her aunt tapped him playfully on the
sleeve. He was far cleverer than they thought. No doubt the
rogue intended to charm them into believing he was harmless
after all.

When her turn came, it was all she could do not to laugh
outright as the colonel lifted her gloved hand to his lips with
studied punctiliousness and murmured a conventional flowery
phrase of greeting. The effect was ruined, however, the
moment he stood up and looked down at her, mocking laughter
in his dark eyes.

"I trust I pass muster, my lady," he drawled, holding her
hand rather longer than was strictly de rigueur.

"How absurd you are, sir," she replied promptly. "You don't
need me to tell you that. Now, please sit down, Colonel, before
I get a crick in my neck." She had become very conscious of
his height towering over her and of the provoking proximity
of his tightly encased thighs, uncomfortably in her direct line
of vision.

"How do you go on at the Abbey?" Lady Octavia enquired
brightly, as soon as the colonel had settled his frame into a
wing-back chair between the two ladies. "I do hope the
chimney in the formal dining-room did not smoke again this
winter. It has never drawn well since the wind knocked it down
in the autumn of 1795, and it had to be rebuilt."

The colonel grinned good-humouredly. "Since I have never
dined there, my lady, I have had no occasion to notice any

deficiency in the draft. But no doubt our good Featherbow would have informed me if there had been anything amiss."

"Well, and so he should," Lady Octavia remarked. "He has been there longer than I can remember." Her voice faltered, and for a terrible moment Penelope thought her aunt was about to say something impossibly nostalgic that might well remind the colonel of their differences.

"And the lambs?" she interrupted quickly. "How is this year's lambing coming along?"

His mocking glance told her all too clearly that he had seen through her ploy, but before he could reply, the door opened and the butler announced, in clearly condemnatory tones, the arrival of Mr. Swathmore. Penelope had been accustomed to seeing her cousin make a complete cake of himself ever since he was old enough to squeeze into a tightly fitted coat, but tonight Geoffrey seemed to have outdone himself. Not only was his coat a bilious green against the pale yellow of his small clothes, but his impossibly high cravat prevented him from moving his head more than an inch in either direction. He pranced into the room looking like nothing so much as a skittish horse in blinkers.

Happily for the success of the evening, Geoffrey paid no attention at all to the colonel and confined himself to boasting of all the daring deeds he had done during his brief sojourn at Oxford. Lady Octavia humoured him and kept his attention sufficiently distracted to allow Penelope to entertain the colonel with accounts of their amusements in Brighton.

It was only after both gentlemen had taken their leave, that Penelope confessed to her aunt that they might expect the colonel to call upon them tomorrow at eleven. She had been unable—and perhaps a little unwilling—to speculate on his reasons for wishing to talk to her, but her aunt had no such reservations.

"What did I tell you, love?" she remarked as they sat over one last cup of tea before retiring for the night. "The smooth rogue is all set for a spring campaign. I wonder what approach he will take this time."

Although she refrained from speculating on this subject, Penelope had a sinking sensation that her new lilac silk had

failed miserably in diverting the wily colonel from any siege he
might be planning against the Ashington ladies.

The following morning dawned cold and blustery, and
Penelope wondered if the weather presaged the outcome of her
interview with Colonel Bellington. She was not fanciful by
nature, but the sudden change from the bracing, sun-lit days
which had preceded the earl's arrival gave a melancholy hue to
her thoughts. She shook them off impatiently and squared her
shoulders as she entered the morning-room to join Lady
Octavia. Her aunt was poring over the latest samples received
from London, in her tenacious search for just the right shade of
red brocade to refurbish the chairs in the dining-room, and she
glanced up in annoyance at the appearance of her niece.

"I declare there is not a decent red among the lot, Penelope.
Whatever are we to do? I had quite set my mind on that colour,
and it oversets me to think of choosing another."

Penelope laughed at her aunt's obvious distress. "We have
much more pressing things to consider this morning, Aunt,"
she said, taking a seat in her favourite puff-pillowed settee
beside the cosy fireplace. "Here it is after ten o'clock already,
and we have not been able to determine what possible reason
the colonel might have for calling on us this morning. I am cast
into a quake at the prospect, let me tell you."

"Fiddle!" Lady Octavia scoffed. "Do not, I pray you, child,
allow yourself to be thrown into high fidgets over that black
rogue. We are quite safe from him here, after all. I fancy he is
merely scouting the ground to see if we have any chinks in our
armour. When he finds we are immune to his advances and
have covered our flanks—"

"*Please,* Aunt!" Penelope cried, dissolving into laughter.
"*Must* you adopt the language of a field marshall when
discussing the colonel? Has it never occurred to you that the
poor man may simply enjoy our company? Or perhaps he is
merely doing his duty as head of the family in looking out for
our welfare. Must you always suspect the worst of him?"

Her aunt raised her eyes from the samples and gazed at
Penelope with a gleam of alarm. "Once a rogue—" she began
sternly.

"Yes, I know, dear. Always a rogue. But I think you are off

the mark this time. The colonel behaved quite unobjectionably last night, and said everything that he ought."

"And you have fallen for the oldest trick in the world, my love," her aunt interrupted brusquely. "I'll admit that he has a smile that would charm the birds out of the trees, in spite of that dreadful scar, but don't believe a word of it, dear. This is merely a dastardly Machiavellian tactic to take us off guard. He must find himself at a disadvantage now that we are no longer at the Abbey. That's as plain as a pikestaff. And he might be contemplating a truce for reasons best known to himself. Fighting does not always take place on the battle-field, Penelope. Remember that."

Penelope was to remember her aunt's admonition only too well an hour later as she sat watching the colonel sip sherry from one of her grandmother's antique crystal glasses. She wondered if he recognised it as one of those she had salvaged from the Abbey during one of their more bellicose encounters. She smiled slightly at the recollection. He was certainly not bellicose at the moment. Lounging against the marble mantel-piece, one booted foot crossed negligently over the other, the earl showed once again that he was perfectly able to carry on the polite conversation expected of morning callers.

So much at ease had her cousin appeared during the initial twenty minutes of his visit, that Penelope had not minded in the least when her aunt excused herself to attend to household duties. Penelope and the colonel conversed companionably for another ten minutes, and she was laughing at one of his wry stories of his years on the Continent, when she saw his smile fade and a sudden wariness appear in his eyes. Had she said anything to offend him? she wondered, casting her mind back over their recent exchange. Or was it possible that the colonel was preparing to take his leave without revealing what her aunt had called the nefarious purpose of his visit?

Determined to satisfy her curiosity and perhaps prove that her aunt's flights of fancy concerning the earl's motives were as rattlebrained as they sounded, Penelope plucked up the courage to ask her question.

"Was there anything in particular you wished to see me about this morning, Colonel?" she enquired. "Yesterday, you seemed to imply—" She paused uncertainly. His eyes had taken on that mocking quality she recognised so well from their previous arguments, and his lips twitched into his infuriatingly sardonic smile.

"Have you given any thought to marriage, Penelope?"

Penelope had been prepared for anything but the point-blank barrage of that startling question, and it took her a moment before she could regain enough composure to reply.

"I was betrothed to Viscount Clayton three years ago," she said coolly, refusing to show the annoyance she felt at his impertinence. "Of course," she added in a neutral voice, "his death put an end to any thoughts of marriage."

"I was referring to the past few months, since you put off your blacks," he said.

"Then the answer is no, I have not," she replied sharply. "And I fail to see that it is any of your concern, Colonel."

"What about that puppy Swathmore?" he demanded, ignoring the set-down. "He seems to consider himself a favoured candidate."

Penelope drew herself up haughtily. "He is mistaken," she snapped. "Geoffrey is in need of a rich wife, it is true, but I have cast no lures out to him or to anyone else. And furthermore, I do not intend to."

"I'm glad to hear it. Swathmore is not the man you need."

Penelope felt her mouth begin to fall open, and she shut it resolutely. Who did this rogue—her aunt was certainly right in that respect—think he was to be telling her what kind of man she needed, or that she needed any man at all for that matter? The very impropriety of the notion made her blush. All his urbane, gentlemanly manners had been a sham, she realised. Once again he had deceived her into trusting him, but the odious colonel had not changed in the least. He was still the rough barbarián upstart they had imagined he would be before they had even set eyes upon him. She would put him in his place immediately.

"I do not need a . . ." she began icily, and then hesitated, unable to bring herself to say something which seemed to have taken on quite another meaning. "I do not need anyone," she concluded hastily, conscious of the laughter in his eyes. "Geoffrey or anyone else."

"You plan to wither away on the shelf, I take it?" The tone

was sarcastic, and Penelope felt her flush deepen. "What are you now, anyway?" he asked carelessly. "Twenty-two? Twenty-three?"

Penelope rose to her feet and gathered the shreds of her dignity about her. "I find this line of interrogation particularly offensive," she said in her most chilling tones. "If you have quite finished, my lord, I propose we conclude this interview immediately."

The colonel grinned and poured himself another glass of sherry.

"As a matter of fact, my dear, I have scarcely begun." He held the golden sherry up to the light and then took a sip with evident relish. "Please sit down and hear me out, Penelope. And I apologise for being so blunt. Your aunt has called me a barbarian, and perhaps she is right. There is no denying I am more at home giving orders to my troops than exchanging pleasantries with ladies in drawing-rooms, and that's the truth."

He smiled at her then, and Penelope was entirely captivated by the sudden boyishness of it. Her anger seemed to melt away miraculously, and she had to force herself to remember why she had asked him to leave. It no longer seemed as important as it had only a moment ago, so she sat down again and allowed the colonel to fill her glass.

"Did I actually hear you mention an apology, Colonel? Or are my ears deceiving me?" she teased, astonished at her own playfulness.

"You are right to take me to task on that point, Penelope," he admitted. "It is not a word I usually employ. But I owe you one now, and perhaps another for frightening you away from the Abbey."

"You did not frighten me away from anywhere," she corrected him. "As I recall the events, I made the decision to come to Brighton for other, more practical reasons. It was obvious to us that you had no notion of the deplorable mustiness of the Dower House, otherwise you would hardly have condemned us to live there."

"I would never condemn you to do anything you were not entirely happy with, Penelope," he said, suddenly serious. "I hope I can trust you to believe me on that head." He looked at her searchingly before continuing, his voice lower now and strangely gentle. "As head of the family, I have certain responsibilities which it has taken me some time to come to terms with. I am speaking in particular of Lady Octavia and yourself, Penelope. It is my duty to look after your welfare, and when I found that you had both quit the Abbey, I realised I had failed that duty."

"Nonsense, my lord," she said softly, much affected by the sincerity of his words. "My aunt and I are accustomed to taking care of ourselves."

He shook his head. "You should not have to do so, my dear. That is my responsibility, and I intend to see to it that neither of you are forced to fend for yourselves ever again."

Penelope could not quite believe her ears and wished fervently that her aunt could have been present to lend this odd scene a measure of reality it seemed to lack. Had she heard aright? she wondered. Was this really their rogue colonel who was saying these civil and quite convincing things to her about responsibility and duty, about his role as head of the family in charge of their welfare? She could only stare at him in wonder. Had their departure from the Abbey finally brought him to his senses? she wondered, wanting to believe but still hearing her aunt's warning ringing in her head.

The colonel had taken up a restless pacing between the hearth and the window, and as he spoke, Penelope found her attention wandering between admiration for his lithe form—displayed to advantage in skin-tight breeches of soft buckskin and the well-cut riding jacket which defined the breadth of his shoulders and tapered hips—and the gist of his words, which flowed around her, confusing her with their soft intensity and the utterly unthinkable shapes they were creating in her mind.

"When I came back from Hampshire and found you gone, Penelope," he was saying, pausing for a moment before swooping off again towards the window, "I realised that I had made a mull of things." He grinned. "You may well smile. It was hard for me to admit it, I will say that, but when I saw how empty the Abbey was without you two ladies, I knew I had to find a way to restore you and Lady Octavia to your home."

Penelope blinked at him in surprise. "I can well believe the place felt empty to you, Colonel," she remarked dryly. "After all, quite half the furnishings are either here with me or packed in boxes in the Dower House. But let me warn you, my lord," she continued archly, "if you are proposing to buy everything back, I shall refuse to part with anything for less than double what I paid you."

He grinned again. "That is not what I intended, but you have put me in mind of something." He thrust a hand into his pocket and pulled out a sheaf of papers, which he tossed onto the rosewood boulle table beside the settee. "These are yours, my dear. I have no need of them, after all. I found my grandfather's estates prospering, and the Abbey rents have come in, as did the interest on the Funds your father invested in. So I want you to have these back. A sign of good faith, shall we say?"

Penelope looked at the little pile of her bank drafts and wondered if she should pinch herself. Was she dreaming? she thought. Which was the real earl? The cynical colonel who had bullied her into purchasing her family treasures with her own fortune? Or the gentleman who stood regarding her with a faintly apprehensive look in his eyes, as though he fully expected her to reject his offer to return these same drafts?

"So you *do* wish to have the furnishings returned?" she enquired tentatively, her gaze steady on his face. Was this another ploy, as her aunt had warned? she wondered, torn with the desire to believe this new colonel, who was a vast improvement over the other, hard, autocratic man she had known at the Abbey.

"Not just the furnishings, Penelope," he said softly. "I want *you* back, too. You and Lady Octavia belong at the Abbey, and I want to be allowed to escort you back home. I feel very strongly that if we join forces, you and I, we can both benefit from the alliance."

"Alliance?" Penelope repeated, feeling that she was missing something. "You are as bad as my aunt, Colonel. Always talking as if she were planning some foreign campaign or other. I'm afraid I don't know much about alliances, sir. Please explain it to me."

Was that a startled glimmer she caught in his dark eyes? she wondered. But it was gone before she could be sure, and then he grinned again, and she forgot it.

"Well, my dear, to be valid and viable, an alliance must offer substantial benefits to both parties." After this auspicious beginning, he faltered, as if unsure how to continue. "As you know, I have holdings in Hampshire which belonged to my grandfather Bellington. Not large by your standards, perhaps, but prosperous if well tended. And there is the rub. My presence is needed in Hampshire almost as much as it is needed at the Abbey. I need someone I can trust to help me with that estate while I am away in Hampshire."

"Don't you have a steward at Bellington Hall?" she enquired, feeling the name roll rather pleasantly off her tongue.

"Not any more. Old John Nelson had been taking care of things for me, but he died this past December. That is one of the reasons I left the Abbey."

Yes, Penelope thought to herself, but she would wager a hundred pounds it was not the only reason. Yet it comforted her to know that she had not been the only cause of the colonel's departure.

"And cannot you hire another steward?"

He looked at her, eyes hooded now, as if unsure of his ground. "Aye, I suppose I could, but it is not something that can be done in a hurry. And besides . . ." His gaze hardened, and Penelope wondered what painful thoughts might be running through his head. "I like to work my own land," he added, almost defiantly.

With admirable forbearance, Penelope did not point out to him that the Abbey was also his own land, as he called it, and as his principal seat, deserved his undivided attention. These observations were not appropriate now, she knew instinctively. Perhaps they never would be with this strange man who was slowly revealing himself to her as never before.

"I see," she said slowly, although she was not sure she did. "So what is this alliance you are talking about? And how does it concern me?" He looked at her rather strangely, she thought, but perhaps she was mistaken.

"It depends entirely on you for its success, Penelope," he said, watching her intently. "If you do not agree to return with me as mistress of Laughton Abbey, if you are not willing to take over the running of the household again and help me manage the estate itself in my absence, if you feel you cannot share this burden with me, then there can be no alliance."

There was something puzzling about this explanation, which

Penelope could not quite put her finger on. "Oh, I see," she repeated. "You are proposing that we return to the way things were before? Well, I see no real objection to that. But I would have to consult with my aunt—"

"Not exactly the way things were before, my dear," he interrupted, and Penelope caught a mixture of amusement and what looked like exasperation in the depth of his eyes as he regarded her steadily. "Not *quite* the same."

She raised a quizzical brow. "No? Then how would it differ? What would you expect me to do that I didn't do before?"

He laughed ruefully at this, and Penelope had the distinct impression that she had embarrassed him. He turned away and went over to stand by the window.

"The alliance I am proposing would require that you come back as the true lady of the manor, Penelope." He turned around and stared directly into her eyes, mesmerizing her with the intensity of his dark gaze.

"As the Countess of Laughton."

CHAPTER NINE

Tentative Surrender

Lady Penelope sat rigid for several moments, staring at him with eyes wide and blank. Then Nicholas saw the gradual dawning of understanding seep into their lilac depths, changing the expression on her upturned face from puzzlement to stark disbelief. So much for his power to sweep the chit off her feet, he mused, cynicism coming to his rescue as it so often did since his accession to the title. He released the breath he had unwittingly been holding and attempted a smile, but his lips were tautly unresponsive; all he felt was the curled scar twitching beside his mouth. A sight to send any gently bred lady into a fit of the vapours, he thought dryly. Of course, Lady Penelope was not given to missish starts, thank the Lord, and she seemed singularly unfazed by his deformities. Was that because she had seen him at his very worst? he wondered, fleetingly disappointed that she would never see him at his best. Not that he had ever been an Adonis, his cynical self pointed out, as Lady Penelope's viscount appeared to have been.

A movement from the settee dispelled these musings abruptly. Lady Penelope rose slowly to her feet, and Nicholas saw anger flicker briefly across her pale face.

"You are jesting, I take it?" Her voice vibrated with contempt.

Her response surprised him. After first conceiving the plan to marry his cousin during that solitary New Year's vigil in his grandmother's rose-garden, Nicholas had gone over every aspect of the proposed alliance with his usual military precision and found it both logically and tactically feasible. Now the chit was accusing him of jesting.

He frowned and was about to return a blistering retort concerning the absolute propriety of his intentions, when he noticed that her fingers, clasped together in front of her, were white knuckled and trembling. Nicholas strode forward, his momentary wrath evaporating.

"I see I must apologise yet again, my dear," he said, a grin softening the irony of his remark. He reached out to clasp her hands and found them icy to the touch. "I am not usually given to jests of any nature, much less in something as important as this." He gazed down at her and for the first time questioned the wisdom of his plans for this particular Ashington lady. It had all seemed so simple three months ago, he remembered, but now as he stood so close to her, it flashed across his mind that perhaps he had miscalculated the power of his enemy. Had he failed to consider his own vulnerability? he wondered. Might not this woman, upon whom he had thought to vent his urge for revenge against the whole Ashington clan, possess the very weapons he was least prepared to overcome?

"Then I can only suppose you to be disguised, my lord," he heard her say in that cool voice of hers. "I can think of no other reason for such an odd start, Colonel." She attempted to withdraw her hands from his grasp, but he held them firmly, searching for the right words to bring about her surrender.

"I am neither jesting nor bosky, Penelope," he said. "And I seek neither to shock you nor insult you. I am sorry if I have done either. My offer is sincere, and I do not make it lightly. An alliance between us has much to recommend it." He paused, unsure of his ground here.

He saw a smile hover in the corners of her mouth. "Name one for me, if you please, Colonel," she retorted gently.

"You and Lady Octavia will be permanently restored—in a legally binding way—to your home, and you would be mistress of your own establishment in every sense of the word. You will not argue with the social advantages of such a position, I trust." Nicholas deliberately kept the cynicism out of his voice.

Penelope gazed at him, all traces of the smile gone. "Lady

Octavia would no doubt agree with you," she said dryly. "For myself, however, I am interested in the advantages *you* hope to obtain from such an arrangement, Colonel."

He hesitated briefly. What response from him would move her into accepting his offer? he wondered. The knowledge that he could not tell this woman the truth about his intentions pricked his consciousness fleetingly, but he brushed it aside. This was no romantic liaison they would be entering into, he reasoned. There would be no need for him to maintain even the illusion of emotional attachment. He would treat her with unswerving respect and courtesy, and spend as much time as he could in Hampshire. If she were like most women, he thought with sudden uneasiness, she would want a family, but that could be arranged some time in the future with no great inconvenience to himself. Inconvenience? his cynical self repeated snidely, and Nicholas felt his gaze slide down the lady's slender throat to rest briefly on the swell of her small perfect breasts, rising decorously from the lace collar of her blue muslin morning gown. Inconvenience indeed. At least he could be honest with himself, the cynic in him said. The prospect of bedding the enemy suddenly acquired a piquancy Nicholas had not anticipated, yet instinct told him that this confession would hardly serve to persuade Lady Penelope to accept his suit.

He raised his eyes to her face and realized that she must have half-guessed at his thoughts, for her lovely face was tinged with pink, and her eyes had turned distant.

"I could boast of having quite the most beautiful wife in the south of England, my dear," he said lightly, seeing the disbelief bloom in her eyes even before the words had left his mouth.

"Spare me the idly flattery, my lord," she said sharply. "I would like to know the truth, if you please."

Aye, and there's the rub, lass, he thought wryly. "I will be expected to take a wife," he began carefully, but she interrupted him immediately.

"There is certainly no shortage of beautiful, highly eligible young ladies willing to jump at the chance to be your countess, my lord," she pointed out. "You have only to show your face in London next month, and you may take your pick of the new crop on the Marriage Mart."

"Show my face, indeed?" he repeated, and when her eyes widened in consternation, he was perversely pleased to have caught her in a faux pas. "You may be right, my dear, but I doubt it. My face is hardly one that young girls see in their dreams at night." He laughed, surprised at his own bitterness.

She must have sensed it, too, for her glance softened. "I beg your pardon, Colonel. I spoke without thinking." She paused, then added with a touch of humour in her voice, "But you may rest assured that young girls rarely marry the men they see in their dreams," she said.

"It is kind of you to lay my fears to rest, Penelope," he remarked curtly, suddenly wishing they did not have to fence like this. "But I am not the man to take a wife fresh out of the schoolroom. And a stranger to boot. As I said before, I need a wife who will accept me, barbarian that I am, as your aunt would say." He grinned at her confusion. "One whom I can trust. One who is familiar with the estate and has its interests at heart. A sensible female who will not wish to spend half the year in London frittering my money away on gewgaws." He stopped abruptly, suddenly realising that the picture he was painting might not be the most appealing to a young woman of wealth, rank, and beauty. "In short," he finished lamely, "a woman like you, Penelope."

During the pause that followed, Nicholas became uncomfortably aware that he had described his cousin far more closely than he had intended. And it had all been true, he saw with surprise. The description of the wife he wanted had suddenly crystallized in his mind as he was speaking. The shape and texture of the woman he had intermittently over the years imagined that he would one day choose for himself had somehow fused with the shapely form of Lady Penelope Ashington. The idea disconcerted him.

Penelope stood gazing up at him, a startled expression in her eyes. Had he exposed too much of the truth? he wondered. He glanced down at their joined hands, and the sight nearly made Nicholas lose his nerve. In an attempt to overcome these misgivings, he raised her fingers to his lips and kissed them, a gesture as foreign to him as the idea that in Penelope he might have found the ideal wife.

To hide his embarrassment, Nicholas released her and

stepped back. "I naturally do not expect you to answer me now, my dear," he said, unwittingly using the curt tone he invariably used with his junior officers when they had failed to live up to his expectations of them.

"May I call on you tomorrow?"

Penelope laughed for the first time since he had broached the topic of an alliance between them. "And you expect me to have your answer for you then, no doubt?"

He was surprised at her perspicacity but detected a note of raillery in her voice. He had indeed expected to receive her acceptance on the morrow. He would have preferred it now, but he knew enough about women—and about this one in particular—not to expect her mind to be entirely pliable to his wishes. But he was a reasonable man. He was prepared to wait until tomorrow, and so he told her.

She laughed again. "Come to dine with us tomorrow, Colonel," she said as if there were nothing else of importance on her mind. "And at least you may hear what Aunt Octavia has to say about your proposed alliance."

Nicholas was not sure he liked the sound of that.

"It's just as I thought," Lady Octavia exclaimed jubilantly when Penelope carried the news of Colonel Bellington's offer into the cosy sitting-room later that morning, where her aunt sat embroidering fat-cheeked cherubs on an altar-cloth. "Didn't I warn you that the rogue had something up his sleeve, dearest? An alliance, indeed! What kind of sapskulls does he think we are to be taken in by such a Banbury tale? It's pockets to let with the scoundrel, I don't doubt. And he expects to mend his fortunes at your expense, Penelope. I forbid you even to consider this so-called alliance. Why, it's positively ludicrous."

Penelope smiled at her aunt's explosive and quite predictable reaction. "I hate to disabuse you, Aunt, but it is not lack of funds that has motivated the earl to make such an unexpected proposal." She fished in the pocket of her gown and pulled out the sheaf of bank drafts. "Look at this, Aunt. He has returned every single draft that I gave him. All of them! I am nearly twenty thousand pounds richer than I thought I was just this morning. He has not cashed a single one. How do you account for that?"

"Pshaw!" came the instant reply. "'Tis but a ploy, child. Give with one hand and take away with the other. The man's a card sharp to boot, for this is a gambler's game, Penelope." She shot a calculating glance at her niece and then resumed her stitching. "You are not contemplating doing anything rash on my behalf, are you, Penny?" she enquired, in quite a different tone.

Penelope did not pretend to misunderstand her aunt's meaning. "I confess that I am still too confused to contemplate anything, Aunt. It all happened so unexpectedly. I don't know what to think. He took me quite by surprise, you see. At first I thought he must be playing some cynical joke on me, but he assured me . . ." She paused, her thoughts reliving jumbled snatches of her interview with the colonel. "Oh, Aunt! I wish that you had been there. He sounded so plausible. So very convincing. And what he said was undeniably true. Such an arrangement would benefit all of us."

"I forbid you to do anything rackety merely because that rascal has made what might appear to be an attractive offer, Penny. And notice that I say *might*, dear. No doubt the silver-tongued rogue is a past master at talking his enemies into weak positions."

"Aunt, please!" Penelope cried, her nerves sorely tried by the events of the past hour. "This is not a military manoeuvre but an offer of marriage. A highly convenient arrangement for all of us, I believe."

Lady Octavia emitted one of her more sonorous snorts. "You are a lackwit if you believe that, Penny. *Everything* that man does is a military operation, take my word for it. And as for convenience, of course it is convenient, but for whom? My lord colonel will acquire a well-born, wealthy, and beautiful wife who—if I understand the conditions correctly—will allow his lordship to waltz off to Hampshire whenever the fancy takes him, leaving you with the running of that large estate again. Where is the convenience for you, dear? I must be getting senile, for I cannot see it."

Penelope's thoughts flew to Laughton Abbey, the home of her happy childhood, and a great wave of nostalgia washed over her. She saw it again in all its splendour, the Long Gallery replete with pictorial history, the State Dining-Room filled

with illustrious guests from London, the Great Hall ringing
with music and the babble of a myriad dancers at one of her
mother's sumptuous New Year's Eve balls. She sighed. Would
she be able to restore this past grandeur? she wondered. Would
she really want to? This last thought, which popped unbidden
into her head, disturbed her. Of course, she did, didn't she? She
was an Ashington, one of the last of that powerful Norman
baron's blood-line. It was her heritage, her pride, her responsibility, her very duty to see that glory restored. Wasn't it? And
if she must marry the renegade colonel to achieve her dream,
why did she hesitate?

"We can go home," she whispered, half to herself. "We can
go home again, Aunt."

Lady Octavia took one look at her niece and laid her
needlework resolutely aside. "Come here, child," she ordered
gently, patting the settee beside her. "I can see that the sly
rogue has overset your good sense by putting the notion in your
head that you can recapture the past." She took one of
Penelope's hands and squeezed it comfortingly. "That is an
impossible dream, my dear, and well he knows it—"

"But I thought you loved the Abbey as I do, Aunt," Penelope
protested, surprised and vaguely alarmed at the drift of her
aunt's argument. "Don't you wish to go home?"

Lady Octavia smiled a little sadly and shook her head. "Of
course, I love the Abbey, dearest. It holds all my childhood
memories, as it does yours. Yet I have discovered something
interesting about myself since you offered me a home with you
here in Brighton. It has suddenly dawned on me what it means
to a woman to make her *own* home. As an unmarried female in
my father's, and later my brother's and nephew's establish-
ments, I had a roof over my head, it is true, and I have taken
that for granted over the years. But I had no part in making the
Abbey a home."

Penelope was appalled at the wistfulness in her aunt's voice.
"Oh, but you did, Aunt," she cried. "I could never have
refurbished the State Dining-Room without you. And you have
helped me with innumerable such tasks over the years, just as
you did for my mother."

"Oh, indeed, yes, dear," her aunt replied quickly. "And I do
not mean to complain about my lot. But our refurbishings of

the Abbey were always directed at restoring or maintaining the past glory, Penny. And I have discovered here in Brighton that I find the grandeur of the past rather oppressive." She remained silent for a moment, and Penelope saw her aunt's blue eyes cloud with memories. This was so unlike her usual cheerfulness that Penelope felt a tremor of fear run through her.

"And I have discovered something else," Lady Octavia murmured, a strange little smile curving her lips. "For the first time in nearly twenty years, I regret turning down that offer from Jonathan Beckwith."

Penelope gaped at her. "You received several offers, as I remember, Aunt, and accepted none of them."

"True, child. But none of those gentlemen could hold a candle to Jonathan. Absolutely ineligible he was, of course—as my father pointed out quite rightly—a mushroom of the worst kind, but so handsome and amusing. And kind, too. He quite dazzled the seventeen-year-old chit I was then. I nearly lost my head as well as my heart, until my father told me of the family curse. I knew then what I had to do, and I turned him down—"

"Beckwith?" Penelope repeated, her eyes widened as she made the connexion. "Surely you cannot mean Edward's uncle Jonathan, can you?"

Lady Octavia smiled again. "Yes, Jonathan Beckwith. He left for India shortly afterwards, I understand. Done quite well for himself, too, as we all know."

"But he was not eligible at the time, so you were forced to turn him down? How sad."

"I was not actually forced, dear. Nothing quite so Gothic. But my father made it clear to me where my duty lay, and I obeyed him. But make no mistake about it, Penny, Jonathan Beckwith is no more eligible today than he was twenty years ago. Nabob or no nabob, he is still a commoner and no fitting match for an Ashington."

"Are you saying that I should not accept the colonel, Aunt?"

"Nothing of the kind, dear. Whatever his faults, the man is an earl now. All I am saying is that you should not allow yourself to be bamboozled into accepting his offer. And if you choose to do so, make sure you do not accept this alliance for the wrong reasons, my dear."

Lady Octavia regarded her steadily. "You cannot live in the past, Penny. You must look at this alliance realistically. The colonel strikes me as a difficult man to live with."

The implications of her aunt's words caused a faint blush to colour Penelope's pale cheeks. She lowered her eyes. "He has said he wishes to spend a considerable part of the year in Hampshire. So he will not be at the Abbey to bother us."

Her aunt made no reply to this, and after a while Penelope raised her eyes and saw an amused expression on Lady Octavia's face. "And is this what you really want, Penelope? Not to be bothered by him, I mean?"

Penelope felt her blush deepen. There was no mistaking the indelicacy of her aunt's question. She rose and wandered over to gaze out at the Steyne, glittering invitingly in the spring sunlight. The colonel's proposed alliance, which had seemed so convenient and reasonable, was suddenly fraught with mysterious undercurrents which threatened to pull her in over her head.

Two mornings later Penelope rose earlier than usual and sat for more than an hour at her window overlooking the river, pondering the unexpected turn her life had taken. Her eyes often strayed to the huge bouquet of lilacs on her dresser, a mute reminder that her understanding of the man who had sent them was woefully deficient. The flowers had arrived yesterday morning, accompanied by a gilt-edged card bearing the bold scrawl she had instantly recognised as her cousin's. He had signed himself Nicholas in a decisive, heavy-handed script that marched across the white surface of the card as if daring anything to stand in its way. The name covered the entire available space, and Penelope could not help thinking that the signature was as invasive and domineering as the man himself. And that was all. Just Nicholas on a pristine field of white. As if the name were sufficient in and of itself. No hint of softness, no weakening of his defenses, no endearment to work its subtle magic on a woman's heart.

Which man would she be accepting? she wondered impatiently, reaching for the bellpull to summon her morning chocolate. The man who carried that strange repressed anger in his heart, or the one whose touch had shaken her as no man—no, not even her beloved Edward—had done before.

Later that morning, as Penelope cantered Bluedevil sedately along the Steyne, she reviewed the colonel's behaviour at dinner the evening before. He had arrived with his usual punctuality, but if he had imagined he would receive an answer to his offer, he was disappointed. Barely ten minutes later, Geoffrey Swathmore had been announced and quite dazzled his aunt and cousins with the account of a bear-baiting he had witnessed that afternoon. As a result, the only private conversation she and the colonel had enjoyed had concerned Penelope's intention to ride the following morning.

So here she was, Penelope thought, not without a glimmer of amusement. Since she rode almost every morning, their encounter—if indeed they did meet—could hardly be termed an assignation, even if the colonel had promised to meet her beside the Steyne—which he had not. There was little doubt in Penelope's mind that what the colonel lacked in romantic ardour as a suitor, he made up in tactical expertise, and the alliance he had proposed between them was, pure and simple, a cease in the hostilities which had marked their relationship in the past. To imagine anything else in the truce he offered would be the height of foolishness, she told herself firmly, guiding Bluedevil past an old-fashioned barouche driven by an ancient coachman evidently more accustomed to country roads than Brighton's crowded thoroughfares. She must not expect more from Nicholas Bellington than he had to give, and what he had, Penelope reminded herself for the tenth time that morning, was Laughton Abbey, the home of her childhood.

"A penny for your thoughts, my dear."

Penelope whirled around, startled out of her reverie by the colonel's voice so close beside her, and Bluedevil took advantage of her distraction to prance sideways nervously.

"Good morning, Colonel," she replied with a smile, bringing Bluedevil expertly back under control. "I am glad to see that you are giving Merrylegs some exercise. He tends to put on weight if allowed to idle for more than a week."

"You did not answer my question." His voice was teasing, but Penelope recognised the unconscious command beneath the pleasantry.

"I was thinking of the Abbey, if you must know."

"Does that signify a capitulation on your part, my dear?"

Penelope frowned at the directness of his attack. "Capitulation?" she repeated coolly. "Must you talk as though we were engaged in a military encounter, Colonel?"

"I am a military man, Penelope."

"And this alliance you talk of, is that just another military encounter for you, Colonel?" she demanded, aware of a bitter undercurrent to her words. She had stopped her horse and swung round to face him as she spoke and was startled to catch a flicker of alarm in his eyes. Before she could be sure of it, he had shuttered them and grinned at her sardonically.

"All life is a series of encounters of one kind or another," he answered without rancour. "Most of them antagonistic, if not downright bellicose, which is merely another term for military."

"I do not wish to spend the rest of my life engaging in military encounters of any kind," Penelope said sharply, urging Bluedevil forward again.

The earl laughed at this. "That is precisely why you should give serious consideration to an alliance between us, my dear. Such an agreement would assure us both a future without strife."

"How can you be sure it would work?" she enquired, voicing one of her most troublesome reservations.

"We can't be absolutely sure, of course," he replied. "But we are not going into this marriage with blinders on, as many couples do who depend solely on physical attraction. Love matches, I believe they are called. You are no schoolroom miss, Penelope, and I am no green youth like our Cousin Geoffrey, whose prime concern at the moment seems to be bear-baiting and curricle racing. I think we stand an excellent chance of being exceedingly comfortable together. What do you say, my dear?"

Penelope glanced at him uneasily. "What do I say?" she repeated. "Do you mean that you want an answer now, Colonel?"

He raised a quizzical eyebrow. "I had hoped to return to the Abbey tomorrow, but I could stay for another day or two if necessary."

"Indeed?" Penelope felt inexplicably peeved at the earl's nonchalant attitude towards her future. It was plain as a pikestaff that he wished to get the matter settled as quickly as possible with little regard for her sensibilities. Did he really expect her to acquiesce to this so-called alliance he was dangling before her with no more consideration than she would give an invitation to a musicale? His presumption that she would fall in with his plans without so much as a murmur of opposition was typical of his overbearing nature, and Penelope felt her temper rise at this exhibition of masculine arrogance.

"Indeed?" she repeated coldly. "In that case, Colonel, I suggest that you do not spend another minute kicking your heels in Brighton on my account. By all means return to the Abbey if your business there is so pressing. I would not wish it rumoured that I kept you from your duties, sir." She nudged the black's flank and the horse broke into a canter, but before Bluedevil had taken more than ten paces, a hand on his bridle brought him to a standstill.

Penelope turned her head and locked gazes with the colonel's opaque stare. She saw that his jaw was dangerously clenched and his mouth set in a taut, stubborn line. Even as she watched, she saw it relax into an amused smile, the gesture reflected in the twist of the scar on his lean cheek. Bluedevil snorted nervously, and Penelope became aware that the colonel's knee was pressed warmly against her own.

"I beg your pardon, Cousin," he said dryly, releasing her bridle and moving his horse away. "I had not taken you for one of those spoiled Incomparables who delight in keeping a man dangling indefinitely—"

"Indefinitely?" Penelope gasped, amused in spite of herself at the man's overwhelming gall. "It has not yet been two days, if my memory does not fail me, Colonel. And you may as well know now that I will not be bullied into making such an important decision on the spur of the moment just because you wish to leave Town. And I have no intention of keeping you dangling—as you call it. It's just that I am not sure in my own mind."

"Then I will stay until you are, my dear," the colonel said lightly.

Penelope was not fooled for a minute by this apparent

surrender. "How much time are you giving me, my lord?" she enquired innocently.

"A sennight should be more than enough."

Penelope raised an eyebrow in mock dismay.

"A fortnight, then," he conceded grudgingly. "But not a moment longer, my girl. Or I shall take you up before me and ride off with you."

"You are not serious, I trust," she replied primly, conscious of a strange flutter in the region of her heart. "Only think of the scandal!"

The colonel did not answer, but his dark eyes glittered dangerously and his mouth curled into a smile which reminded Penelope quite forcibly that she was dealing with a rogue who would—if Aunt Octavia was to be believed—stop at nothing to get what he wanted.

The notion that the colonel wanted her—regardless of his reasons—brought a blush of excitement to Penelope's pale cheeks.

CHAPTER TEN

Shattered Truce

"What I most regret about this whole affair," Lady Octavia declared in lugubrious tones, "is that we shall miss Lady Bradford's dinner-dance next Wednesday."

Penelope, who had been gazing out of the window of the travelling chaise at the wet, bedraggled hedgerows, turned to her aunt in surprise. "You have never cared a fig for Lady Bradford, Aunt," she exclaimed, her own melancholy momentarily displaced by the incongruity of Lady Octavia's remark. "And if I remember correctly, you made all sorts of excuses to decline her invitation."

"She always serves those delicious lobster patties, dear," her aunt replied prosaically. "I grant you that the champagne is invariably inferior, but the patties make up for the tediousness of having to listen to Amelia Bradford puff up that pimply-faced chit of hers. How she ever hopes to settle the poor girl creditably is beyond me."

The mention of marriage caused Penelope to recall her own impending nuptials. She turned back to the window, all interest in Lady Bradford's daughter dissipating as memories of the past week crowded back to haunt her. The Sussex countryside, green and lush with new spring growth, lay shrouded in a dense, misty drizzle. Penelope wondered if these April showers, traditionally linked with the blooming of the wild flowers along the hedgerows, presaged a similar burst of colour in her own life. The Ashington chaise had just passed through the village of Broadwater and was even now turning north toward

Findon. Ashington lay a scant four miles farther north across the South Downs, and a mile beyond the village she could see—in her mind's eye—the stately wrought-iron gates of Laughton Abbey open to welcome her back.

Had she made the right decision? she wondered, snuggling deeper into the warmth of the rug the colonel had provided for her comfort. She had asked herself the same question countless times over the past two days, but the answer was always elusive. At times it had seemed so right. Where else would she be as happy as at the Abbey? she reasoned. Then her aunt's warning about the colonel's real motives would return to tease her, and Penelope would question her own reasons for accepting the colonel's offer. Was she prepared to accept his conditions? Could she be content with an absentee husband? An unconsummated marriage? And what about a family? She had dreamed of a large family with Edward, but it was not Edward she was about to wed. Would Nicholas—she had begun calling him thus in her mind—wish for an heir? Surely he would, she thought. The question was, When would he make such a decision? Penelope felt a tremor of apprehension at the thought of sharing such intimacies with the colonel.

"Are you cold, dear?" Lady Octavia asked solicitously.

"Oh, no, Aunt." Penelope forced her stiff lips into a smile. "Merely having second thoughts again. I would never have believed I could be so missish, if you must know the awful truth."

"You are anything but missish, dear," her aunt replied sternly. "Personally, I think you are incredibly brave to take on such a challenge. But there is still time to cry off, you know. I wouldn't hesitate for a moment if I had any doubts at all, Penny. And if that rogue kicks up a dust, well, the devil fly away with him, I say."

Penelope had to laugh to her aunt's vehemence. It was a relief to know that she was not quite alone in this new venture. "You are such a comfort to me, Aunt," she said, her voice husky with emotion. "I can't thank you enough for letting me uproot you again—"

"Nonsense, child," Lady Octavia interrupted, her eyes suspiciously damp. "You are all the family I have, now that poor Neville is no longer with us," she added, fishing in her reticule for a handkerchief which she used to blow her nose vigorously. "But let's not turn into a pair of watering-pots, dear. That's enough to make even the colonel quake in his boots." She stuffed the damp handkerchief away and patted her niece's clasped hands affectionately. "Don't take on so, there's a good lass. I believe that, in spite of all my reservations about that scoundrel, you have made the proper choice, dear. He is more of a gentleman than I gave him credit for, and at least we can be sure—if Mr. Hamilton has drawn up the marriage settlements as he said he would—that your fortune is protected."

Penelope sighed. Mr. Hamilton had indeed been more than kind during his brief stay in Brighton last week. She had summoned him from London when she decided to accept the colonel's offer, and the solicitor had been instrumental in arranging the settlements to her advantage. She had been pleasantly surprised when the colonel made no objection to any of Mr. Hamilton's suggestions and signed every document the solicitor put before him.

"Yes," she said after a pause. "Mr. Hamilton's approval of the settlements set my mind at rest in one aspect at least. Our esteemed colonel is not the fortune hunter we had at first supposed."

"Perhaps not," her aunt agreed, albeit reluctantly. "But I cannot like all this haste, Penny. Why cannot he wait for the banns to be read like a decent Christian? There is something unsavoury about a special licence, I always say. It is almost as though he wants to legshackle you before you can change your mind. Reverend Matthews will be quite upset, I'm warning you. He will want to see you married properly, child, and I must say that I agree with him."

"I *will* be married properly," Penelope explained for perhaps the fifth time since Colonel Bellington had first revealed his intention of not waiting the required three readings of the banns. "The license is perfectly legal, you know."

"But wouldn't you rather tie the knot in the traditional way?"

Penelope shrugged. "I cannot say I care one way or the other, Aunt. At least I will be married at Ashington chapel and not in Brighton, as he wished. That is quite enough tradition for me."

"Well, you *should* care, Penelope." Lady Octavia snorted

indignantly. "A ramshackle business if ever I saw one. But just what one might expect from an encroaching upstart, of course. We should not forget that, for all his insinuating charm— which he is not above turning on when it suits him—the colonel is still the wily rogue who descended upon us last July. And don't you ever forget it, my girl."

Penelope sighed. "I will have to set aside some of my reservations about our cousin if this marriage is to work, Aunt," she protested. "And indeed, I have already done so. He has been everything that is charming and considerate since he arrived in Brighton last week. Why, you yourself remarked upon it, Aunt."

Lady Octavia emitted another of her expressive snorts. "Fiddle!" she exclaimed impatiently. "Of course the rascal has behaved himself. Charm is more effective than a sword in the kind of skirmish he is engaged in with you, Penny. All I ask is that you be on your guard, my dear. And do not, for the love of heaven, imagine for a moment that our so charming colonel has developed a sudden *tendre* for you. This alliance is clearly a convenience for him, and if you allow yourself to believe otherwise, he will break your heart, love."

"Are you saying I am making a mistake in wedding the colonel?" Penelope demanded sharply. "I thought we had decided that it was the sensible thing to do, Aunt."

Lady Octavia leaned over to pat her niece's gloved hands comfortingly. "Of course, it is the sensible thing to do, dearest. I still say so. But I want to remind you that there is nothing romantical about the colonel. He is not Edward, you know."

Penelope turned to gaze out at the bedraggled countryside. No, indeed, she thought. And her aunt was right. There was nothing romantical about Nicholas Bellington, and she would do well to remember it.

She was reminded of it an hour later as he helped the ladies descend from the coach and ushered them into the Abbey with a gleam of what might have been triumph in his expression. She forgot it momentarily during the two busy days following her return, as she and Lady Octavia supervised the preparations for the wedding. But her aunt's words flooded back to harrow her like so many Furies as she stood beside her bridegroom in the twelfth-century Norman chapel in the little village of

Ashington on that sunny April morning, dressed in a wedding-gown hastily designed and executed by Madame Dumont, and felt his strong hands slip the wedding band onto her finger.

As she looked down at the engraved gold band, Penelope had the strangest sensation that she was now well and truly the colonel's captive. He had won, she thought, her hand if not her heart as Edward had done. For a few precious moments, she allowed herself to pretend that it was Edward standing there, holding her hands gently in his. Edward, she thought, with a rush of nostalgia. The golden god she had dreamed of—first as a school girl, and later as a young woman. Caught up in the make-believe, she raised her eyes to the man beside her and caught her breath in dismay. What she saw was not the blue eyes of her romantic fantasies, but the dark gaze of a stranger, fixed upon her with alarming intentness. Was that a glint of cynicism in their inscrutable depths? she wondered. Or was this merely the foolishness of her overwrought nerves?

And then he raised her veil, and after a slight pause—could it be that he was reluctant to kiss her?—he bent to place cool lips against hers. The brief kiss was over before Penelope had time to savour the novelty of being kissed by a man other than Edward, and then the organ struck up and she found herself walking down the aisle on the arm of a man who was still very much an enigma to her.

In the flurry of congratulations following the simple ceremony, Nicholas caught himself glancing down at the glowing face of his new bride and wondering if perhaps he had committed a serious tactical error in placing himself in what might prove to be a vulnerable position. He had been strangely reluctant to raise Penelope's veil and seal their vows with the traditional kiss, and when he looked down into her lilac eyes, he realised why. The unpredictable chit had given him her trust. He could see it reflected in her wide, innocent gaze as she raised her face for his kiss. She had capitulated—perhaps not consciously, but Nicholas had been in enough skirmishes in his time to recognise capitulation when he saw it. And he had seen it in Lady Penelope Ashington's every unconscious gesture as she stood by the altar awaiting his kiss. It had been implicit in her warm, liquid gaze and in the softness of her full lips. He had felt its heady effect in the way her body swayed almost imperceptibly towards him. Nicholas had had to steel himself against the impulse to defy decorum and crush her against his chest to brand her with a kiss that would leave no doubt in her mind that she was now his.

But he had conquered these disruptive impulses and merely touched her lips with his, wondering cynically what the lady would say if she knew how close she had come to breaching his defenses. As they walked down the aisle together and out into the April sunshine, Nicholas had been acutely conscious of Penelope's small hand in the crook of his arm. He glanced down at her again as they stood together on the small chapel portico to receive the first of the many well-wishers who crowded around them, and could not resist a smile at the ease of his victory.

"You may well smile, lad," Sir James Swathmore exclaimed jovially, thumping the earl on the back in high good humour. "You have run away with the prize of the Season, m'lad. I don't have to tell you that our Penelope is a jewel past price, and if you fail to make her the happiest lass in Sussex, I shall personally demand to see your seconds. I'm warning you."

Nicholas shook the baronet's hand and smiled. "I shall certainly try my best, sir," he replied. Privately, he liked Sir James better than any of Penelope's relatives, in spite of his being a quite inferior candidate for an Ashington, as Lady Octavia was in the habit of reminding him. Knowing that Lady Octavia also lumped him in the same category of undesirable connexions, Nicholas had a special affinity for the bluff, friendly baronet, who seemed to bear his sister-in-law no ill will for her unflattering opinion of him. Sir James obviously doted on his niece, not having a single daughter of his own, in a houseful of boys, and had been overjoyed when she asked him to stand in place of her father at the ceremony.

"It does my heart good to see the lass so happy," the baronet added in a more serious tone. "She has had enough unhappiness to last a lifetime already."

Nicholas felt the older man observing him shrewdly, but before he could think of a reassuring response, he found himself embraced enthusiastically by Lady Swathmore, whose eyes were still moist with emotion.

"My dear boy," she exclaimed in tremulous accents. "We are all so delighted that our darling Penny has found a champion worthy of her at last," she twitted, planting an uninhibited kiss on the colonel's scarred cheek. "I never did care much for that Hayward fellow," she confided, sotto voce, glancing nervously at her niece, who was deep in conversation with a neighbour. "Rather a namby-pamby creature, if you ask me. And much more beautiful than any man has a right to be. Now, you," she added, giving Nicholas a frankly appraising look, "are more the thing. Yes," she smiled saucily, "much more the thing. Don't you agree, James?"

"Hush, my dear," the baronet replied with a good-natured grin. "You will embarrass the colonel, lass. Please forgive my wife, m'lord," he added, turning to Nicholas. "She is a trifle outspoken. Like all the Ashingtons, I might add. Why, our own Penny is no shrinking violet, as you probably know already. And as for Octavia—"

"What about Octavia?" enquired that lady forcefully. "Never say you are slandering me behind my back, James Swathmore, for I'll not have it. Do you hear me?"

"Of course, he hears you, Octavia," her sister cut in serenely. "So does everyone else, dear. Please don't start one of your brangles with James at Penny's wedding. You will only upset her and make a cake of yourself."

"I never brangle with Lady Octavia," Sir James remarked in great good humour. "I wouldn't dare, for one thing."

Before Lady Octavia could take offense at this impertinence, Lady Swathmore had taken her sister firmly by the arm and bustled her into their waiting carriage. "Come, James," she said peremptorily to her husband. "It's time for us to be on our way. I am sure there must be a dozen things to see to at the Abbey."

After the jostle and babble of the crowded church-yard, the inside of the Laughton carriage seemed unnaturally quiet. Nicholas had deliberately taken a seat opposite his new countess, who gazed in apparent absorption at the passing countryside. He allowed his eyes to rove slowly over her face and slim figure until they came to rest on her gloved hands, clasped tightly in her lap. So, he mused, the chit is not as calm as she would have him believe. The evidence of Penelope's distress should have gratified him. Was it not in a way a mute acknowledgement of his power over her? But for some odd reason, the sight of those small hands which, even as he looked, trembled slightly—as if she could feel his predatory stare—caused a rush of tenderness quite foreign to his nature to well up in his chest.

What the devil was wrong with him? he wondered, turning to stare moodily out of the window. He had just completed a highly successful campaign to bring the last of the cursed Ashington line into his power and, quite inexplicably, he was beset by scruples. There was no place for scruples in his campaign against the Ashingtons, he reminded himself grimly. And the sooner he shattered any misconceptions his new bride might have about the kind of alliance she had entered into, the better it would be for both of them.

"I shall be leaving for Hampshire as soon as possible," he heard himself say in a voice that sounded harsh even to his own ears. "I have already spoken to Stevens about hiring an assistant steward to assist him in running the estate. That will take some of the burden off you."

He heard her gasp and knew she had turned to stare at him. "So soon?" she whispered, and for the briefest moment Nicholas allowed himself to savour the implications of her words. Would she miss him? he thought. Did she want him to stay? Or perhaps she was disappointed that he would not be in her bed tonight? He withdrew his gaze from the damp hedgerows and stared at her. No, his cynical self cut in firmly. He would do well to stay clear of that trap. Lascivious thoughts led to lascivious deeds, and a man could lose his senses and his freedom by treading that treacherous path. And his heart, too, of course, if he were fool enough to fall for a woman's wiles, which could enslave him forever. That would never do for Colonel Nicholas Bellington, he thought, ruthlessly pushing to the back of his mind all tender fantasies about this woman who was now his wife.

He became aware that his scrutiny had brought a pinkness to her pale cheeks that was highly becoming. He smiled thinly at the perversity of his thoughts. The sooner he could get away from the Abbey, the safer he would be from the temptations of the flesh, which seemed to assail him with alarming persistency ever since he had conceived his plan to wed his cousin.

A normal enough masculine urge, he reasoned, and one that could be effectively assuaged by some willing country lass over in Hampshire. The sooner the better, his cynical self amended.

"Yes," he replied at last. "The sooner the better," he added with deliberate cynicism. "Do you have any objection, my dear?"

He watched with a sense of loss as the light died out of her magnificent lilac eyes, and her lips drew into a taut, angry line. Then her chin rose and her eyes took on the glint of battle.

"Oh! Am I allowed to object, my lord? How diverting! Of course, I have no objection to your instant departure, my lord. And, as you say, the sooner the better," she added mockingly.

Nicholas turned back to the window, but he had the distinct impression that the first skirmish of his married life had gone to his wife.

In the weeks that followed, Penelope was to remember these angry words with shame and regret. They had set the tone of her relationship with the colonel during those first two days of their marriage, and Penelope, hurt more than she cared to admit by his apparent rejection, had been unable to bring herself to make the slightest push to bridge the abyss that seemed to yawn ever wider between them.

She had known instinctively that he would not come to her that first night but had lacked the courage to resist Alice when the abigail insisted that she wear one of her prettiest nightrails. There had, Penelope recalled, been the vague understanding between them that theirs would be a marriage in name only until a more appropriate time. Those had been the colonel's words, she remembered, but the exact nature of that appropriate time had never been determined. There had been something in his glances during the ceremony, however, that had caused Penelope's blood to race. Was he regretting his decision—it had certainly not been hers—to postpone their intimacies? she wondered, startled at the indecorous yearnings of her own body. But she had been wrong, of course, misled by those same romantical fantasies Aunt Octavia had warned her against.

Nicholas had not come. His sudden coolness in the carriage had told her that he wouldn't, as had his apparent desire to shake the dust of Laughton Abbey from his boots. But even though she had known he would not come, Penelope had not slept until the grey light of dawn filtered between the curtains. And she had awakened at her usual time, bleary-eyed and unrested as if she had indeed spent the entire night in sweet debauchery. She smiled wryly at the thought and waited quite half an hour for Peggy to bring up her chocolate before she remembered that the servants would in future expect their mistress to ring for them. Married ladies, her aunt had carefully explained to her several days ago, might not wish to be interrupted at inappropriate times. Penelope remembered that she had giggled at her aunt's refusal to explain exactly what time might be inappropriate for a married lady to be interrupted.

But the colonel was not there with her to be interrupted, and this was not her old room, where there had been no need to ring for her chocolate. Peggy might have burst in there as she normally did every morning, her round face perennially cheerful, her soft country voice greeting her mistress before she opened the curtains to another day. But the colonel had ordered the countess's suite made ready for her, and Penelope found the luxurious boudoir she had loved so much in the past unaccountably menacing. It had been her mother's room, of course, and her grandmother's, and all those other females who had carried the name of Countess of Laughton. And now it was hers. A room separated from the earl's rooms by an intimate sitting-room. She wondered why he had bothered. For appearance sake, she assumed. Or perhaps he wanted her close by in case he felt an urge . . . But no, she chided herself. She was being nonsensical again.

Penelope sighed and reached for the bell-pull. Her first day as a married lady would be, she suspected, much like any other. She felt a sudden reluctance to face the man who had given her the sleepless night and on impulse requested her breakfast in bed when Peggy appeared with her chocolate. . . .

CHAPTER ELEVEN

Close Encounter

As Bluedevil cantered through the brilliant yellow carpet of buttercups in the south meadow, Penelope let the fresh beauty of the countryside wash her mind clear of the unpleasantness of her recent visit to Clayton Manor. Charlotte had been less than civil to her for some time now, she admitted reluctantly, and her petulance had sorely tried Penelope's patience and deprived her of the pleasure and comfort she had hoped to derive from her friend's company. Of course, it should have been evident to her over the past months that Charlotte no longer considered herself Penelope's friend. Not only had she refused to visit the Abbey since the colonel's arrival, she had also failed to acknowledge Penelope's invitation to spend a few weeks with her in Brighton. Upon learning of Penelope's forthcoming nuptials, Lady Charlotte had thrown a tantrum the likes of which Penelope devoutly hoped she would never have to witness again. Although she had tried to find excuses for her friend's invective, Penelope had been sorely tempted to box Charlotte's pretty ears for her.

The fact that Charlotte still wore deep mourning for her lost love should have warned her, Penelope thought, when she had visited Clayton Manor with the glad tidings of her return to the Abbey as its permanent mistress. She had wished to patch up their differences and recapture the closeness they had shared as girls together. But Charlotte had received her with nothing approaching her previous warmth, and announced that wild horses could not drag her into the chapel to lend her countenance to a union she considered frankly scandalous.

She made no further attempt to see Charlotte. That part of her past was definitely over, as was her easy companionship with her brother, and the romantical dreams of a life with Edward she had—until recently—carried in her heart. She had put it all aside when she married Nicholas, and she owed it to him to do her best to live up to the alliance they had made with each other.

As that first week turned into a second, and then into a third, Penelope found herself throwing all her energies into estate business. The spring was a busy time of year, and there were moments—as she rode from one corner of Ashington land to the other supervising the tilling and planting, the culling of herds, the sale of new lambs, the yearly dredging and restocking of the artificial lake, and endless other tasks which demanded her attention—when she could almost forget that Colonel Bellington had come into her life at all. But the memory of his lean countenance and dark gaze would return in full force the moment she entered her bed-chamber every evening to dress for dinner. Why this should be Penelope did not clearly understand since, to her knowledge, he had never set foot in her room.

Perhaps it was her persistent desire to see him there that coloured her imagination, she thought, one evening towards the end of May, as she stood before her cheval mirror watching Alice adjust the folds of the new evening-gown Madame Dumont had sent up from Brighton the week before. It was a highly flattering deep lilac silk, cut—Madame Dumont had assured her ladyship—in the very latest fashion of slim elegance, which clung suggestively to her small hips and made her feel for all the world like a wanton seductress. The colour gave her eyes a darker hue than usual and emphasized the pale gold of her hair. Penelope examined her reflection in the mirror with a glow of satisfaction as Alice clasped a single string of pearls round her neck.

"You look dazzling tonight, m'lady," the abigail remarked, gazing critically at her mistress. "Madame has outdone herself this time. It's a pity his lordship ain't here to feast his eyes on you."

"Oh, but he is," came an amused voice from the doorway. "And you are right, Alice. Her ladyship is a rare sight indeed for weary eyes."

Penelope whirled to face him—as Alice bobbed a curtsy and slipped away—her breath caught in her throat at the picture her husband presented lounging at his ease in the doorway of her boudoir. She had the odd impression that he was taller than she remembered, which was nonsensical, of course. She stood, paralysed by conflicting emotions, as his gaze slid slowly down her while a lazy grin made the curled scar jump erratically. And then he was looking straight into her eyes, his own inscrutable.

"Delectable, my dear," he drawled. "One might almost suspect that you were expecting me."

Was that a hint of censure she heard? she wondered. Whatever maggot he had in his head must be stamped out instantly, she decided. Nothing must be allowed to spoil the sweetest, most deliciously intimate moment they had ever shared. She smiled at him.

"Nicholas!" she breathed, knowing her happiness was there for him to see in her smile and in her eyes, and not caring a fig if she was making a cake of herself. "Welcome home." She was beset by an insane urge to throw herself into his arms, but caution came to her rescue. "And of course, I expected you, my lord." Involuntarily, she took a step towards him. "I expect you every night . . . that is every evening," she corrected herself quickly when she saw the arrested look in his eyes. "Since you did not tell us exactly when you would return. There is a place set for you even now at the dinner-table," she rushed on, conscious of her overheated cheeks. "I trust you have a good appetite, my lord."

There was a definite pause, during which Penelope's heart seemed to do a furious jig in her breast as the colonel's eyes roved over her again, and a slow smile began at one corner of his mouth, softening the lean planes of his face and expanding until it glowed wickedly in the dark depths of his eyes.

"Yes, indeed, my love," he drawled softly. "I am fair consumed with hunger."

A rush of emotion such as she had never experienced before caused Penelope to gasp for breath. Her eyes, riveted by a force stronger than her own will, refused to disengage from the glittering, amused gaze of her husband. Even as she watched, mesmerized into acquiescence by the latent power of the man who appraised her so blatantly, Penelope saw the amusement gradually faded, replaced by another emotion she had never seen in any man's eyes before. It spoke to her of danger and desire; it threatened and thrilled her simultaneously; it warned her to run away even as it pulled her towards him; it was predatory yet intensely pleasurable. Conscious of her bones slowly melting away and her vision blurring, Penelope put out a hand to grasp the back of a spindle-legged chair. Her mouth felt dry and she could not swallow, but she knew, beyond a shadow of a doubt, that she wanted Nicholas to gaze at her with this same hunger in his eyes for the rest of her life.

After what seemed like an eternity, breeding came to her rescue, and Penelope forced herself to break the spell. "Perhaps you will want to change for dinner then, my lord," she murmured in a voice that sounded nothing like her own.

The amusement suddenly reappeared on his face, and Penelope wondered if she had dreamed that other, soul-shattering glance they had exchanged. No, she thought—determined to keep the memory of that precious moment alive whatever the cost—she could feel every inch of her body still quivering from the sensual invasion of it. Heaven help her, she mused, if he could make her feel so positively wanton with his eyes, what might he not do with his lips, his hands, his . . . ? Instinctively, she jerked her mind away from those dangerous ruminations and stepped towards the door, studiously avoiding his eyes.

"I shall await you downstairs, my lord."

"Don't go!"

The urgency in his voice brought her up short, and she glanced at him, half expecting—perhaps hoping—to see that smouldering look in his eyes again. But he was grinning at her.

"At least not until I give you this, Penelope. It belonged to my grandmother." He pulled a small box from his coat pocket and held it out to her.

Penelope stared at it in amazement. His grandmother? He was giving her something that had belonged to his grandmother? This didn't make any sense, but she reached for it before he changed his mind. It was an old jeweller's box, its corners rubbed shiny by fingers long dead, and Penelope was unprepared for the radiant perfection of the jewel that glittered in the candlelight as soon as she opened the shabby box: an amethyst, large as a damson stone and faceted to catch every glimmer of light in the room. How appropriate, she thought, that the setting was so simple, unencrusted with the usual diamonds, which could only have detracted from the marvellous rich colour of the stone. Caught up in the wonder of it and mesmerized by the scintillating lilac warmth, Penelope was startled when he spoke.

"You will want to have it reset, no doubt," he said. "It's unfashionably plain, I'm afraid."

"Oh, no!" Penelope cried, her reticence forgotten. "It is absolutely beautiful just the way it is. I . . . I am d-delighted that you want me to have it, my lord."

He was grinning at her again, and Penelope felt suddenly light-headed as he took the box from her limp fingers. Wordlessly she extended her left hand, and the colonel slipped the ring slowly onto her third finger until it nestled beside her wedding band. It was a perfect fit. She sighed in contentment as she looked down at her hand resting so naturally in his warm palm.

"So you like it?" he asked in a husky voice.

Her eyes flew to his face. "Oh, yes," she breathed rapturously, unable to keep the utter happiness she was feeling out of her voice. "I love it. And I can't thank you enough, my lord—"

"Nicholas."

"I can't even begin to thank you, N-Nicholas. I really can't. It's too lovely for words."

He raised her hand and placed a warm, infinitely sensuous kiss on her fingers. Penelope closed her eyes and prayed that this whole incident would not turn out to be a dream.

"Oh, I'm sure we can think of something far more agreeable than mere words, my love. What do you say?"

Penelope opened her eyes abruptly and stared up at her husband, certain that her mind had been playing tricks on her. Had he just said what she thought she had heard? she wondered. He stood far too close to her, holding her hand in both of his. No wonder she could not think clearly. And then, without warning, that look was back in his eyes again, and she knew he had indeed suggested that they kiss. Of course, she had imagined kissing the colonel several times in her more romantical moments, and she had always managed to acquit herself admirably well in such encounters, she recalled. Now that the actual act was upon her, however, Penelope couldn't for the life of her move a single muscle.

"That is if you have no objection, my love," he murmured with deceptive meekness, although Penelope was quite sure he was going to kiss her come hell or high water.

"Objection?" she breathed helplessly, inwardly cringing at her own lack of resolution. "Well, I think— "

"Splendid decision, my love," he cut in, taking her chin firmly in one hand and tilting it up at a convenient angle. And before Penelope could think up a suitable protest, his mouth was on hers, warm and tentative and infinitely tender. Penelope was effectively silenced.

After a few moments, however, a nagging sense of incompleteness assailed her. In her imaginary embraces, the gentleman had never been quite as tame as this, she remembered. She had imagined him to be a good deal more enthusiastic, not to say downright aggressive. Tentatively, Penelope leaned into him, a soft moan escaping her as she opened her lips invitingly. The result was instantaneous. She found herself clamped against the colonel's hard body with a ruthlessness that knocked the breath out of her. His mouth was no longer either tentative or tender. He took full advantage of her invitation and invaded her mouth as she never dreamed of being invaded. Never in her most daring fantasies had she imagined an assault as wildly sensuous, as demanding, as frankly possessive as that first kiss from her husband.

She had no idea how long it lasted, but when it ended—as suddenly as it had begun—it left her whole body heavy and tingling with desire, and Penelope knew she had set her foot on a path from which she had no wish to turn back. Her every nerve protested when the colonel released her abruptly and strode over to the door.

"I shall be late for dinner if I don't hurry," he threw over his shoulder before closing the door sharply behind him.

*   *   *

Nicholas had no recollection of crossing the intervening sitting-room, nor did he recall entering his own bed-chamber and closing the door. What stood in his mind all too clearly was the reason for his abrupt retreat from his wife's boudoir. As he slowly regained his composure, his first sensation was one of breathlessness. His heart pounded as it always had during countless skirmishes with the French, and he found his back pressed against his closed door as though the whole French army threatened to break it down.

Slowing releasing his breath, Nicholas relaxed his rigid muscles and stepped away from the door. He ran a hand over his eyes. Good God! he thought, noting that it trembled slightly. What had he done? Mechanically he rang for Bates, and as the old valet helped him out of his travel-stained clothes, Nicholas reviewed the recent scene with his wife and his own ignominious retreat.

He had only meant to give Penelope the ring, he reasoned. Ah, yes, he thought, his grandmother's favourite ring. That had started this whole business. No sooner had he set eyes upon it less than a week ago, as he rummaged through his grandfather's safety-box looking for the deed to a long ago acquired piece of farmland, than he was beset by a vivid and quite nostalgic vision of his wife's eyes. The thought of taking the amethyst ring back to Laughton Abbey and presenting it to her had seemed the natural thing to do at the time. Nicholas did not recall how long he had sat there at his grandfather's carved Sheraton desk, but he did remember the deep sense of nostalgia that had swept over him as the image of his grandmother invaded his consciousness, overlapped by that of the other woman in his life, one who resembled her in so many ways.

The notion had immediately struck him as ridiculous. What could the wealthy, top-lofty, pampered Lady Penelope Ashington possibly have in common with his precious, unpretentious grandmother? The thought was almost sacrilegious. But the more he thought about it, the more Nicholas became convinced that the uncanny resemblance went much deeper than the pale halo of hair and lilac eyes. There was a determination about Penelope, a steadfast and wholehearted dedication to her family heritage—however mistaken he considered her loyalties—that reminded him of his grandmother's life-long dedication to his grandfather, the man who had given up his home, family, and the Ashington heritage to live a quiet country life with the woman he loved.

Nicholas stood patiently while Bates deftly arranged the folds of his cravat into a perfect fall. Yes, he thought, it had seemed so appropriate that his grandmother's ring go to Penelope that Nicholas had not stopped to consider the ramifications of such a gift. In truth, the idea had taken such a hold on his imagination that he had cut short his stay at Bellington Hall and posted back to the Abbey with the express purpose of watching his wife's eyes light up at the sight of the amethyst ring. Not until he was halfway to Ashington did it occur to him that this gesture on his part might well be misconstrued as a weakening of his defences. He had brushed the thought aside, strangely reluctant to think of anything but Lady Penelope's eyes turning dark violet with emotion. And like a fool he had not given a thought to his own reaction.

He had arrived later than expected, shortly before the dinner hour and, after a brusque enquiry from a startled Featherbow, had gone straight up to visit his wife. He had found her dressing for dinner and had stood in the open doorway of her boudoir for several moments, enthralled at the sight of her fresh loveliness. He had not remembered quite how very lovely she was, he realised with no little amusement. The deep lilac gown she wore, cut low across her small bosom, emphasized her slim form in a way that quickened his blood. He had been amused by his instant arousal until her eyes, wide and startled, locked with his. Then some inner emotion had shifted radically, and Nicholas had been gripped by conflicting urges of tenderness and lust.

To hide this unexpected rush of emotion, he had pulled the ring out of his pocket and given it to Penelope. Her reaction was everything he had hoped for, and when he slipped his grandmother's ring onto her finger, he was struck—for the first time since their wedding—with the shattering realisation that this desirable woman was his. To have and to hold, he thought, with a flush of his habitual cynicism. To touch, to kiss, to bed as he suddenly desired to do with a fierceness which startled him. He looked down at her small hand, lying so confidently in his own, and tried to tell himself that these marital intimacies were not, and should not, be part of his original plan to destroy the Ashingtons. How could he destroy this woman, as he had intended to do, if he developed a *tendre* for the wench like any star-struck moonling?

Quite without warning, he found himself pressing his wife's fingers lingeringly against his mouth. The softness of her skin against his lips conjured up visions of other soft parts of her which were his for the taking. To divert his mind from these lascivious thoughts, Nicholas had said something outrageous. He no longer remembered what it was, but it had caused Penelope to colour up adorably and stutter in confusion.

And then he had kissed her, with a restraint and tenderness quite foreign to his nature. She made no move to pull away, and he touched her lips gently with his own, marvelling at their softness and warmth. Her trust and compliance delighted him, and he had just steeled himself to end the embrace, when Penelope moaned softly under his mouth and swayed against him. But it was her parted lips that undid his careful control. Before he could think rationally, he had crushed her in his arms, revelling in the soft shape of her against his own sudden harshness. Time stood still, and he experienced the odd sensation of being both the conqueror and the vanquished. The blood rang in his ears as he invaded the sweet warmth of his wife's mouth, and the whisper of the lilac silk intoxicated his senses as he ran his hand down her back to draw her body closer into the curve of his own.

It was at this precise moment of imminent capitulation to the demands of his senses that Nicholas heard the amused murmur of his cynical self reminding him that only a fool would believe that a woman's body might be invaded with impunity. Such a victory, this snide voice insisted—if indeed bedding one's own wife could rightly be considered such—could only be obtained at the expense of a man's own defences. And it was this life-long habit of military training that cooled his blood and made Nicholas draw back from an encounter which had, only moments before, seemed inevitable.

He had dropped his arms abruptly and turned away, with some patently feeble excuse of having to dress for dinner. And now, he thought wryly, shrugging his broad shoulders into the

new evening coat Bates was holding for him, he would have to
convince his wife, whose eyes had been misty with surrender,
that he had no intention of deviating from the terms of the
alliance they had entered into.

Nicholas wondered, as he trod down the wide staircase to
join the ladies in the drawing-room, what kind of fool he was
to have imagined that he could vanquish the enemy with a
wedding band.

Although Penelope had dreaded facing the colonel again
after their passionate interlude, his demeanour over the dinner-
table laid those fears to rest. As the evening wore on, however,
and the earl gave no sign—either by speaking glances from his
dark eyes or any softening of his saturnine expression—that
the kiss they had shared meant anything to him, Penelope did
not know whether to be relieved or offended. How fortunate,
she thought, as she stood by the pianoforte later that evening
turning the music for her aunt, that she had not mentioned the
colonel's amorous advances to Lady Octavia. Her aunt had
greatly admired the amethyst ring, of course, but when she
fixed her blue eyes on her niece expectantly, Penelope had
shied away from revealing her wanton encouragement of the
colonel's attentions. Which was all for the best, she thought,
since the dratted man seemed bent on pretending that nothing
untoward had occurred between them. Well, two can play that
game, my lord, she told herself, angry at her own naive hope
that perhaps the colonel might have more than a military
interest in their alliance after all.

"Why don't you entertain us with one of those lovely French
lullabies you sing so well, Penny?" Lady Octavia remarked as
she came to the end of the country dance she had been playing.
"I doubt Lord Laughton even knows you have a sweet singing
voice."

"And I doubt the colonel has any interest in French lullabies,
Aunt," Penelope retorted rather ungraciously.

"Then you are mistaken, my dear," drawled that gentleman,
who stood lounging against the mantelpiece. "There is nothing
I would enjoy more than hearing you sing, Penelope."

Penelope met her husband's eyes directly for the first time
that evening and felt a sharp stab of disappointment at finding

no hint in them of that intense stare hat had turned her bones to jelly. Instead, she detected a hint of cynicism and a perverse intent to bait her.

"I am sorry to disappoint you, my lord," she answered coolly, refusing to be cowed. "But I do not feel like singing this evening. Some other time, Aunt," she added, casting a glittering smile at Lady Octavia, who was regarding her in astonishment.

Feeling an odd rush of longing for something she could not quite put her finger on but which definitely concerned the colonel, Penelope took refuge in icy politeness. Turning back to the cause of her vague unhappiness, Penelope addressed him with deliberate sweetness.

"How soon will you be returning to Hampshire, my lord?" she asked, conscious of her aunt's sudden intake of breath.

The colonel gazed at her steadily, and Penelope saw his lazy amusement disappear abruptly.

"Very soon, I would imagine, my dear," he replied in clipped accents. "Very soon indeed. Now, if you ladies will excuse me, I have papers to go through before I retire."

"What was that all about?" Lady Octavia demanded as soon as the door closed behind the earl. "It is not like you to be so impolite, dear. You sounded for all the world as though you wished to see the last of the rogue."

"And so I do, Aunt," Penelope replied briefly, not sure that this was strictly true.

She was even less sure the following afternoon when the colonel caught up with her as she was cantering back from a visit to an outlying tenant farm.

Penelope glanced at him surreptitiously from beneath her lashes. She had been feeling definitely guilt-ridden over her rudeness of the previous evening and this seemed to be a heaven-sent opportunity to cleanse her conscience.

"About last night," she began impulsively. "I really did not mean to sound quite so . . . so—"

"So dismissive?" he offered helpfully, amusement crinkling the corners of his eyes.

"Well, yes," Penelope acknowledged. "Aunt Octavia said I sounded quite rude, and I wish to apologise for it. I did not mean to send you packing quite so soon," she added, unable to resist the temptation to tease.

This sally was greeted with a shout of laughter, and the tension between them eased noticeably. So much in charity was she with the colonel in his present benign mood, that Penelope was easily persuaded to sing for him that evening. The following evening she discovered that her husband had a pleasant baritone and insisted that he sing a duet with her. Their evenings *en famille* thus began to take on a sense of harmony which Penelope found increasingly appealing. They also formed the habit of breakfasting together long before Lady Octavia left her rooms, and it was here one morning two weeks after his return to the Abbey that the colonel informed her that he would be leaving for Bellington Hall that afternoon.

True to his word, however, the colonel was gone less than a fortnight this time, and before Penelope had reached the point of admitting to herself that she missed him, she saw him striding towards her one afternoon as she worked in the rose-garden.

She knew he was going to kiss her the moment she saw the eagerness in his step and the light in his eyes, and she fought to control the wild surge of delight which threatened to betray her into an unbecoming display of emotions. Feigning a composure she was far from feeling, Penelope set down her basket, gloves, and secateurs, and brushed a stray curl out of her eyes.

"You look positively charming, my dear," he murmured, ignoring her proffered cheek in favour of her lips, while he brushed fleetingly with his.

Penelope blushed and glanced self-consciously around her, acutely aware of the colonel's hand on her waist, and wondering how many of the servants had witnessed his lapse from decorum.

"I have extended the rose-garden with some new varieties the head-gardener obtained for me over near Petworth, my lord," Penelope explained breathlessly, gesturing at the newly turned earth. "Roses are quite my favourites, you should know."

"I am glad to hear it, Penelope," he drawled, smiling down into her eyes in a way that set her blood singing. "You must see the roses my grandmother planted at Bellington Hall. They are rightly famous in the neighbourhood and in full bloom at this time of year."

Bellington Hall? Penelope thought incredulously. Was he

actually suggesting that she visit his home in Hampshire? she wondered. Or is this merely a polite, meaningless observation?

"I trust you had a good journey, my lord," she murmured, stooping to pick up her basket. "The weather has been so fine that Aunt Octavia and I have taken to having our tea served on the terrace overlooking the lake. I hope you will join us, Colonel."

"I would prefer Nicholas, if you have no objection, my dear."

Sensing that he was teasing her, Penelope laughed. "I hope you will join us, Nicholas," she repeated.

"I would be delighted, my dear. Here, let me carry that for you," he added, taking the basket from her and offering his arm.

Penelope was surprised and pleased at the ease with which they fell back into their comfortable routine. Even Lady Octavia remarked on the colonel's mellow demeanour, which not even the arrival one afternoon of the Swathmores, for a family dinner, seemed to ruffle. Not that Geoffrey didn't do his damnedest to make his host wish him in Jericho, Penelope thought, after her cousin had uttered his umpteenth fulsome compliment designed to put even a hardened society matron to the blush.

The colonel had continued his conversation with Sir James as though supremely unconcerned with Geoffrey and his overblown flattery, a feat which threw the latter into such a fit of the sullens that his mother felt obliged to apologise to her host for her son's childish behaviour.

As spring slipped into summer, and the colonel's absences from the Abbey became less prolonged, Penelope began to feel that complete happiness was almost within her grasp. It was true that the colonel was still—most perversely, she thought— her husband in name only. But that would change in time. Penelope was certain of it. Didn't he kiss her every time he arrived back from Hampshire? Kisses that were becoming gradually warmer and more sensual? None had yet come close to rivalling that first one, of course, but she was optimistic that, given time, the colonel would kiss her that fiercely again. And now he had taken to kissing her when he left as well. Surely that augured well for their future together, she thought.

By mid-July, Penelope was certain that her marriage would soon be more than a convenience for the colonel, for he informed her upon returning from Hampshire that he intended to spend the rest of the summer at the Abbey.

"That is, my dear," he said with a new playfulness that Penelope found most endearing, "if you have no objections."

Rejoicing at the thought of what the summer months might bring, Penelope blushed. "None that I can think of at the moment, my lord," she replied gaily. "Of course, we may well be invaded by friends and relatives. Have you no friends you wish to invite down for a stay in the country?"

The colonel assured her that there would be plenty of time for house-parties in the holiday season, and Penelope was secretly glad that she would have the whole summer to charm her husband into a more satisfying relationship. Such was her confidence that Fate had finally smiled on her that Penelope was only mildly surprised, during the last week in July, to find a note from Charlotte awaiting her upon her return from a ride to the village.

Could it be, she thought complacently as she joined Lady Octavia in the morning-room, that her friend had finally come to see the error of her ways? She devoutly hoped so, for of all things, she would have liked to share her new happiness with Charlotte.

"Well?" her aunt prodded, when Penelope sat staring at the missive in her lap, as if turned to stone. "What does the lass say, Penny?"

"Oh, Aunt!" she cried, her voice strangled with emotion. "Something terrible has happened." And without a further word, Penelope jumped up and rushed out of the room. She must tell Nicholas, she thought, her mind in a turmoil. He would help her cope with this disastrous news. Blindly she ran down the hall and burst into the study, where she knew the colonel spent much of his time.

"Nicholas!" she cried, standing in the doorway, Charlotte's letter clutched in her hand. "Oh, Nicholas!" She seemed unable to say any more for her throat was constricted with emotion. The colonel stood up and came quickly across to her, taking the letter from her nerveless fingers.

He perused its contents swiftly and then raised his eyes, their dark, enigmatic gaze riveted on her face. Penelope felt a thousand questions hovering in the air between them. If only she knew the answers, she thought, she would not feel so helpless at the force of destiny which had suddenly shaken the very roots of her being.

"What shall I do, Nicholas?" she whispered, her voice a weak thread. "Whatever shall I do?"

The colonel regarded her for several seconds in stony silence. When he spoke, his voice was harsher than she had heard it in months. "What should you do? Why, nothing, of course. What can they expect from you at this late date? You are my wife, Penelope. And I sincerely hope you will not forget that vital fact."

Penelope felt overcome by dizziness. Of course, what had she expected him to say? There was no going back. She was the Countess of Laughton now, married and forever cut off from all the things that might have been. As Nicholas had said, there was no changing that vital fact.

Even as she stood staring into the expressionless depths of her husband's eyes, Penelope heard Featherbow's discreet cough behind her. She tensed and reached out instinctively for the colonel's support.

"The Viscount Clayton, milord," the butler said in an emotionless voice before disappearing soundlessly, leaving the visitor standing in the open doorway.

Penelope forced herself to turn around. He hadn't changed a bit in the three years he had been gone. He was still the Greek god she had worshiped as a schoolroom chit. His golden hair still curled about his finely boned head in elegant disarray. His nose still had that classical cast to it, and his eyes were still the brilliant cornflower blue which had caused her so many sleepless nights as a romantical young girl.

She stood enthralled as the man she had long imagined dead slowly took shape before her in every glorious detail. "Edward," she murmured disjointedly and swayed towards him. She felt the colonel's hand tighten on her arm, and she swayed back against his chest, as if seeking some kind of shelter from the storm of emotions which raged in her heart.

Edward Hayward stepped into the room, his blue eyes accusing. With a moan of anguish, Penelope gave in to the dizziness and felt herself falling into blackness, accompanied by the angry murmur of masculine voices.

CHAPTER TWELVE

Surprise Attack

Nicholas scooped his wife up in his arms and glared ferociously at the blond stranger, who had sprung forward as Penelope crumpled, obviously with the same intention in mind. The seconds ticked by in uncomfortable silence as the two men stood gazing warily at each other.

The viscount's eyes fell to Penelope's pale face, and Nicholas deliberately settled her more closely against his chest. A fierce sense of possessiveness such as he had never experienced before welled up inside him. This woman was *his*, he thought, conscious of the warmth of her body resting so lightly in his arms. Wisps of her glorious pale gold hair had come loose across his sleeve, and he could smell the faint lilac perfume she used. His heart contracted painfully. This woman was his wife, he thought again, and no man—certainly not this obscenely handsome viscount from the past—was going to take her away from him.

"I would thank you not to frighten my wife out of her wits in the future," he growled menacingly. "In fact, you might stay away indefinitely, since there is nothing here for you any longer."

The viscount seemed not to hear this piece of deliberate rudeness, and his gaze, which bored fiercely into the colonel's, held such real anguish that Nicholas felt a flash of pity for the man.

"So it's true?" he snapped harshly. "Penny really did marry a nobody, and a damned soldier to boot." He drew himself up, and his aristocratic lip curled disdainfully. "I refused to believe it when my sister told me. It's not like Penny to disregard what is due to her name. Had she waited another few months, things—"

"Well, she didn't," Nicholas snarled, his temper simmering dangerously. And perhaps that would teach Clayton not to take a woman like this for granted, he thought cynically. He could have married her three years ago. Three lost years when he might have enjoyed her . . . Nicholas shied away from imagining the delights the viscount might have enjoyed with Penelope had he never left England to travel to India.

"And now, if you will excuse me," he said bluntly, glancing at the door.

After one last lingering look at the unconscious countess, the viscount turned on his heel and left without a word.

A few moments later, Nicholas had reached his wife's room and laid her still form on the brocade counterpane of the huge four-poster. He sat beside her and took her limp hand in his. Gently he brushed a pale gold strand from her forehead, revelling in the smooth coolness of her skin. Her lashes curled, long and silky, against her cheek, and something caught in Nicholas's throat at the sight of her vulnerability. She was completely at his mercy, his cynical self whispered snidely, and the thought aroused all his predatory instincts. He allowed his invasive gaze to poise on her mouth, softly relaxed and innocent enough to tempt a man to acts of madness. He tore his eyes away and let them wander leisurely down her body. The clinging summer muslin hid little of her womanly charms, and Nicholas could well imagine the delights in store for the man lucky enough to lay claim to them. And that man would be none other than Colonel Nicholas Bellington, he thought with a perverse thrill of pleasure. That damned soldier nobody, as Clayton had called him. He grinned sardonically as he watched the gentle rise and fall of his wife's breasts. His hand ached to curl around their softness and to slip leisurely down her flank to encircle the small waist, then over the gently swelling hip and down the long length of leg, clearly discernible through the thin gown.

These pleasant ruminations were abruptly interrupted when Penelope shifted. Nicholas looked up and found his wife gazing at him, a hint of fear moving behind her lilac eyes. He smiled encouragingly at her, cursing himself for not curbing his lascivious thoughts sooner.

"How do you feel, sweetheart?" he murmured, watching her keenly.

Penelope looked about her nervously. "Where is he?" she asked tremulously. "I must ask him about Neville."

For some reason Penelope's question drove every tender thought from Nicholas's mind. So the silly chit was panting to see her golden boy returned from the grave, was she? Well, he thought grimly, he had news for her. The viscount would not come skulking around the Abbey again. Not if he could help it. She had made her bed and would have to lie on it, whether she liked it or not.

"If you are referring to Viscount Clayton, my dear," he said silkily, "he has gone back where he belongs." He had a hard time restraining himself from adding that no wife of his would spend her time languishing over that indecently handsome coxcomb. Something of his violent thoughts must have shown in his eyes, however, for Penelope dropped her gaze, but not before he had glimpsed the shimmer of tears in them. He felt immediately contrite and would have wished nothing better than to kiss away his wife's pain. But he knew this was not the moment. Penelope was too distraught by the viscount's sudden reappearance, and Nicholas himself too full of murderous urges against this man who had disrupted the growing harmony at the Abbey.

He carried her unresisting fingers to his lips and kissed them. "He is gone, Penelope. There is no reason to be frightened."

"I need to talk to him," she murmured. "To explain—"

"There is nothing to explain," Nicholas cut in harshly. "What possible explanation could he expect after leaving you to kick your heels for three years? No, there is nothing to explain, my dear. So don't worry your pretty head about the wandering viscount. He no longer signifies."

Penelope appeared not to have heard him. "I should have waited," she whispered, so softly that Nicholas had to bend forward to catch her words. They struck both fear and fury into his heart. Fighting to maintain his outward calm, Nicholas released his wife's fingers and stood up slowly. He gazed down into her troubled eyes and wondered if she saw him at all.

"Perhaps you should have," he said bleakly. "That might have been better for both of us."

Unable to keep his features passive a moment longer, Nicholas turned and strode out of his wife's boudoir, his mind a snakepit of conflicting emotions.

Penelope closed her eyes with a sigh. Edward was back. She marvelled at the thought, letting the realisation of this miracle seep into every fibre of her being. The impossible had happened. Her lost love had come back, hale and hearty, and had rushed over to see her, Penelope Ashington, his affianced bride. She sighed again at the enveloping sweetness of the vision, but something was distorting the rosy perfection of his fantasy, and Penelope felt the image of Edward Hayward fade gradually into an indistinguishable misty silhouette in her consciousness. She struggled to recapture the intoxicating moment when she had gazed into those brilliant blue eyes, but the vision escaped her. Instead, she felt herself pierced by a dark, hot gaze that glared at her possessively, hungrily, almost violently. She shuddered and opened her eyes. She was alone, but she could feel the presence of Nicholas Bellington as if he were still sitting beside her. The imprint of him was there on her bed. Her fingers were still warm from his touch. His anger still lingered in the room behind him.

And then everything came back to her in its proper dimension. Of course, she thought, the shock of coming face-to-face with the past had addled her brains. She was no longer the Penelope Ashington that Edward had left behind three years ago. In fact—and the thought struck her for the first time as faintly ominous—she was not an Ashington at all any more. She was Penelope Bellington now, the Countess of Laughton, a married lady who had no business swooning at the sight of a Greek god from the past.

And Nicholas? she thought, suddenly aware of the unpleasant effects on the colonel of Edward's reappearance. Where was he? He had been with her only minutes ago, she was sure of it. She had opened her eyes to find his enigmatic gaze upon her, and then she had muttered something—whatever had she said?—and the colonel had left abruptly. And what of Neville? Where was her brother?

A sudden rush of anxiety made her sit up and swing her legs to the floor. She paused, overcome by dizziness. Before she could find the strength to rise, the door burst open and her aunt sailed in, followed closely by Alice with a bowl of lavender water.

"My dear child," Lady Octavia exclaimed, motioning to the abigail to put the bowl on a delicate rose-wood table beside the bed. "I cannot believe my ears. Featherbow informed me that Edward was here. Is it true, love?" Her blue eyes regarded Penelope sharply. "I see it is. Come, Penelope. Lie down again and I will bathe your face. You look as though you have seen a ghost."

"I have," Penelope said miserably. "And I think Nicholas is furious with me. I must have said something quite rattlebrained when I saw Edward standing there."

"He will get over it," Lady Octavia said, briskly dismissing the colonel and his sensibilities. "Now, get back into bed, Penny."

"Has he gone?" Penelope asked, allowing herself to be undressed and settled beneath the cool sheets.

"If you mean Edward, love, of course he's gone. You didn't expect that colonel of yours to offer him a glass of brandy in the library, now did you?"

No, thought Penelope, she could not imagine the irate colonel doing anything quite so civil. She only hoped the two men had not come to fisticuffs. The idea of Nicholas bloodying Edward's perfectly classical nose appalled her, and she glanced apprehensively at her aunt.

"He was not rude to Edward, I trust," she murmured.

Lady Octavia chortled. "My dear girl, you are a ninny to be sure. If you gave the matter any thought at all, you would know that Edward is more the type to expend energy on offensive rhetoric than the colonel. Edward was always a great one for talk; the colonel, on the other hand, is more likely to darken a man's daylights for him if push came to shove."

She smiled at the accuracy of her aunt's description of the two men. "I really should talk to Edward, though. Don't you think so, Aunt? To explain how . . . that is, why—"

"Nonsense, child," Lady Octavia exclaimed brusquely. "If you know what's good for you, Penelope, you will steer clear of Edward Hayward."

"But I am bound to meet him everywhere, Aunt," she wailed, despair making her petulant. "What am I to do?"

"I think you are making a fuss over nothing, dear. Just remember that you are Lady Laughton now, and your betrothal to Edward is a thing of the past."

Penelope tried to keep her aunt's words in mind as she went about her daily routine as though nothing had happened to mar the smooth surface of her life at the Abbey. She soon discovered that although the surface of her life appeared tranquil, the inner discord created by Edward's return made itself felt almost immediately. Gone was the comfortable companionship she had shared with the colonel, who seemed to have retreated behind a barricade of silence. No longer did they enjoy their musical evenings together. Instead of accompanying the ladies to the drawing-room after dinner, as had been his wont, the colonel now retired immediately to the library, pleading the need to go over estate affairs.

Much as she tried to ignore it, Penelope was lonely for her husband's company. She missed the easy camaraderie they had shared riding about the estate in the afternoons; she missed his teasing and the lazy smile that softened his dark eyes and made her heart skip. Most of all she missed the man whose hands on her waist as he lifted her from Bluedevil's back left a tingling imprint on her skin which accompanied her to bed every night.

This man whom Penelope was beginning to fear she needed more than she had realised was gone, replaced by the stern autocrat who had arrived at Laughton Abbey over a year ago, bent on destroying every vestige of Ashington heritage. All her dreams of creating a real family with the taciturn colonel began to evaporate as the days went by and he maintained a cool distance that chilled Penelope's heart. Even their rare excursions together became nightmares of nervous tension.

The first Sunday after Edward's return had been particular stressful to her. Naturally the Haywards had attended the service; how could she expect them not to? She had dreaded this first public confrontation with her former intended, but could think of no good reason to stay away. Besides, it would never-do for Charlotte to think that she was a coward, would it? So she had put on her best morning-gown and a new bonnet which the modiste in Brighton had assured her was all the crack, and sat through the service, hearing barely a word of the vicar's sermon. Inevitably, Edward had come over to greet the party from the Abbey and to offer his condolences as soon as they left the little chapel. Lady Octavia had saved the day by throwing her arms enthusiastically around Edward and prattling on to cover the awkward silence. But as soon as Edward had turned to her, Penelope felt the firm grasp of her husband's fingers on her arm. Reminded thus forcibly of her new responsibilities, and conscious of Charlotte's gimlet stare, Penelope was able to utter the expected civilities in a cool, controlled voice which hid the wild churning of her emotions. Poor Neville, she thought. Weakened by malaria and abandoned by the bandits—according to the viscount's story— three months into their captivity, who could doubt the reality of his death now? When she felt the colonel's grip on her arm tighten almost painfully, she smiled graciously and accompanied him to their waiting carriage.

It was not until several days later, during which the colonel had become—if that were possible—even more taciturn, that Penelope began to see a pattern to his perversity. His moods definitely became blacker and his face more tightly chiseled after each public encounter with the viscount. At first she attributed this discovery to coincidence, but when she mentioned it to Lady Octavia, her aunt confirmed her suspicions.

"The man's absolutely rabid with jealousy, my girl, as if you didn't know," her aunt snorted disgustedly as the two ladies sat on the south terrace drinking their afternoon tea. "And I wouldn't like to be in Edward's shoes if the colonel finds him poaching on his preserve," she added with a meaningful glance at her niece. "Ah!" she exclaimed when Penelope flushed guiltily. "Don't tell me you have been such a fool as to meet clandestinely with the viscount? Of all the totty-headed starts, child. The colonel is not a man to take such games lightly, Penelope. You are really a fool if you believe you can hoodwink him."

"I believe nothing of the sort," she replied angrily. "But how can I avoid speaking to Edward when I meet him in the village? Can you tell me that, Aunt?"

Her aunt brushed the question aside impatiently. "How many of these *innocent* encounters have there been, Penelope?" she demanded, setting her empty cup down with a clatter.

Startled by her aunt's vehemence, Penelope answered reluctantly. "Only three so far. He was there again yesterday when I rode in to change your books at the circulating library. Charlotte was with him, and I couldn't very well avoid their company on the ride home without appearing positively rude."

This reasoning sounded plausible enough to pacify even the colonel, but Penelope carefully omitted the less innocent fact that she had encountered Edward Hayward several times over the past weeks while out riding on Ashington land. It was not until after the third such seemingly haphazard meeting that she began to suspect they were premeditated. The encounters had occurred far enough removed from the Abbey to minimize detection, but when the viscount continued to accost her, Penelope became uneasy. It was not that Edward ever did anything to alarm her, at least not anything that she could take exception to. He was always pleasantly attentive, and Penelope—who missed the stimulating male companionship the colonel had provided—found herself falling insidiously into her comfortable childhood relationship with her former betrothed.

This misconception of the viscount's motives vanished quite suddenly late one afternoon as Penelope dismounted to tighten a loose girth. Bluedevil suddenly pricked up his ears and whinnied, and Penelope glanced over her shoulder to see Edward cantering up behind her. He swung off his horse and came over to make the adjustment she had been struggling with, and then, instead of lifting her back into the saddle as she had anticipated, he took her waist between his hands and pulled her roughly against him.

The nostalgia of being in his arms again swept over her, momentarily depriving her of the will to resist. Only when the warmth of his mouth shocked her into awareness did Penelope push blindly against his chest and wrench her face away.

"No, Edward!" she cried angrily. "Whatever are you thinking of? Release me instantly."

He laughed and pulled her closer, nuzzling her neck and murmuring endearments. "Nonsense, my darling Penny," he whispered into her ear. "I never should have left you to go to India three years ago. You cannot imagine how often I have dreamed of holding you in my arms again, sweetheart. Every day I spent as a captive in that dreadful nest of thieves and murderers, I dreamed of this moment. Tell me you've missed me, too, darling. I know you have. I don't believe this cock-and-bull notion that you have given your heart to a half-pay officer from the wrong side of the family."

"Edward," she gasped, struggling to disentangle herself from his overheated embrace. "You are mad! I am a married woman now, and I won't be subjected to this indecency. Let me go, I say. At once!"

Whatever else she meant to say was lost as the viscount claimed her lips in an ever more ardent kiss. Penelope, now thoroughly alarmed, squirmed in vain to escape, but her efforts only seemed to incense the viscount more.

"Tell me you still love me, Penny," he begged. "I know you cannot feel anything but contempt for that low-born husband of yours." He held her so tightly now that Penelope had difficulty breathing. "Please, love. Say it's me you want. You are such an innocent, darling. Anyone can see you don't love that soldier of yours. I've been watching you, dearest. It's in your eyes. Charlotte tells me it's a marriage of convenience you have with him and that you only accepted him to save the Abbey." His ran his lips down her neck as he spoke, and Penelope could scarcely tell what she found most despicable—Edward's wet kisses or his ugly words.

"Let me go," she whimpered, fright making her incoherent. "*Please*, Edward. Don't do this. *Please!*"

His only response was a deep chuckle against her neck. "Don't be a goose, Penny. And don't tremble so, sweetheart. I wouldn't hurt you for the world. I love you, darling. Now, tell me the truth. Is Charlotte right? Are you married in name only, my pet?"

He raised his head and stared down at her, his brilliant blue eyes dark with passion and something else. Could it be triumph? she wondered. Was Edward exulting in this invasion he was practicing on another man's—what had Aunt Octavia called it?—preserve. Yes, that was it. She belonged to Nicholas, and Edward was doubtless enjoying this incursion into the colonel's preserve. The thought made her feel slightly sick. She had been naive indeed to think that Edward was different from any other man. His motives were transparent to her now. He wanted her because she belonged to another man. She glared back at him defiantly, glad that her courage was returning.

"That's no concern of yours, Edward," she said with icy precision. "Now, do as I ask and let me go."

He merely grinned at her, his hands slipping suggestively down her back. "It's true, isn't it, Penny? You *are* still an innocent? That nodcock cares so little for you, he has not touched you. Am I not right? No doubt he favours serving wenches and has no experience with ladies. Well, so much the better, dearest. I can help you get an annulment, my sweet, and that will show the upstart that he has no place among us. He's as common as they come, everyone can see it."

"No!" Penelope hissed, her anger now thoroughly aroused. "You really are mad if you think I will be a party to such treachery."

The viscount seemed not to hear her. "Just tell me that the marriage is not yet consummated, and I will do the rest, Penny. I can claim that you had a prior contract with me, which is the truth. That is reason enough for an annulment, I wouldn't doubt, my love."

Penelope was beginning to fear she would be carried off by force, when Bluedevil lifted his black head from munching grass and pricked his ears nervously.

"Someone is watching us, Edward," she whispered urgently. "Let's get away from here."

"Very well, my dear," he replied, obligingly lifting her up onto Bluedevil's back, before turning to grasp the reins of his gelding. Penelope did not wait. As soon as Edward's back was turned, she clapped her heel to Bluedevil's side and raced back to the Abbey without a backward glance.

As she pulled the winded horse to a standstill in the safety of the stable-yard, Penelope found she was trembling violently and knew that it was not her unpleasant experience with Edward that had turned her fingers to ice. No, she thought, handing the reins to Jeremy, her fear of Edward was nothing

compared to that which assailed her at the thought of facing the
cold contempt in her husband's eyes if he ever learned of her
indiscretion.

Penelope managed to get up to her room unobserved and
slipped out of her riding-habit, determined to rest for an hour
or two before she must face her husband over the dinner-table.
Although her emotions were raw from Edward's unexpected
and unwelcome assault, she was unable to relax, and after half
an hour of twisting and turning on her crumpled bed, she rose
and sat by the open window, wrapped in her favourite lavender
silk robe.

Gingerly she touched her lips, and as her fingers probed their
puffy contours, the vision of another man's assault on them
came crowding back into her mind. But how different that had
been, she mused, luxuriating in the tingle of desire that flowed
through her at the memory of the colonel's kisses that evening
he had presented her with the amethyst ring. She glanced down
at it now, glowing luminously on her finger, and wished she
might recapture the closeness she had shared with her husband
in that memorable encounter.

She sighed, dragging her thoughts back to the recent fracas
with Edward. How revolted, how absolutely violated she had
felt in his embrace, she mused. How could that be? If anyone
had told her that she would find Edward's kisses disagreeable
in the extreme, she would have laughed in his face. Wasn't the
viscount her golden Greek hero, the shining knight of her
childhood who had finally claimed her—a romantical chit
hardly worthy of his regard—for his bride?

Penelope shuddered. It had been an appalling experience,
one which she would never, *never* wish to repeat with any man.
The incongruity of this fervent wish burst suddenly upon her,
and Penelope paused again as another unsettling thought
invaded her mind. Hadn't the colonel practiced just such an
ardent, vaguely licentious invasion upon her person? she
mused. And she had been anything but revolted, hadn't she?
The memory of her own wanton eagerness to experience the
tantalizing hardness of his body against hers swept over her,
causing her cheeks to grow warm. But that was different, she
tried to tell herself. The colonel was her husband, and husbands

had the right to that kind of intimacy. And to much more, a little voice whispered insidiously, but she brushed the thought aside.

Penelope was struggling to regain her composure in the face of these unladylike thoughts, when Lady Octavia burst into the room.

"My dear Penelope," she gushed, bustling over to place a small, plump hand on her niece's forehead. "You are not coming down with something, are you? It seems to me that you are running a fever, love. Hadn't you better go straight to bed? I'll have Featherbow bring up your dinner on a tray."

Her aunt's genuine affection had always touched Penelope, but this afternoon, in her present state of agitation, Lady Octavia's kindly ministration undid her. Uncharacteristically, she burst into tears, and by the time her aunt had restored her to a semblance of her normal composure, Penelope had blurted out the whole dreadful tale of Edward's perfidy and her own fear of the colonel's fury.

Her ladyship regarded Penelope speculatively for a long time. "Assuming that the colonel has no desire to let the viscount steal you away from him," she said without round-aboutation, "then you must put an end to these clandestine meetings and let Edward know—by giving him the cut direct if necessary—that you will be no party to such a ramshackle and highly scandalous affair. But first, my dear," she added, her stern countenance softening as she regarded her niece, "you must go to the colonel with the whole story."

Penelope gasped in horror. "You cannot be serious, Aunt. He would *never* forgive me." She shuddered at the thought of the blistering tongue-lashing such an act would call down on her head from the irate colonel.

"If you meant what you said about not wanting to end your marriage, my dear, you must do so immediately. Think how much worse it would be if the colonel found out about your little trysts with Edward from some busybody."

Much as Penelope hated to admit it, her aunt's advice made sense and had the advantage of forcing the colonel to talk to her. Having screwed up her courage to the sticking point, and rigged herself out in her most seductive evening gown, Penelope suffered a sharp setback when Featherbow announced to the ladies in the drawing-room that the earl would not dine at home that evening. Lord Laughton had, the butler informed the startled ladies, merely ridden over to the village that afternoon and intended to dine there.

"Let us know the moment he returns, Featherbow," Lady Octavia instructed, murmuring waspishly to Penelope as soon as they were alone that one could always count on gentlemen to be anywhere but where they should be when they were needed. Penelope had to smile at her aunt's pithy recriminations, but by the time the last course was removed, she felt her courage flagging.

"Never fear, my love," Lady Octavia remarked bracingly after they were ensconced comfortably in the drawing-room once more. "Perhaps his lordship will be mellowed by old Ben Lockley's best brandy if he takes his dinner at the Blue Boar Inn. I have heard that it is a superior brew."

Penelope could not help smiling at her aunt's comment. "Perhaps I should not inquire too closely how you know that Mr. Lockley's brandy is superior, Aunt," she said, glad to have a momentary distraction from the task that lay ahead of her.

She never did learn the answer to her teasing query, for at that moment Featherbow entered to inform the ladies that his lordship had returned and was requesting the presence of Lady Laughton in the library.

CHAPTER THIRTEEN

Unconditional Surrender

Any hope she may have entertained that the interview might be a civil one fled precipitously at the first sight of the colonel's grim countenance. He looked tired, Penelope thought, noticing the dark shadows under his eyes as she advanced into the room, but his cold stare made her shiver with apprehension.

She managed a tentative smile. "Good evening, my lord," she said, glad to hear that her voice sounded stronger than she felt. "And I am glad that you sent for me, because I had a particular desire to speak with you myself tonight." She paused, one hand resting lightly on the back of a Queen Anne chair. She felt herself stiffen as his dark gaze raked her insolently, and steeled herself to endure some scathing insult, which would doubtless reduce her courage to ashes. She was not disappointed.

"Very charming, my dear," he drawled. "Very charming indeed. I see you have set out to seduce me into witless submission as you seem to have done with Clayton. I warn you, Penelope, I am not so easily gammoned as his lordship."

Penelope straightened her back and gave the colonel a level stare. "If you have called me in to grind your teeth at me in this odious way, I shall leave you, my lord," she said stiffly. "What I have to say to you can wait till tomorrow."

"What I have to say to you *cannot*," he replied shortly. "Sit down." He motioned to the leather settee.

Ignoring the rude delivery of this request, Penelope sank

gratefully down on the straight-backed chair instead, her legs
jellified with panic.

"Now," he said, pouring himself another glass of brandy.
"What is it you wish to speak to me about?"

Penelope took a deep breath to steady her racing pulse and
looked up into the colonel's flinty eyes. "It's about Edward,"
she blurted out before she could lose her nerve.

"What about him?"

The harshness of his voice made her quail, but Penelope
rushed on. "I cannot seem to escape his presence," she
murmured, not sure how to avoid making Edward into a villain.
"He appears everywhere I go. At the library, the vicarage, the
tenant farms, even here on the estate—"

"The puppy has dared to accost you on the estate?" the
colonel demanded sharply.

"There's a short-cut from the village across the south
meadow—" she began, unwilling—now that the moment had
arrived—to unleash the colonel's ire.

"Answer my question," he snapped, in his most quelling
military tone.

"Yes," she said bluntly, then added hastily as the colonel's
brows slanted into a thunderous scowl, "but until this afternoon
there was never any question of impropriety."

"And this afternoon?" he said in a deceptively soft voice.
His eyes bored into her so accusingly that Penelope felt as
though she were undergoing a court-martial.

She took another deep breath and plunged on. "This afternoon everything changed," she whispered. "He kissed me."

This confession was followed by an uncomfortable silence
as Penelope tried in vain to read her husband's thoughts behind
the glittering eyes which had not ceased to regard her fixedly.
Why didn't he show anger, or contempt, or some emotion she
could recognise? she thought. She could deal with these
emotions, had even expected them. But this sudden icy
withdrawal disconcerted her and gave her a distinct feeling of
doom.

Then suddenly the colonel smiled, and Penelope felt a
tremor of fear at the lack of warmth in the smile. "And exactly
what kind of *encouragement* did you give him, my dear?" he
drawled softly.

Penelope jumped to her feet, glad to be released from the paralysis of apprehension which had gripped her. "That was unkind of you, sir," she retorted angrily. "If you know anything about me at all, you must know that I would never sink to such despicable depths. *Never!*"

"Ah, but there you have it, my dear. I know very little about you, you see. What little I have learned warns me that you value blue blood and impeccable lineage above everything else, which undoubtedly includes me." There was so much bitterness in his voice that Penelope felt her heart wrench. It distressed her that the colonel could think her so lost to all sense of decency that she could betray her marriage vows. She had not intended to reveal the depths of Edward's iniquity, but in view of the colonel's suspicions, she would have to. Suddenly it was of vital importance to her to let her husband know she was true to him and to no other.

"You are wrong about me," she said calmly, although her whole body was trembling with emotion. "I am not such a callous, heartless creature as you seem to think. I begged Edward most earnestly not to insult me with attentions that were abhorrent to me. And when he made his unspeakable suggestion, I was positively rude to him. But he wouldn't listen."

"And what suggestion was that?"

Penelope noticed that the scar on the colonel's cheek was twitching and curling beside his tautly clenched mouth. In a surge of unexpected tenderness, she felt the urge to reach out and still the tortuous jumping with her fingers, to stroke the pale, jagged line back into place along the colonel's weathered cheek. The emotion shocked her and made her blush.

"Edward seemed to be under the illusion that I would welcome an annulment to our marriage," she answered slowly.

"An annulment?" he repeated harshly.

"Yes," Penelope said. "He had heard from Charlotte that ours was a marriage of convenience. Which should not amaze you," she added, conscious of her own bitterness. "All the servants here must know, so it is not surprising that it is common knowledge in the neighbourhood."

When he made no reply to this revelation, Penelope added self-consciously. "He assumed that I was an innocent. In fact, he seemed to know I was. How he could is a mystery to me."

The colonel's lips twisted briefly into a semblance of a smile. "It is written in your eyes, my dear."

The endearment, however insincere, bolstered Penelope's courage. "He said that since I had had a prior contract with him, he could take care of everything. Our betrothal *was* official, you know."

"And what was your reply?"

"I told him that he was mad to suggest it," she replied with spirit.

"Am I to understand that you do not wish for an annulment?" There was a different quality to his voice, she noticed. It had lost its hard edge, and his smile was less cynical.

Penelope stared into the colonel's dark eyes for several moments, wishing that things were not so strained between them. If only he were not so dauntingly stern and cynical, she thought. It was almost as though he did not wish to encourage any intimacy between them. He never spoke of his family, except for his grandmother, and her only briefly. She wondered suddenly—with a tug of jealousy—if he had ever loved a woman. There was no doubt in her mind that women had loved him, for he must have been a handsome figure of a man before his face was marred so drastically. And even the terrible scar had not really detracted from his harsh good looks, for it added a dash of mystery and danger which she considered highly attractive. She was brought back from her romantical musing by the colonel's voice.

"Well?" he said, his eyes filled with an emotion which might have been anxiety, Penelope thought in surprise.

"No, I do not," she declared calmly.

"Are you quite sure of that, my dear?"

Penelope was certain—well, almost certain—that this time the endearment was genuine. The thought filled her with such delight and relief that she gave him her most glittering smile. "Absolutely sure, my lord," she said gaily, feeling her muscles relax as a warm glow of happiness flooded through her body. She had brushed through this dreadful interview without drawing the colonel's wrath down on her head, and felt as though an enormous weight had been lifted from her heart. He had believed her. Perhaps now they could return to their comfortable relationship, she thought. Perhaps now he would become, once again, the man she had missed so much. The man who had become so necessary to her well-being.

He placed his glass on the mantelpiece and stepped across the Oriental carpet to stand beside her. "In that case you can have no objection to scotching any further misunderstandings about where your loyalties lie, can you, my love?" The seductive smile that curled his lips should have told her that she was in danger, but Penelope was too happy to hear the teasing in his voice to pay attention.

"Of course not, my lord," she replied without thinking. "What do you wish me to do?"

No sooner had these words left her lips than Penelope realised their implications, and the smile trembling on her lips froze. Any hope she may have had that she had misconstrued the colonel's meaning died at the flare of desire she glimpsed in his eyes. She lowered her own quickly, half hoping that she had mistaken the matter. Her heart, however, fluttered wildly, and she knew that deep inside she wanted that predatory look in his eyes to be real, to be for her. She glanced up at him through her lashes and knew that her heart had won out over her more rational caution. The look in the colonel's eyes was unmistakably hot, and his lips were parted in a frankly sensuous smile that made Penelope forget how recently she had sworn never to permit another man to assault her.

She felt his finger under her chin and raised her head as if in a trance, keeping her lashes lowered.

"I had hoped to hear you say that, Penelope, my love," he said caressingly. "We need to pool our forces to deflect this dastardly attack on our alliance."

Penelope was momentarily confused. What was he talking about? she wondered, trying to make sense of this military jargon. Her emotions were in such a state of turmoil that she could think of little else besides the fact that she wanted him to kiss her. Most desperately she wanted him to kiss her. She literally ached with wanting it so much.

"Don't you agree, my love?"

How could she refuse him anything when he called her his love in that tone of voice? "Yes," she murmured eagerly, not sure quite what he meant and not really caring. "Yes, of course, I do."

He stroked her cheek gently and she heard him laugh softly. "Look at me, Penny," he said. And when she obediently raised her lashes, he smiled as if at some private joke. "Yes, there it is for all the world to see," he murmured. "Your innocence, my love," he explained in answer to her puzzled look. "That should be our first skirmish, don't you think? Together we can demolish it. No one will dare question your loyalty again, my love, after we have accomplished that mission."

"Oh!" she exclaimed weakly, when the import of his words began to sink in. "I see." She felt a rush of colour stain her cheeks as she saw all too clearly what the colonel was suggesting. Before she could protest, however, he lowered his head and brushed her lips leisurely with his. Penelope's senses reeled anew, and she offered no resistance when the colonel's arm encircled her waist. She relaxed gratefully against him, for her legs felt unaccountably rubbery.

"I'm glad you do, sweetheart. And the sooner we start the better, wouldn't you say?" He raised his head and glanced at the ormolu clock on the mantel. "It is almost eleven now, Penelope. What do you say if I come up to you in half an hour?"

Penelope marvelled at the smoothness with which the rogue had manoeuvred her into a position where surrender seemed the only option. Of course, she told herself candidly, there was not a single fibre in her entire body which did not welcome the surrender she was about to make. Quite the opposite, if truth were told. Her blood was tingling feverishly with anticipation.

The colonel coaxed her towards the door, one arm lightly around her waist. He opened the door and looked down at her, a quizzical smile on his lips and a devilish light dancing in his eyes.

"Half an hour, then, my love? That is," he added with a heart-stopping caress in his voice, "if you have no objection, my lady?"

Penelope looked up at him fleetingly and wondered how any woman with an ounce of romantical blood in her veins could object to being seduced by such a man. And that was his intention, she acknowledged, and it was her own shameless desire to allow herself to be seduced.

"No objection at all, my lord," she replied breathlessly, slipping out of his hold to run helter-skelter up to her room.

No objection whatsoever, her heart repeated over and over. No objection whatsoever.

As the door closed behind his wife, Nicholas strolled back to retrieve his glass from the mantelpiece. When he lifted the decanter to pour himself some more brandy, his hand trembled visibly, and he realised that during the past half hour he had been holding his emotions under tight control. He sighed and flung himself down in the leather armchair, stretching his long legs out before him. First there had been that wild surge of anger at the thought of Penelope kissing another man. He had lashed out at her, accusing her of encouraging the viscount, he remembered, feeling a twinge of remorse at the memory of the hurt in her lilac eyes. And then there was that stab of cold fear that had pierced his heart at the mention of annulment. The knave had schemed to take Penelope away from him, he thought, shaken out of his complacency at his success in bringing the two Ashington women back into his power.

Nicholas groaned softly and took a gulp of brandy. That victory had been doubled-edged, all right, he admitted, his thoughts going back to that delightful interlude in Penelope's boudoir when he had first tasted her lips himself. He could hardly blame the viscount for wanting to possess all of her, could he? He had wanted to do so himself that evening. And he could have done so easily, he thought, smiling at the memory of his wife's unexpected warmth. She had been more than receptive to his kisses, and her tiny moan of pleasure had set his blood on fire. It was fear—or was it cowardice?—that had held him back. He feared the insidious power of this woman's femininity, he had finally admitted to himself. Fear of becoming addicted to the sweet allure of her body which promised delights he had tried not to think about. The thought of her lying there, two unlocked doors away, had caused him to curse the day he had set eyes upon her golden loveliness. He had fled to Hampshire to counteract the feeling of being caught in a vortex of uncontrollable passion. Nicholas had never liked losing control of his life, much less of his emotions. That was not his style at all, and he fought it with every ounce of discipline he possessed. But it had not been enough. He had been drawn back to the Abbey from the safety of Bellington Hall by the memory of two lilac eyes, eyes which filled with laughter and warm greeting every time he returned to her.

But now his hand had been forced. Clayton had challenged him, threatened his marriage to Penelope, who had come to mean so much to him. The realisation that he cared for his wife more than he ever intended to had dawned upon the colonel quite suddenly and with shattering force that afternoon she had swooned into his arms. As he had held her limp body against his chest and seen that pale gold hair spread over his shoulder, Nicholas remembered feeling the whole foundation of his world shake. He had not bargained on this insidious affection for the enemy which threatened to undo all his carefully laid plans. The alliance he had envisioned should have made Penelope his possession, virtually his prisoner according to the laws of the land, but he had reckoned without her courage, her loyalty, and her trust. And also her sweet, delectable self, he thought, staring at the amber liquid in his glass.

He glanced at the clock for the third time. The minute hand seemed to be taking an inordinately long time to count off the thirty minutes he had promised her. Nicholas grimaced at his own impatience. He was behaving like a moonling on his first assignation. It would be wiser to consider this night's work as part of his plan to humiliate the Ashingtons. After all, the purpose of this whole manoeuvre was to seduce Penelope into bedding the grandson and great-grandson of a Cit, wasn't it? Not for the first time since entering into this alliance with Lady Penelope, Nicholas wondered if his motives were as clear-cut as they had seemed six months ago when the notion had first occurred to him. Didn't he owe it to his grandmother to see the Ashingtons brought as low as they could get? he thought. And hadn't Penelope's own great-grandmother decreed that marriage to a Cit was lower than the Ashington's could bring themselves to countenance?

Nicholas's thoughts veered suddenly into the past. His dear grandmother, whom he had always considered a lady in spite of being the daughter of old Adrian Bellington, the sea trader turned country gentleman, had taught him to be proud of this sea-faring side of his family. He had never cared a fig about being a commoner. Unlike Sir Adrian Bellington—as the old man liked to be styled, Nicholas recalled, after he had purchased the obscure baronetcy with his opulent fortune— titles meant nothing to Nicholas. But the old sea captain had not been attuned to the land, and in spite of his desire to leave a legacy of gentility for his only daughter, he had frittered away his hard-earned blunt in well-meaning but ineffectual schemes to find a place for his family among the local gentry.

Predictably, it had been David Ashington who had given the Bellingtons the social status they sought, when he met little Annie Bellington at an assembly in Brighton and married her, in spite of the disapproval of his grand family. Nicholas's mother, whom he remembered only vaguely, had followed her father's good example and married back into the Bellington side of the family. Since a tragic boating accident at Brighton one summer had deprived him of both parents at an early age, Nicholas had even a fainter recollection of his father, who had been his mother's cousin. He often wondered what his life might have been like had his parents survived to provide the love and tenderness of a normal childhood. As it was, his happiest memories were irrevocably centered on his doting grandparents, and the story of their humiliation at the hands of the Ashingtons of Laughton Abbey had shaped his life.

Nicholas sighed and glanced again at the clock. Another ten minutes to go, he thought restlessly. All this reminiscing had done nothing to clarify the confusion he felt at what he was about to do. It was all very well to take refuge in his military strategies, or to blame the viscount for forcing his hand. But part of him rejected these excuses, and a voice within him—no longer either cynical or logical—warned him that he was so anxious to seduce his wife, not because he wanted to claim her as his possession, but because she had captured his heart.

Dismissing this notion as preposterous, Nicholas rose abruptly to his feet and placed his glass back on the mantel-piece. It still lacked five minutes to the appointed hour, but by the time he got up to his room and out of his clothes . . .

He refused to think any further, and as he took the stairs two at a time, his heart was beating with something other than military fervour.

The almost full-blown summer moon lit the Abbey grounds with a silvery brightness. Leaning on the ancient stone parapet which encircled the small terrace attached to her boudoir, Penelope gazed out at the fairylike scene and felt a glow of happiness at the bounty of the Fates who had blessed her with the clear bright beauty of this spectacular night. If she had planned it—which of course she hadn't—she could not have wished for a lovelier night for her own seduction, she mused, conscious of a sense of mystery and unreality enveloping her there in the moonlight. The perfume of the honeysuckle, whose vines had climbed in tangled luxuriance up the supporting trellis and entwined themselves, like so many lovers' arms, around the columns of the parapet, intoxicated her with its sweetness. The scene appeared almost staged, and Penelope marvelled at it. She glanced down at the lawns below, as if Romeo himself might appear at any moment to climb up and claim her bed.

The magic of the moon stirred her imagination, and Penelope wondered if it had been just such a moonlit night which had prompted the legendary Lady Mathilde, rebellious daughter of the notorious duc de Saxe, to elope with her Norman baron lover. A night like this could encourage madness, Penelope mused, searching the pools of darkness under the huge oaks which dotted the park. A warrior on horseback could easily hide beneath such an oak, she thought. Or had he cantered on his big black war-horse right up to his lady's window to plead the urgency of his love? Penelope could imagine the softening of the stern visage of that long ago lover and the warm pleading in his dark eyes. And Lady Mathilde? Penelope wondered. What midsummer madness had moved her to entrust her person to the dark, fearsome warrior who braved her father's wrath to seek her love?

Penelope experienced a delicious frisson of excitement at the thought of Mathilde's daring. How romantic it all seemed now, but had the lady given any thought to the dangers inherent in her rash decision to defy her father's command? Had she trusted her warrior lover to keep her safe from the duc's rage?

Had she known herself to be so loved and cherished that she threw discretion to the winds and sacrificed rank and wealth to follow the dictates of her heart? That must have been the case, Penelope sighed, wishing that she had been called upon to make such a sacrifice for the man she loved.

The suspicion that she was indeed in love with the colonel had occurred to her before, but tonight, under the enchanting influence of the summer moon, Penelope admitted for the first time that she had lost her heart entirely to the dark warrior she herself had married. She understood, with a flash of clarity, how Lady Mathilde had given her heart unreservedly to just such as man as Colonel Bellington. A man bred as a warrior but with a soft chink in his armour through which an enterprising lady might reach his heart. Penelope prayed that she had found that chink in her husband's armour. Tonight, she thought, with a wave of desire, would give her the answer to her heart's dilemma.

It was a sense of his presence rather than any betraying sound which made Penelope whirl around. There in the shadow of the open window stood a masculine figure which might well have been that rogue baron who had come to steal Lady Mathilde's heart away. Tall and dark, eyes shadowed and unreadable, he radiated power and dominance as that daring warrior must have so many centuries ago. Caught between dream and reality, Penelope stared at him in wonder. His clothes—form-revealing breeches and a shirt festooned with elegant lace ruffles—proclaimed him a man of her own time, but to her feverish imagination he represented that warrior lover she had been dreaming about. And he had come for her.

Impelled by a recklessness she attributed to the influence of the moon in the limpid sky above, Penelope flashed him a melting smile and held out her arms. In an instant the man stepped across the space between them and took her hands in his, holding them against his chest and smiling down at her with a tenderness that quite undid her. At this distance, barely inches from her own face, the colonel's features were softened by the moonlight, and the fire in his eyes promised all the love and cherishing Penelope yearned for. Without a doubt, she thought, gazing spellbound up into her husband's dark eyes, the rogue baron had employed just such a loving glance to bring Lady Mathilde willingly into his arms.

"Oh, Nicholas," she sighed, dropping her eyes to the colonel's lips, which curled provocatively at the corners and, even as she stared, parted to reveal the gleam of his teeth in a seductive smile. Penelope felt deliciously decadent as her own lips parted in shameless response, and the colonel, correctly interpreting her invitation, lowered his dark head and covered her mouth with his.

Abandoning herself to the heady embrace, Penelope slipped her arms up to bring his lips more firmly against hers. She felt his hands possess her waist and heard his sudden intake of breath as his fingers slid over her silk-covered skin. She leaned into him, knowing from that other time what tempestuous passion she would be releasing and not caring what happened so long as he continued to create those tantalizing sensations on her body with his hands. And then his hand covered her breast, and she let out a long sigh, revelling in her power to turn this rogue soldier of hers into a lover much as Mathilde must have done with her forbidden warrior.

Nothing else mattered now, Penelope thought, making no protest as the colonel slipped her robe off her shoulders and let it slither to the terrace floor. Her shoulders felt cool in the moonlight, and she wondered if Nicholas would remove her filmy nightrail, too. What would it feel like, she wondered, to stand naked in the moonlight and watch the passion flare in her lover's eyes as he gazed at her?

Appalled at her own wantonness, Penelope shuddered in the colonel's arms. Instantly he raised his head and regarded her searchingly.

"Cold, sweetheart?"

Choked with emotion, Penelope shook her head.

He grinned. "Having second thoughts, Penny?"

This notion was so far from the truth that Penelope had the grace to blush and lower her eyes. "Nothing so missish, my lord," she murmured demurely.

He regarded her for a moment before lowering his head again to whisper against her parted lips. "Then I can think of only one other reason for this trembling, my love," he murmured between tender assaults on her eager lips. "You are impatient to take possession of this poor battle-scarred soldier. Is that it, love?"

Penelope reacted instinctively to this remark in which she detected a reticence and uncertainty she had never heard in the colonel's voice before. She reached up to his face and trailed her fingers gently down the length of his sabre wound until they reached the curl beside his mouth. There she paused, feeling the scar jump beneath her fingertips.

"I *like* your scar," she confessed quickly, before modesty could prevent her.

Nicholas raised his head and stared down at her for several moments, an arrested look in his eyes. Then he grinned and kissed her soundly.

"I'm glad to hear it, my love. But I have other scars, as you know. And I think the time has come to reacquaint you with them. That is"—and here his voice assumed the teasing quality she loved—"if you have no objections, my lady?"

Penelope felt her heart swell with love, and she smiled mistily up at him as he picked her up and held her for a moment cradled against him.

"None that I can think of, my lord," she replied softly, reaching up to kiss the tantalizing curl beside his mouth.

"None at all," she sighed, no longer envious of Lady Mathilde and her warrior lover since she would soon—very soon indeed, she thought, feeling her husband's arms tighten around her—have one of her own.

CHAPTER FOURTEEN

Counter Attack

Penelope stirred in the big bed, feeling deliciously drowsy. The pale morning light filtering through the carelessly drawn curtains assured her that the day was still young. She yawned and turned away to burrow her head in the covers which seemed unusually tangled. Tangled? Suddenly she was wide awake, and her eyes flew to the pillow next to hers. The unmistakable imprint of a head married its plump contours, and she blushed hotly as the whole delightful experience of the previous night came flooding back. So she had not dreamed it, after all, she mused, vaguely remembering the full moon and visions of the black knight riding off with a duke's daughter. Gingerly she reached out and touched the indented pillow. To her intense surprise and concusion, the feathers still retained the fading warmth of the man who had slept there all night. Well, she corrected herself guiltily, he had not slept all night, *she* could swear to that.

Momentarily diverted by immodest memories of just what Nicholas had been doing in her bed last night in lieu of sleeping, Penelope snuggled down beneath the covers, feeling comfortably lethargic. It was then she discovered that she was not wearing her nightrail. Of course, she remembered, Nicholas had stripped it off her after he laid her on the bed last night, just before he had taken off his own clothes and—

Penelope sat up abruptly, holding the covers against her breasts. She must get up, she thought apprehensively. Nicholas might come back. The thought of having to face her husband unclothed in the light of day unnerved her. Last night the moonlight shining in upon her bed from the open windows had lent a dreamlike quality to their nakedness, but Penelope quailed at the notion of displaying herself by daylight.

Glancing warily at the door to their sitting-room, Penelope scrambled out of bed and searched for her clothes. She soon discovered that whereas her emotional self was fairly glutted with satisfaction, her body was stiff and not a little sore. She stretched tentatively to flex her muscles and pulled on the nightrail which, together with her lilac silk robe, had been placed over a chair by the bed. So he had retrieved the robe from the terrace floor where it had fallen last night, she mused, inordinately pleased at this thoughtfulness on the part of her warrior lover. "*Her lover,*" she repeated aloud, savouring the sound of the words on her tongue. She was now Nicholas's wife in more than just name. Now she was truly the Countess of Laughton, mistress of Laughton Abbey.

For some odd reason, this latter idea did not satisfy her as she had imagined it would. Her pleasure and happiness, she realised with unprecedented clarity, sprang from her new and intimate relationship with her husband rather than from her position as his countess. Now that she had breached his last defences, Penelope decided, she could start on the next phase of her campaign: to provide Nicholas with a warm and loving family and an heir to carry on his name.

For a fleeting moment, an unwelcome thought caused a shadow to mar the contented future she saw ahead of her. It would be the Bellington name that she would perpetuate, and her son would be the first in a new line of Bellingtons to rule as masters of the Ashington estates. With Neville's death, the Ashington line had died out. How ironic, she thought, that the descendant of that black sheep banished so long ago by their common great-grandmother should be the man to displace the Ashingtons in history. And she, Penelope Ashington, was destined to help him do so. That unbending and heartless Lady Laughton must be trembling in her grave with frustration, Penelope thought, not without a glimmer of amusement at the hand the Fates had dealt her.

Penelope deliberately dawdled over her bath and tried on three morning dresses before settling on a pale blue muslin

embroidered with forget-me-nots around the hem. She instructed Alice, who was beginning to regard her oddly, to
arrange her hair simply, tied back with a velvet riband. Her
object was to have the breakfast-room to herself, but no sooner
had Featherbow informed her that his lordship had left with the
estate foreman an hour ago, than Penelope wished she had
dared come down earlier to greet her husband. Unable to stand
the thought of trying to act as though nothing momentous had
happened, Penelope opted to take her breakfast upstairs in
Lady Octavia's sitting-room. Her aunt, she felt sure, would
provide the necessary counterbalance to her own light-
headedness.

"Well, that rogue is not such a lack-wit as I had imagined,"
Lady Octavia declared with her usual bluntness, when she
learned the outcome of Penelope's interview with the colonel.
"And about time, too, I should say. That will spike young
Hayward's guns for him and no mistake. Annulment indeed!"
she snorted disgustedly. "Shame on him! No gentleman would
dare to hold a lady to a contract that must surely have been
considered void after news of his death reached us. Did he
expect you to be a mind-reader? But at least some good has
come from all this farradiddle, my dear," she added, throwing
a speaking glance at her niece. "Before you know it, we'll have
the Abbey halls swarming with little Ashingtons again. I shall
look forward to it, Penelope."

Penelope blushed furiously before it dawned on her what
Lady Octavia had said. "Bellingtons, you mean, don't you,
Aunt?" she murmured. "Little Bellingtons they will be, if and
when they arrive."

"That's exactly what I said, dear," her aunt protested
brazenly. "Little Bellingtons. It's been a long time since the
Abbey has sounded like a real home with children playing, and
running up and down the stairs, and creating the general
mayhem that you and Neville did when you were children,
dear.

Penelope was to remember her aunt's words in the weeks
that followed, for it seemed evident to her that Nicholas was
also eager to populate the Abbey with little Bellingtons. On
that second evening, as she waited nervously on the moonlit
terrace, half afraid that he would not come, his dark figure had

appeared again in the doorway, and Penelope had reached out to him impulsively, her heart full of joy. As the days went by and the intimacy of Nicholas's nightly visits became increasingly essential to her happiness, Penelope wondered at the strange twists of Fate which had brought the colonel to her doorstep last summer. She had had to lose a brother and her betrothed in order to gain a husband and lover. If she had been forced to make a choice between them a year ago, she knew without a doubt that she would have rejected the taciturn stranger her aunt had called rogue and scoundrel. And now here she was, she thought, curled up in the arms of that same rogue, satiated with his love-making, a woman more content and fulfilled than she had ever believed possible.

Occasionally, when she was alone, Penelope had what seemed like a premonition that this blissful existence was part of a dream that she had wandered into by mistake. Lady Octavia scoffed at this piece of downright foolishness, as she called it, and Penelope's fears were temporarily assuaged. The life they led was entirely too idyllic, she said to her aunt one afternoon several weeks later, as the two ladies sat drinking their tea on the south terrace.

"Fiddlesticks, child," her aunt scoffed, vigorously buttering a warm scone and slathering it with strawberry jam. "You must be increasing already, my dear, if you are so mopish and off your food. Here," she added, offering the scone she had just prepared to her niece. "Try these scones, love, they are simply marvellous."

Penelope regarded the offering with distaste and blushed rosily at Lady Octavia's blunt comment. It had become her aunt's habit of late to bring up the subject of babies at every opportunity, as if by talking about it constantly, she could make the happy event she so wished for happen.

"No, thank you, Aunt," Penelope said with a brief shake of her head. "I'm not really hungry." She sighed and considered her aunt's words. Perhaps her upset stomach over the past week was not caused by her overindulgence in plums and gooseberries as she had imagined. And yesterday she had felt positively nauseated at the thought of drinking her chocolate. This morning she had felt better, but no sooner had she finished her chocolate than she had to reach for the chamber pot. Alice had helped her back into bed and wiped her clammy face with a damp cloth, but when Penelope attributed her sickness to the green gooseberries, her abigail had laughed outright.

"What ails you, milady, is something a good deal more permanent than gooseberries," she declared, her rosy face wreathed in smiles.

Penelope had stared in disbelief at the beaming abigail. "That is impossible," she protested weakly, still feeling the effects of her churning stomach. "It's too soon, Alice. You must be mistaken."

"Nonsense," replied the abigail, sounding distinctly like Lady Octavia. "It only takes once, milady," she added slyly. "And I would wager my best bonnet on it."

Penelope had sworn her abigail to silence until she could be quite sure that her indisposition was indeed not caused by the gooseberries. She had been sorely tempted to confide in Nicholas, but what if she were mistaken? she thought. How foolish she would appear. She had decided to wait for another week before sharing her secret with the colonel, but she was beginning to believe that Lady Octavia's wish was about to come true.

That afternoon as she sat watching her aunt demolish a second scone lavishly smothered with jam, Penelope considered whether or not she should give Lady Octavia a hint of what was afoot. She decided against it, however, when she remembered that the Swathmores were coming for dinner that evening. Her aunt might not be able to restrain her enthusiasm, and Penelope was not yet prepared to have the entire family informed of her suspected condition. Besides, if it were true, as she devoutly hoped it was, she really owed it to Nicholas to tell him first.

Lost in these happy ruminations, Penelope was startled to see her aunt's hand, firmly clutching yet another buttered scone, pause half-way to her open mouth. A strangled cry escaped Lady Octavia's lips, and she struggled to rise, dropping the untouched scone on the terrace floor. Her aunt's eyes, fixed on some point behind Penelope's back, were wide and starting from her head as though she had seen a ghost.

"My dear Octavia," a warm, jovial voice called out loudly from the doorway. "What a delightful sight you are for these poor eyes of mine, my dear. Still lovely as ever, I see."

Penelope's first thought was that Featherbow had grossly neglected his duty in allowing this stranger to wander calmly into the house and disturb their privacy. In the next instant, however, she realized that this could be no stranger for he had addressed her aunt in an alarmingly familiar way. Since Lady Octavia appeared, for the first time Penelope could ever remember, quite incapable of speech, she turned to observe the newcomer.

The man who stood framed in the open doorway deprived Penelope of speech herself. He was a large gentleman—no, she thought, "gentleman" was perhaps not the correct term—a large man, both in girth as well as height. His face was florid and comfortably round, liberally marked with deep laugh lines around a generous mouth which, even now, was split in a friendly grin. His eyes—what she could see of them between the folds of his ample cheeks and the overhanging growth of grizzled eyebrows—were startlingly blue and twinkled at her with uninhibited amusement and delight. His dress was what Penelope would have described as exuberant rather than gaudy. His well-tailored yet comfortable coat of brown broadcloth had evidently long since abandoned its original purpose of confining the considerable bulk of the man and now gaped open rather informally, only partially obscuring his colourful waistcoat in an improbable shade of purple striped satin. His large, powerful, and—Penelope had to admit—rather well-shaped legs were encased in tight-fitting breeches of the palest yellow, and his boots, evidently the work of a master boot-maker, gleamed in the sunshine.

As Penelope watched, powerless to utter the most trivial of greetings, the stranger strode purposefully over to their table and grasped Lady Octavia's fingers none too gently in his huge hand.

"My dearest Octavia," he began, regarding her keenly. "I am most delighted to renew our acquaintance. I trust you have not forgotten an old friend, my lady." He raised her aunt's limp fingers to his lips and bestowed an enthusiastic and rather noisy kiss upon them.

To her utter amazement, Penelope saw her aunt blush scarlet and murmur something totally incoherent.

Penelope felt it incumbent upon her to come to her aunt's rescue. "I don't believe I have had the pleasure," she began in her coolest manner.

Undaunted by this chilly reception, the rotund gentleman fixed her with his blue stare, and his smile widened. "Why, I am Jonathan Beckwith, quite at your service, my dear," he exclaimed with a heartiness Penelope found quite daunting. "And you must be Penelope—Lady Penelope I should say, my dear. Please excuse an old man his eccentricities. I have heard so much about you from dear Neville that I feel quite related to you. Only in a manner of speaking of course," he added with a great guffaw of laughter at her startled reaction.

But Penelope's sudden pallor had not resulted from the newcomer's quite inappropriate familiarity.

"From Neville, did you say, sir?" she managed to choke out.

"Why yes," Mr. Beckwith confirmed with a nod. "I have had the great pleasure of accompanying his lordship home from India."

If Mr. Beckwith had divested himself of his elegant yellow breeches on the terrace, the effect could not have been more devastating on the two ladies. Penelope, who had risen slowly to her feet at this alarming news, met her aunt's astonished gaze across the table. For a second that seemed like an eternity, the effect of Neville's resurrection—if indeed this turned out to be the truth—flashed through her mind. Her first thought was for Nicholas, and she winced inwardly at the devastating effect Neville's reappearance would have on the colonel. Her heart cringed at the thought of his humiliation. Before she could stop herself, she blurted out her fear and frustration.

"That is impossible, sir," she cried, conscious of the panic in her voice. "Neville is *dead*."

Mr. Beckwith regarded her affectionately. "You may have thought so, my dear. But I assure you that the lad is very much alive. Rather under the weather, I'll admit, from his harrowing experience, but alive nevertheless."

"He is *here*?" Penelope felt as though the safe, comfortable world she had thought to build for herself and Nicholas were tottering around her.

"Yes, here," Mr. Beckwith repeated kindly, taking her limp hand in his huge paw and squeezing it gently.

"And very anxious to see you, my dear, I am sure."

Penelope would always remember the afternoon of Neville's return as the worst hours she had spent in her entire life. Not only was the household staff understandably at sixes and sevens with the sudden reappearance of their old master, but the unflappable Featherbow deserted his post in an uncharacteristic display of nerves which almost reduced Penelope to tears. Lady Octavia was no help either, since the jovial presence of Mr. Beckwith seemed to throw her aunt into a befuddled and incoherent state quite unlike her practical self. When that gentleman refused to leave his dearest Octavia's side for a moment, Penelope felt abandoned and adrift in her hour of greatest need.

Happy as she was to have her beloved brother restored to her so miraculously, getting a feverish and wasted Neville—whom she hardly recognised as her robust, hearty brother—settled into one of the guest-rooms tested Penelope's patience to the breaking point. Although glad to see his sister, Neville was peevish and petulant as Penelope had never seen him, and seemed to be pathetically eager to discuss the quite appalling foreign diseases he had suffered and his timely rescue by two British missionaries. Nothing would do for the returning earl but to inspect his own bed-chamber, as he called it. And in truth it was now legally his again, Penelope had to admit, although Nicholas had occupied it for over a year now, and the traces of his presence were everywhere. Neville took instant exception to the blue coat and discarded buckskins draped over the back of a chair, and Penelope could not prevent him from opening various drawers and exclaiming angrily at the upstart who had presumed to invade the sanctity of his chambers.

"And I suppose you are installed in the countess's rooms, Penny," he enquired petulantly as she accompanied him to the guest-room she had ordered prepared for him.

"Where else would I be, Neville?" she responded more sharply than she had intented. "I am married to the colonel, you know."

Neville's thin lips curled in disgust. "I can't imagine why you married the rogue, Penny," he commented, disregarding the warning glitter in Penelope's eyes. "The man's a damned commoner. I didn't believe it when Aunt Octavia told me how things stood here at the Abbey."

"We all thought you were dead," she replied coolly.

"Well, I ain't, Sis. And you can tell that dashed redcoat of yours that I want my room back."

Willing herself to make allowances for his poor health, Penelope turned a deaf ear to this rudeness. "I am sure that Nicholas will be happy to move as soon as he comes back, dear. So don't fret yourself," she added soothingly.

"Oh, no, he won't," Neville replied snappishly. "He ain't going to be at all happy to discover he's no longer the Earl of Laughton. Where is the blighter anyway? Why isn't he here to welcome me back?"

Penelope disregarded Neville's last, absurd question. Her brother was probably right, she thought. Nicholas was not going to like this new development at the Abbey. She didn't like it herself, she admitted, dismayed that she could not feel undivided loyalty to her brother. On one hand, she could hardly wish that Neville's reported death had been true, but on the other, she wished with all her heart that Nicholas might be spared the humiliation that awaited him upon his return.

Neville also tired easily, Penelope discovered. One moment he was engaged in a lively conversation—mostly about the atrocities he had suffered while a captive of the Indian bandits—and the next he fell into a lethargy and demanded, in a thread of a voice like that of a man twice his age, to be assisted up to his bed. Penelope breathed a sigh of relief when she had seen her brother safely confined to his room and instructed his old valet—who had been thrown into a state of acute agitation at his master's reappearance—to sit with him until she could send for the doctor. When he arrived, Dr. Kentwick was visibly shocked at the appearance of the patient and, after a thorough examination, privately informed Penelope that the earl's recuperation would be lengthy and not entirely guaranteed unless his lordship remained in bed and followed strict instructions.

No sooner had the doctor departed than Penelope, who had descended to the kitchens to ascertain whether the dinner preparations were going forward as planned, was informed by a still-agitated Featherbow that Viscount Clayton and Miss Hayward had called and were waiting in the Yellow Saloon.

"Oh, no! I can't see them now, Featherbow," Penelope exclaimed, her nerves ragged.

"And so I informed the viscount, milady," Featherbow

pointed out fatalistically. "But it appears that Miss Hayward is particularly anxious to see his lordship."

"Well, she cannot do so," Penelope snapped. "His lordship is in bed, and it is hardly fitting for her to pay a call on him there."

"Shall I inform her of this, milady?" Featherbow enquired woodenly.

Penelope shook her head in exasperation. "No, Featherbow. I shall do so myself. Inform my aunt if you please and send in some refreshments."

Twenty minutes later, having managed to pacify the cook, who had gone into spasms at the news of the earl's return, and to threaten the housemaids with instant dismissal if they did not stop bursting into tears at regular intervals, Penelope entered the Yellow Saloon in no mood to tolerate Charlotte's hysterics.

She saw at once that she was not to escape them, however. No sooner had she stepped across the threshold than Charlotte gave a small shriek and ran to clasp Penelope's hands.

"How is he, Penny?" she cried, her face showing the ravages of tears. "Do tell me how my darling Neville is." Her mouth contorted into a weak smile. "I *must* see him," she continued, veering into another channel of thought. "I simply cannot wait another minute to see my darling. Has he asked for me? I don't doubt it for a moment, of course. *Do* let me see him, Penny. I cannot *bear* it, truly I cannot." She raised a fragile hand and pressed it melodramatically against her forehead.

Penelope looked over Charlotte's bent head and caught her aunt's eye. The apprehension she read there caused her to curb her temper. She disengaged her hands from Charlotte's frantic grasp. "Neville is sleeping at the moment," she replied coolly. "Dr. Kentwick administered a dose of laudanum and ordered complete rest for at least a week. He cannot be disturbed."

Edward had approached during this conversation, and when Penelope turned reluctantly to greet him, she did not like what she saw in his eyes.

"We came as soon as we heard of Neville's return," he said smoothly. "Charlotte was most anxious to be reunited with her betrothed. Unlike another lady I could mention," he added *sotto voce*, his smile never leaving his face.

"We thought you were both dead," Penelope was provoked into saying.

"*You* may have done so," Charlotte intervened sharply. "But I never did. I *never* lost hope that my dear Neville would come back to me." She sobbed audibly and reached for her handkerchief. "If you had had the same faith in my brother, Penny, none of this would have happened."

Not having a very clear idea of what Charlotte was referring to, Penelope gestured towards the brocade settee.

Charlotte refused to be mollified. "I shan't leave until I see Neville," she declared. Penelope experienced a flicker of apprehension at the thought of the uneasy future awaiting this petulant miss and her equally petulant brother.

"And what you find to smirk at in this affair is beyond me," Charlotte complained. "After all, you are no longer a countess, are you? *I* shall be the countess here, not *you*," she added maliciously. "Isn't that right, Edward?"

"Quite correct, my love. And Penelope will not be a viscountess either unless she has reconsidered my offer to pursue an annulment." He regarded her quizzically, evidently enjoying her discomfiture.

"Well, I have *not*," Penelope stated firmly. "Nor have I any intention of doing so." She could not quite believe that Charlotte—the Charlotte whom she had known all her life as a loving, if somewhat rattlebrained, bosom-bow—could have spoken such spiteful words. Edward's attack she could understand; she had already seen his true colours.

"A baronet, I hear? If indeed he is even that," Charlotte continued, seemingly enjoying Penelope's distress. "I presume he has a farm or some such place of his own? You will be removing there, I imagine. I cannot believe that you would want to remain at the Abbey. Especially after Neville and I are married. As we shall be just as soon as the poor dear is feeling more the thing."

Penelope felt an overwhelming desire to slap Charlotte's smirk off her face for her, but a glance at her aunt restrained her, and she smiled grimly instead. After what seemed like an age, she was able to excuse herself on the pretext of looking in on the invalid and was about to flee up to her room to bathe her throbbing head, when a carriage was heard pulling up before the door.

Before she could escape, Featherbow had thrown open the door, and her Aunt Henrietta, followed by Sir James and

Cousin Geoffrey, crowded into the hall, all exclaiming at once about the fortunate turn of events that had brought Neville home safe and sound.

"Oh, you poor thing!" Lady Swathmore exclaimed, enveloping her niece in a comforting embrace. "You look fit to be tied, dear. I cannot believe that Neville is actually home again."

"Neither can I," Penelope said simply, too tired to hide her anxiety any longer. "Edward and Charlotte are here," she added glumly. "I hope you don't mind, Aunt. Everything is just too much." Her voice broke, and it was only her firm determination not to be a complete ninny that saved her from bursting into tears. "Nicholas does not know yet," she whispered, glad to be able to share her fears with her aunt. "I cannot imagine . . . I don't know what . . . Oh, Aunt!" she blurted out. "I am not making any sense, am I?"

"No, dear, you are not. But you may safely leave the Haywards to me. Do they stay for dinner?"

"I don't know," Penelope replied truthfully. "I hope not. I simply cannot bear a whole evening of Charlotte's gloating."

"Gloating?" Lady Swathmore raised imperious eyebrows. "How *dare* she. Let me deal with that pretentious chit, my dear. You run upstairs and rest. You look completely rattled. Where is Octavia? Why hasn't she taken charge of things?"

Penelope suddenly remembered the large gentleman in the purple waistcoat. "There is a Mr. Beckwith here as well," she explained. "Edward's uncle. He was the one who brought Neville home from India. Most kind of him, I'm sure, and I have yet to thank him. But his sudden appearance has left Aunt Octavia most unlike herself."

"Beckwith?" Lady Swathmore murmured. "Ay, of course! Jonathan Beckwith. An old beau of Octavia's. Quite besotted with him she was at one time. I remember him well. A rather pleasant fellow, if a trifle too hearty for my taste. Never mind Mr. Beckwith, Penny. I will take care of him, too."

Thankful that the task of entertaining the odd assortment of guests gathered in the Yellow Saloon had been shifted to her aunt's stalwart shoulders, Penelope ran upstairs and threw herself on her bed.

She must conserve her strength, she thought. The worst was yet to come.

CHAPTER FIFTEEN

Renewed Hostilities

Although Penelope had been unable to sleep, she felt rather more composed an hour later when Alice came upstairs to help her dress for dinner. Much as she dreaded the ordeal of sitting through a whole evening playing a role that already felt decidedly awkward, Penelope was momentarily cheered at the picture she presented in her new green satin gown, the tiny puffed sleeves and plunging décolletage of which gave the illusion of a cool elegance she was far from feeling. Alice was putting the finishing touches to her toilette when the sitting-room door flew open, and the colonel strode into her boudoir.

His thunderous expression told her that her worst fears had been realised. Nicholas had learned of his sudden change in status, and the shock had aroused all the old animosity towards the Ashingtons that Penelope had striven for so many months to obliterate.

"Featherbow informs me that your brother is returned." His voice was harsh and so cold that it sent a chill snaking down Penelope's spine. He stared at her for a moment as though she were a stranger. "Is that true?"

Penelope moved towards him, but an almost feral glint in his eyes stopped her abruptly. He had withdrawn from her, she thought. He was once again that hostile, bitter stranger who had arrived on her doorstep over a year ago, bent on revenge against the family who had humiliated his grandmother. She would have to be strong and patient, she realised despondently. All the ground she had gained in her relationship with her husband had been lost in one fell swoop. At least it would be useless she could find a way to break down this new barricade she sensed the colonel had thrown up around himself.

"Yes, it is true that Neville is returned," she replied calmly. "The news was a great shock to me, too, Nicholas." She paused. There were so many things she wanted to say to this man who was obviously still reeling under the shock of finding out that he was no longer the Earl of Laughton. She could only imagine how painful it must be to his pride. Once again an Ashington had humiliated a Bellington, much as that stiff-necked ancestor had humiliated his grandmother. No wonder he looked blue-devilled, she thought.

His lips curled mirthlessly. "I imagine it must have been very lowering to discover you are married to a mere baronet instead of an earl," he remarked cuttingly. "Poor Penelope," he added with heavy sarcasm that seared her through to the core. "What a comedown, indeed." His scar, a stark white slash across his taut face, jumped with tension.

"So I have been informed already," Penelope retaliated, hurt beyond measure by this unexpected attack.

He seemed not to hear her, and Penelope saw that his eyes were focused on some distant, unpleasant scene.

"I must talk to him," he said abruptly, disregarding her anguished expression. "Settle things between us." Before she could think up an excuse to stop him, the colonel was gone, leaving Penelope with a sense of having failed him in some unspecified way.

She gave up any thought of going down to dinner and sent Alice to inform Lady Octavia of her decision. Then she spent a harrowing thirty minutes pacing her room, speculating on the disastrous interview taking place between her husband and her brother. As the minutes ticked by, and thirty minutes became forty and then sixty, Penelope was wracked with growing anxiety. What had happened between the two men? she wondered. Had her brother said something disparaging, perhaps insulting? She had to admit that, given his present debilitated health, it was highly likely that Neville had not guarded his tongue. She shuddered at the thought of the colonel's inevitable reaction to such odious treatment at the hands of yet another Ashington.

After a whole hour had passed, Penelope became desperate. Setting modesty aside, she entered their private sitting-room and tapped sharply on the colonel's door. After a second rap, the door was opened by the giant Samuel, who regarded her without expression.

"Yes, milady?"

"I wish to speak with the colonel," she said forcefully, prepared to do battle with the huge manservant.

To her surprise, Samuel offered no resistance. He swung open the door and revealed to her startled gaze a chaos that spoke only too clearly of a hasty yet well-organized retreat. The huge four-poster was piled with coats, breeches, and waistcoats, while the armchair beside the bed had been draped with numerous cravats, shirts, and other unmentionables. On the floor, two half-filled trunks gaped open, while several smaller portmanteaux occupied the settee, waiting their turn to be stuffed with the scattered apparel.

At first Penelope thought the colonel must still be with her brother, a thought that petrified her. Then she saw his tall figure standing by the far window, and relief swept over her. She stepped quickly around the trunks and moved to stand beside him, but the colonel gave no indication that he was aware of her presence. Tentatively she placed her hand on his sleeve, only to withdraw it abruptly when he turned towards her, pale and silent, his face harsh with repressed fury.

"Well?" He turned back to the window as he spoke.

Penelope was trembling with apprehension but refused to be daunted by his cavalier reception. "You have spoken with Neville, I take it?"

"Yes."

After it became obvious he was not about to elaborate, Penelope spoke again. "What did he say?" she murmured. "What arrangements did he make for us?" Penelope wished she had had time to prepare her brother for his inevitable confrontation with the colonel. Perhaps he might have been persuaded to let them have the Dower House. But no, that would never have worked, she realised. Not only was the Dower House in disrepair, but Nicholas would never, *never* agree to accept such a concession. Not after having spent a year as master of Laughton Abbey. And Penelope couldn't blame him. She wouldn't accept it herself; in fact, she remembered, she had not accepted it when the colonel had suggested that she and Lady Octavia take up residence there.

When at last the colonel spoke, Penelope knew that Neville had behaved with the predictable petulance of an invalid. "Your esteemed brother was good enough to inform me that he requires the use of his bed-chamber."

Penelope gazed at her husband's stern profile and quailed at the humiliation her brother's thoughtless request must have caused him. As her eyes tenderly recorded every curve and plane of his beloved face, Penelope recalled the countless times she had kissed that very same curling scar which was now contorted with tension. What would happen, she wondered daringly, if she should reach up to kiss it again now? Would he thrust her aside in disgust because he imagined her loyalties lay with her brother? Or would he be reminded of the erotic urges she had invariably unleashed in him every time she kissed his scar? But Penelope could not bring herself to risk the third possibility, that he would remain impervious to her loving touch. Such indifference would destroy all her dreams, and she shrank from putting her feminine powers to the test. It was then she recalled the house in Brighton.

"We can remove to Brighton," she exclaimed hopefully. "I confess, I am not comfortable here myself."

"You may do as you choose," he replied with a finality that withered her hopes. Was he implying that they would not be together? she wondered. A frisson of fear touched her heart. But she refused to believe him capable of casting her off in the heat of his anger. She was his wife, she told herself desperately. They had shared the same bed for several months now, and he had seemed satisfied. Much more than satisfied, she thought wryly. She had made him happy, hadn't she? And then a terrible thought struck her. Was her seduction and this cruel casting off merely part of a prior plan to humiliate her? she wondered. No, it couldn't be. The man she loved was not the same rogue who had come seeking revenge a year ago. Was he?

"And you, my lord," she asked softly. "Do you not care for Brighton?"

"No." The categorial denial seemed to slam a door in her

face. But there was worse to come. "I shall go back home to Hampshire."

And there it was, Penelope realised numbly. Home for Nicholas was not, and probably never had been, here at the Abbey with her. He would return to Bellington Hall and take up his life there as if nothing had happened. And what about her? Penelope waited for several moments, praying with all her heart that he would say the magic words, *home to Hampshire with you*. But he never did. Penelope felt her misery well up inside her, a tearing, tangible thing that was splitting her apart. *Inside her?* It was then the notion struck her that inside her she held the most powerful weapon of all, one which would reduce this man's defences to rubble. What man, she thought in sudden euphoria, could resist the obligation to his own blood? His own son? All she had to do to make the colonel hers again was to inform him that he was to become a father.

Before she could open her mouth to pronounce her own magic words, however, an unpleasant thought stopped her. Did she really want a husband who tolerated her merely because she carried his child? a perverse voice whispered. She knew the answer before the question was fully formulated. And the answer was no. She would not sink to using such feminine wiles to trap the colonel into a union he obvious was only too eager to escape. And he did wish to escape it, that was patently clear to her.

Penelope pulled what tatters of pride she had left around her. "Then I shall wish you a pleasant journey, my lord," she remarked in a steady voice. Without waiting for a reply, she turned on her heel and walked blindly towards the door, which Samuel was holding open for her.

The sight of the large sergeant reminded her of something she must do. One last gesture of defiance, she thought ruefully. She paused before the manservant and pulled off the amethyst ring Nicholas had given her. "Here, Samuel," she said softly. "Return this to your master, if you please. I won't be needing it any longer."

She placed the treasured ring—a ring she had always considered a token of Nicolas's love—into Samuel's huge palm and walked out, steeling her heart against the avalanche of emotion which threatened to smother her.

*   *   *

Although the events of the day had left her exhausted in both body and spirit, Penelope spent a restless night. When she couldn't bear her own despondent reverie any longer, she rose and began emptying her drawers and clothes-press, piling the gowns on the bed in readiness for the morning, when she had instructed Featherbow to have her trunks brought down from the attic.

She heard the grandfather clock in the hall below strike three and, on impulse, threw open the glass doors to her terrace. The moon was on the wane, she noticed, a sliver of fading light, perhaps an omen of her own life. She shivered at the hint of approaching autumn in the cool breeze that fluttered her thin nightrail. How different from the bright moonlit splendour of that summer night when Nicholas had come to claim her. Although it had been barely three months ago, that night seemed a million years away now, lost in the mists of history. Penelope shivered again. She leaned on the parapet. There was nothing romantical about the scene this morning, she thought. No black knight waiting in the shadows to carry away his lady love.

She glanced towards the colonel's rooms and saw a faint light flickering out into the grey dawn. Had Nicholas been unable to sleep either? she wondered. The urge to go to him, to beg him not to abandon her here, where life had suddenly become intolerable, swept over her. But of course, that was impossible. Penelope swallowed and blinked back her tears. What was the use of crying? she thought. He didn't care for her, perhaps never had cared for her. She had been deceiving herself to think that Nicholas had begun to love her, to need her as much as she needed him.

Disgusted at this uncharacteristic lapse into self-pity, Penelope went back to her dresser and pulled open the top drawer with unnecessary force. She stared down at the jumble of brushes and combs, pins, ribands, scarves, handkerchiefs, perfume bottles, and other knickknacks. She closed the drawer again sharply, wondering how soon she might decently ring for Alice. The clock on her mantel chimed the quarter hour. Penelope sighed and sat down in her armchair, wrapping a blanket around her cold knees.

Twenty minutes later a noise in the hallway startled her, and she heard the unmistakable sounds of his feet passing her door and fading away down the staircase. He was gone, she thought dejectedly. Deep in her heart Penelope had refused to believe that Nicholas would abandon her, but when the echo of his feet had faded, and a dreadful empty silence settled down around her, she discarded that fantasy. Resolutely throwing off her maudlin lethargy, Penelope jumped up and rang for Alice.

From that point on, Penelope tried not to look back. When a sleepy-faced Alice appeared, Penelope calmly gave her instructions for an immediate departure. She would not stay a minute longer than necessary, she thought, and if her aunt chose not to accompany her—as Penelope had a serious suspicion she would—then she would go to Brighton on her own.

Lady Octavia proved her wrong, however, and when Penelope sought her out in her bed-chamber, where that lady was enjoying an early cup of chocolate, her aunt did not hesitate.

"Of course I will accompany you, Penelope!" she exclaimed, throwing off the covers and ringing for her abigail. "What a peagoose you are, child, to imagine I would fail you at a time like this."

"I did not wish to tear you away from Mr. Beckwith," Penelope remarked slyly.

"Fiddle!" Lady Octavia replied stoutly. "The devil fly away with men," she muttered, flinging open her wardrobe to examine its contents with a critical eye. "If Mr. Beckwith wishes to see me, he will have to come to Brighton to do so," she added, selecting a modish travelling gown in green lusting.

Vastly encouraged by her aunt's enthusiastic support, Penelope ordered the light travelling chaise for ten o'clock and went off to inform her brother of her decision to leave the Abbey. She had suffered serious pangs of conscience at leaving him to the mercy of the officious Charlotte, who had sworn to spend her days at the Abbey nursing her darling Neville. But Neville seemed oddly relieved that she was removing to Brighton, a circumstance which added to Penelope's sense of ill use, while making it easier for her to leave.

"This part of Sussex is beginning to feel rather familiar, dear," Lady Octavia remarked sardonically, as their chaise rattled along the coastal road later that day. "And we will arrive just in time to enjoy the seasonal activities. I trust Madame Dumont has received a new selection of materials, Penelope, for I feel an urge to refurbish my wardrobe."

Penelope regarded her aunt with amusement. "In the event that a certain gentleman should take it into his head to visit Brighton, I presume?" she enquired. Although it had been difficult for her to reconcile the Aunt Octavia who had condemned the colonel's lack of pedigree with the lady who seemed to welcome Mr. Beckwith's fulsome flattery, Penelope was delighted at the way Lady Octavia had blossomed under these attentions.

"Pooh! I am much too old for such frippery," Lady Octavia retorted, although her heightened colour belied her words. "I intend to spend my time making up baby clothes," she added, somewhat defiantly. "Although I did have the presence of mind to bring along some of the items I made for you and Neville when your mother was increasing, Penny."

As it happened, Penelope found her exile—as she privately called it—in Brighton more pleasurable than she had expected. Had it not been for the dull ache which plagued her every time she thought of Nicholas—which she did far too often— Penelope might have considered herself entirely content. Lady Octavia contributed greatly to her feeling of well-being, for she fussed over her niece and coddled her excessively. When their tranquility was shattered—a scant week after their arrival—by the eruption into the breakfast-room one morning of the portly figure of Mr. Beckwith, however, Penelope immediately realised that her aunt's attention would have to be shared with that jovial gentleman.

While it soon became apparent that Mr. Beckwith was a serious admirer of Lady Octavia's, he also proved to be an agreeable escort, who insisted upon lavishing attention on both ladies. It came as no surprise to Penelope when her Aunt's beau—as Penelope privately referred to the jolly visitor— announced that he intended to purchase a house in Brighton.

"I expect you will receive an offer from him any day now," Penelope teased her aunt one afternoon two months after their return to Brighton. "Why else would a bachelor require a house on the Marine Parade?"

"Rubbish, child!" her aunt exclaimed blushingly. "No doubt the poor man wishes to set down roots after all those years away in India. He certainly has the fortune to do so now. And perhaps he will seek out a wife, but it won't be me, dear. I've been an ape-leader these twenty years or more."

The wistful note in her aunt's voice told Penelope more clearly than words that Lady Octavia still harboured a secret *tendre* for the nabob from India, and she hoped that Mr. Beckwith, who had invited them to inspect his newly purchased residence that afternoon, would not disappoint her.

Any fears Penelope had that Mr. Beckwith would not come up to scratch were dispelled as he conducted them through the elegantly furnished house, pausing at every step to seek her aunt's approval on the renovations he had ordered. So Penelope was feeling unusually content with the world as they entered Mr. Beckwith's shiny new barouche for the drive home.

And then her own private loneliness was abruptly brought home to her. Who should she see approaching the carriage with giant strides but Sergeant Hardy. Her heart—which she had naively imagined on the mend—lurched uncomfortably.

"Samuel!" she called out, before she could control this unladylike outburst.

The giant came to a halt and hesitated, his black eyes flickering over her uncertainly. As he approached, Penelope dismissed the idea that an army sergeant would notice anything amiss in her increasing girth and flashed him an eager smile.

"It's good to see you again, Samuel," she said, once the manservant stood respectfully before her. "I trust everything is well at Bellington Hall?"

She would not—or perhaps could not, she thought—bring herself to ask about the colonel, but Lady Octavia, ever attentive to her niece's moods, had no such reservations.

"And how is that rascally master of yours?" she demanded peremptorily. "Haven't seen hair nor hide of him in weeks. What's the rogue up to anyway? Nothing good, if I know anything about it."

The bearded giant grinned impudently at Lady Octavia's stricture. "The colonel is busy with the harvesting, milady," he replied in his slow Scots drawl.

And that was that, Penelope thought despondently, as they

drove home later that afternoon. Perhaps she *should* have told Nicholas about the baby, she mused. She might not have regained her husband's regard, but surely Nicholas would have taken her to Bellington Hall with him had he known about her condition.

Then again, perhaps not, Penelope told herself realistically. Nicholas might not have cared about the child either. She felt a megrim coming on at this melancholy thought, and the spirited chatter of her companions only made her more conscious of her own unhappy state.

In the days that followed, Penelope noticed that Lady Octavia had blossomed under Mr. Beckwith's increasing attentions into an attractive woman. Love definitely agreed with her aunt, Penelope thought one afternoon, as she sat in her drawing-room trying unsuccessfully to finish one of Mrs. Radcliffe's novels she had picked up at the subscription library a week ago. Whereas love did not agree with her at all. In fact it made her increasingly miserable. Much like the hen-witted heroine of this novel, she thought. What reader with any sensibility could work up an enthusiasm for such a spineless creature? she wondered. The poor woman's life seemed to be one long string of tragedies. Penelope had enough tragedies of her own and was about to give up on Mrs. Radcliffe's tearful heroine and ring for tea, when she heard happy voices in the hall.

The door opened to admit a radiant Lady Octavia, and as soon as she saw her aunt's face, Penelope knew that something momentous had occurred. Lady Octavia fairly floated across the room, a beaming Mr. Beckwith, looking like the proverbial cat who ate the cream, in her wake.

"My dearest Penelope," her aunt trilled, obviously in high gig. "You will never guess." She grasped her niece's hands and pulled her to her feet, embracing her warmly.

Penelope smiled. "I believe I can, Aunt," she said. "But tell me anyway." She knew she had guessed correctly when she caught Mr. Beckwith's amused glance over her aunt's shoulder, and he winked.

"It must be as plain as a pikestaff how the land lies between your aunt and me," that gentleman cut in. "And this afternoon, as we were discussing the colour for the new curtains in the library at my— that is to say, our new house, I popped the question, and Octavia has accepted me."

"I shall ask Hunter to bring up a bottle of that French champagne you liked so much, Aunt," Penelope said with a smile. "Congratulations are definitely in order." But before she could reach the bell, there was a scratching at the door and the butler appeared to announce that a gentleman had called to see her ladyship.

"Did he give his name, Hunter?" Penelope enquired, wondering which of their Brighton friends could be calling at this hour.

"Yes, milady," the butler replied. "Sir Nicholas Bellington."

CHAPTER SIXTEEN

Lady Victorious

There was a moment of absolute silence in the drawing-room while Hunter waited impassively for his instructions. Penelope froze. Everyone in the room must surely hear the thudding of her heart, she thought distractedly. She saw her aunt glance at her expectantly, but her lips refused to move. Slowly she sat down again, her knees trembling.

"Show him in, Hunter," Lady Octavia said finally. "And bring up a bottle of the French champagne, if you please."

Penelope felt a shot of panic race through her body. What was Nicholas doing *here*? she wondered, clasping her suddenly frigid hands together in her lap. Her heart whispered that perhaps he had missed her, but her mind ruthlessly dismissed such fantasies. She would *not,* she told herself firmly, make a cake of herself over a man who had abandoned her so cavalierly last summer. She listened to the butler open the door and announce his name before she turned around.

The sight of him wrenched at her heart, and she felt incapable of uttering a word. Luckily Mr. Beckwith suffered no such inhibitions.

"Well met, my boy," he exclaimed in his jovial voice, advancing to shake the colonel's hand vigorously. "You have arrived just in time to help us celebrate a momentous event, sir. I am about to put my neck in the noose, so to speak."

"Jonathan!" Lady Octavia cried in mock horror, but Penelope saw that her aunt was gazing at her future husband with a besotted expression on her face. For a fleeting moment,

193

Penelope envied her aunt, and then she recollected that Lady Octavia had waited over twenty years to find the love of her life. Penelope had found hers last summer, but it had eluded her, she thought, watching her husband unexpectedly kiss her aunt's blushing cheek.

She rose awkwardly to her feet and steeled herself to pretend indifference towards the man who had given her the best and worst moments of her life. Nicholas's dark gaze flickered over her briefly, and then he stepped forward and took both her hands in his.

"I am happy to see you looking so well, Penelope." His voice was cool, polite, and impersonal. Her heart shrivelled at the sound.

Liar! Penelope thought testily, lowering her eyes from his piercing scrutiny. If he expected her to believe that bouncer, he must have left his wits in Hampshire. The colonel raised her hands to his lips, and Penelope was acutely conscious of the clean, masculine scent of his black hair so close to her nose, and the warmth of his lips caressing her fingers. She would have to keep her distance, she thought, panic threatening to overset her again. Or she would find herself wanting to touch him, and that urge could only lead to disaster, for mere touching would never be enough for her. She blushed at the memory of the wanton intimacies that touching Nicholas could provoke.

"I need to speak with you, my dear," he said, squeezing her fingers gently.

She flashed him a startled glance. "We are about to toast the newly affianced couple," she said defiantly. "Perhaps later—"

"Oh, don't be a peagoose, Penny. If dear Nicholas has come all the way from Hampshire to see you, it must be urgent. We shall await you in the library, dear. Come, Jonathan," she added, herding her betrothed towards the door, "we will open the champagne without them."

Penelope could only shrink at her aunt's blatant betrayal. *Dear Nicholas,* indeed! Not so long ago he had been a black rogue and a scoundrel. And her aunt must know that the last thing Penelope wanted was to be left alone with her husband. But her protests went unheeded, so she took refuge in anger to cover her trepidation.

"I trust your business with me is indeed urgent, Colonel," she said politely, striving to maintain at least an outward appearance of calm.

Nicholas regarded her for a moment, a frown banishing the tentative smile in his eyes. "Why didn't you tell me, Penelope?"

Penelope's heart turned over. How characteristic of the man to cross swords with her, she thought bleakly. He had come about the child—Samuel must have observed her condition after all. She had been foolish beyond reason to imagine that Nicholas cared a fig about the mother. She wished he had stayed away; but here he was, at daggers drawn with her once again. But Penelope had learned how to thwart the colonel's frontal attacks, and she drew on her anger to lend her courage.

"Tell you what, sir?" she asked blandly. The effect of this deliberate prevarication was instantaneous.

He took her roughly by the shoulders and glared down at her. "Don't provoke me, Penelope," he growled. "Why didn't you tell me three months ago that you are carrying my child?"

Penelope met his dark gaze calmly. Something in his expression belied his angry tone. Could it be that her irate husband was not as indifferent to her as she had feared? No! she told her eager heart firmly. Stop this senseless dreaming at once. It could only bring more heartache. Penelope gave him a cool smile.

"I concluded that anything concerning me could hardly be of interest to you, since you ran off and abandoned—"

"Ran off?" he cut in, his frown deepening alarmingly. "Don't pretend I had any choice but to leave the Abbey, Penelope. That damned brother of yours practically ordered me off his land. It's a wonder I didn't throttle the bastard."

Penelope could well imagine how close Neville had come to such a fate, but the colonel's revelation did not surprise her. "That hardly explains why you abandoned me," she pointed out. "I naturally assumed—"

"Abandoned you?" he interrupted once more. "What in blue blazes are you talking about, woman?" He released her abruptly and began to pace about the room. "You returned my ring, madam. I naturally took that as a confirmation of what your brother told me."

Penelope felt suddenly apprehensive. "And what exactly *did* my brother tell you?"

"Nothing that I didn't already know, I suppose. Although I had hoped that we . . ." He broke off and glanced at her enigmatically. "He told me that you would never be happy living anywhere but at the Abbey. He assured me that you had admitted as much to him, that you felt your marriage to me was a mistake." The bitter echo in his voice surprised her; she frowned. There was something here that didn't make sense, she thought.

Nicholas came to a halt before her and regarded her broodingly. "Your brother categorically refused to recognise the marriage," he said slowly and deliberately.

Penelope gasped. "Neville would never do anything so *archaic*," she protested, although a flash of insight told her differently.

The colonel shrugged. "He did so, nevertheless." His lips twitched into a faint smile that caused Penelope's heart to flutter alarmingly. "And furthermore, he threatened to disown you if I insisted upon inflicting what he called my 'upstart, encroaching presence' on any of the Ashingtons again." His grin broadened, but Penelope saw no humour in his eyes.

Her mind still reeling from her brother's treachery, Penelope grasped at the one fact she was certain of. "But Neville must be mad! I am not an Ashington any longer," she pointed out. "I am a Bellington."

"Not according to your esteemed brother," the colonel replied curtly.

And you, Nicholas? she wanted to scream at the top of her voice. How could he believe that she was anything but his wife, a Bellington? If she were ever to find happiness again, she must demand an answer to that question.

"And what do *you* think, Nicholas?" she murmured, so softly that she wondered if he had heard.

He had heard, for he placed his hands on her shoulders again and stared into her eyes. "I think you are a Bellington, Penelope." He grinned suddenly with real amusement this time, and Penelope's heart leaped into her throat. "In fact, my girl, I know damned well you are a Bellington. And now that you are carrying my child, I have come to take you to

Bellington Hall. I want my son to be born in *my* house, not here in Brighton. Which reminds me, what the blazes are you doing in Brighton anyway? Your bother objects to the idea of having a Bellington born at his precious Abbey, does he?"

Penelope felt as though her heart had dropped to the pit of her stomach again. Lulled by the warmth of Nicholas's hands on her shoulders, she took a moment to realise the full impact of his words. With a sigh of despair, she jerked away and hurried to the window, willing herself not to give rein to her chaotic emotions. It was as she had feared. He wanted the child. A son to carry on the Bellington name, she supposed. How ironic that neither her brother nor her husband seemed to want *her*. And now that Aunt Octavia was getting married, she would be alone. Except for her baby, she thought. And now Nicholas intended to take that small comfort away from her.

The colonel came up behind her and tried to turn her around, but she resisted him, reluctant to reveal the misery in her heart.

"Have I said anything to upset you, Penelope?" he said anxiously. "I give you my word that you will be free to leave as soon as the child is settled."

Upset her? Lord in Heaven, she thought, men could be such utter lack-wits at times. She had no wish to be "free," as he called it. And what kind of a mother did he think she was to go off and leave her baby?

"I realise that Bellington Hall is nowhere near as grand as the Abbey, but I——"

"And if I do not wish to go?" she interrupted, feeling her temper rising at such obtuseness.

Nicholas turned her to face him, but she refused to meet his gaze. "Do not defy me on this, my dear. It's not every day that a man becomes a father. And it's important to me that the child grow up at Bellington."

"And it is not every day that a woman becomes a mother," she snapped back, thoroughly aggrieved at this senseless argument. "And furthermore," she added spiritedly, "it is important to me that the child grow up with his mother."

"Ah. So you wish to raise the child at the Abbey, is that it?" The bitterness was back in his voice, and Penelope glanced up into dark eyes that glittered with cynicism instead of the warmth she yearned to find in them. How could this man not guess what she was so shamelessly hinting at? she wondered. She would give anything to be mistress of Bellington Hall and Nicholas's wife again. But how to tell him so?

"The Abbey is no longer my home," she said flatly. "*This* is the only home I have now." She saw disbelief flicker in his eyes, followed by something else she dared not name.

"That is not what your brother told me."

"Neville lied to you. He as good as accused me of bringing disgrace to the family, which is complete nonsense, of course. And Charlotte snubbed me most odiously. I also had no choice but to leave."

He gave a deprecating laugh. "History repeats itself, my dear. Some things never change, do they? It's my grandmother's story all over again, isn't it?"

"The Ashington curse you mean, don't you?"

He looked momentarily surprised, and then replied with a warmer smile. "The duc de Saxe's daughter and the lowly Norman baron? Perhaps you are right. He must have been a daring rogue at that. I envy him."

"He was one of William's most valiant soldiers," she said softly, gazing entranced at her husband's eyes roved longingly over her face. "He cared not a wit for the old duc's stuffy traditions."

"And what about you, Penelope?" he asked, his eyes lingering on her mouth. "Does it distress you to be cut off from your family's stuffy traditions?"

The answer that came instantly to her lips was not one she had ever imagined herself giving. "Oh, no!" She smiled up into his eyes. She was quite certain by now that he wanted to kiss her, and the thought delighted her. "Aunt Octavia will be cut off, too, just as soon as Neville hears she is marrying a thoroughly ineligible suitor. But she doesn't seem to mind a bit." She paused, then lowered her lashes before adding shyly, "She is in love with her nabob, you see."

"I see," he said, a sardonic smile curving his lips.

Penelope pretended not to notice when Nicholas slipped an arm about her waist and drew her gently against his tall frame. "Just as our great-uncle David consigned his family to the devil when he fell in love with your grandmother," she added in a rush, determined not to think of the tremors of excitement that were making her bones melt.

"I see," he repeated, this time so close that Penelope felt the heady warmth of his breath on her cheek.

Nicholas took her chin in his hand and tilted her face up at a convenient angle. "I am beginning to see that I have behaved like a dashed slow-top." His thumb brushed lightly over her lower lip, and Penelope closed her eyes and relaxed against him. "Tell me, sweetheart. If I had asked you three months ago to come away to Hampshire with me, would you have consigned your family to the devil for me?"

The answer to this was so self-evident that, once again, Penelope marvelled at the obtuseness of men. She felt a slow smile pull at her mouth. Now that the moment of truth had arrived, she had a perverse desire to savour it to its fullest. She looked into the colonel's eyes, and the shadow of anxiety she saw there brought her a moment of triumph and delight. He was not quite sure of her answer, she thought, unable to resist the temptation to tease him a moment longer.

"Perhaps," she said slowly, watching the flare of desire in the depths of his eyes. "*If* you had asked me, sir. But you didn't, did you?"

"No, and more fool me, my love. But I am asking you now, Penelope. Will you come to Hampshire with me? Bellington Hall is badly in need of a mistress." The tingle of his lips as he trailed them down her neck made Penelope shudder with delight. "And, incidentally, so am I, sweetheart."

Penelope felt his lips travel slowly up her neck again, pause briefly to caress her ear, and then move across her cheek towards her eager mouth. It was all she could do not to turn her lips to meet his. And then his smiling mouth was hovering over hers, his dark eyes dancing.

"If you are suggesting a new alliance, Colonel," Penelope said archly, placing her hands defensively against his chest. "We shall have to discuss the terms, won't we?"

Nicholas looked taken aback for a moment, then he laughed and tightened his arm about her. "This is no alliance, my pet. This is complete and total surrender I am proposing." He kissed the corner of her mouth, and Penelope had to steel herself against his insidious invasion. Yes, she thought happily.

She had surrendered her heart to him months ago. But what about his?

"Whose surrender do you mean, sir?" she demanded.

He heaved a mock sigh and gave her a crooked grin that made her feel suddenly giddy with joy. "Mine, of course, you naughty minx. As if you didn't know. You have me cut off, outmanoeuvred, outgunned, vanquished, conquered, and defeated—in short, completely and utterly routed, my love. Now I know exactly how Napoleon must have felt after Waterloo. What more can I say?"

"I would like you to translate that into plain English, if you please."

The amused look he gave her was so revealing of love and tenderness that Penelope caught her breath in wonder.

"I'm better in action than juggling fancy phrases, my Lady Victorious. So *this* is approximately what I mean," he murmured and captured her lips in a kiss that spoke more of passionate invasion and erotic assault than of surrender. But as she felt her last defences fall before the heady onslaught of her soldier lover, Penelope sighed contentedly.

Something told her that their battling days were indeed over.